Blackman's
Coffin

Blackman's Coffin

Mark de Castrique

WORLDWIDE®

TORONTO • NEW YORK • LONDON
AMSTERDAM • PARIS • SYDNEY • HAMBURG
STOCKHOLM • ATHENS • TOKYO • MILAN
MADRID • WARSAW • BUDAPEST • AUCKLAND

In Memory of Doug Marlette
Who encouraged me to march to my own drummer
While he ran to his own symphony

Recycling programs
for this product may
not exist in your area.

Blackman's Coffin

A Worldwide Mystery/June 2017

First published by Poisoned Pen Press

ISBN-13: 978-0-373-28412-2

Acknowledgments

Research resources for this book came from a variety of individuals whose support proved invaluable. Thanks to Dr. Tom Buter of OrthoCarolina; Kale Hinnant, Rob Reps, and Bill Arrowood of W.T. Hinnant Artificial Limb Company; Ted Mitchell of the Thomas Wolfe Memorial and editor of *Thomas Wolfe—An Illustrated Biography*; and Dr. Kevin G. Steward, coauthor of *Exploring the Geology of the Carolinas*. Any errors of fact are mine. I'm grateful to the many "hosts" of the Biltmore Estate who made my visits so enjoyable.

Although historical figures and real places appear in the novel, the events are fictitious. Special thanks to Kale, Ted, and Kevin for appearing as themselves, and to Linda and Bob Newcomb for introducing me to Thomas Wolfe's brother Fred.

Creating a novel isn't done in isolation. Thanks to Steve Greene for his storytelling insights, my wife, Linda, daughters, Lindsay and Melissa, and son-in-law, Pete, for critical reading of the manuscript, my agent, Linda Allen, and Barbara Peters, Rob Rosenwald, and the Poisoned Pen Press staff for bringing *Blackman's Coffin* to the reader.

Finally, I'm indebted to the late Donald Lee Moore, a mountain gentleman who told me the story of accompanying his father as they transported the body of an African American man out of the North Carolina mountains in 1919 when no other white funeral home would provide the service. His family's kindness during those shameful times provided the seed of the story.

ONE

I FELT A hand on my shoulder, shaking me awake.

"Now you can pass as a local. They've all got one leg shorter than the other. Comes from being raised on the side of a mountain." The woman sitting beside my hospital bed laughed at her own joke and then offered me a paper bag.

"Who the hell are you?" I pushed the control to incline the bed to where I could see her eye to eye. I didn't need someone waking me up and rubbing my nose in my predicament.

She tossed the bag onto my chest. "Tikima Robertson. Marine Corps—retired. Never got over it so now I come to the V.A. hospital to harass the leathernecks who feel sorry for themselves." She gave a salute. The dark metal hook at the end of her forearm brushed her arched eyebrow. "What I figure is if the Marines had had a few more good women, we'd have been out of Iraq three years ago."

"Then let me be the first to encourage you to re-up." I glanced down at the bag and saw a hardback copy of Elmore Leonard's *Up in Honey's Room*. I'm a Leonard fan and the gift cooled my anger a few degrees.

"I would have reenlisted, but when I type I tear up the computer keyboard." She waved the prosthetic hook in front of me. "So the Corps didn't want me back in public disinformation."

I snapped off the sheet and uncovered my maimed left leg.

She looked where the stump ended just below the knee. "Not so bad. But you can't use one of these back scratchers. You'll snag the carpet every time you walk."

I smiled. "You're full of black humor, aren't you?"

"That's what a black woman's for. Keep a black man from taking himself too seriously, even if he's white like you, Chief Warrant Officer Sam Blackman."

I raised my hands in mock surrender. "I give up. What do you want?"

"Give up? Well, if I didn't already know it, you just proved you're Army. And a glorified MP, not even a real soldier."

My temper flared. I lifted the book and shoved it toward her. "No thanks. I don't want your gift or your insults. And we all turned into MPs over there. One god-damned police force trying to separate people who only hate us a little more than they hate each other."

Tikima flinched and looked away. I held the book over the edge of the bed, waiting for her to take it.

She sighed and turned to me. "Sorry. That was uncalled for. Sometimes I try too hard to make a connection." She stood. "But keep the book. Ain't Mr. Leonard's fault I got no tact."

Her apology sounded straight from the heart.

"Wait a minute. You're not getting off so easy." I nodded to the chair. "No woman walks out on Sam Blackman."

She hesitated a moment and then the twinkle returned to her eyes. "Is that an order?"

"Yes, from a glorified MP. Do I have to handcuff you?"

"It helps to have hands." She scooted the chair nearer and sat.

I gave her a closer look. Tikima had dark smooth skin and a shapely figure that her khaki pants suit couldn't hide. She wore her curly black hair cropped close to her head. Her ringless left hand rested in her lap as a cradle for the hook. I have difficulty estimating a woman's age, but I guessed she was in her mid-thirties, a couple of years older than me.

She cleared her throat as if to start our conversation anew. "So, have you found a guy in here with only a left foot so you can go in on shoes together?"

"No. But I left a request back in Amputee Alley at Walter Reed to be on the lookout for a prospect."

"Came through there myself three years ago. They tried to give me one of those new fake arms they claim looks real. Black plastic supposed to match my skin. My skin's no more black than yours is white. I looked like I'd stolen the arm off Darth Vader. I said forget this, give me something that works."

Tikima lifted her arm. The hook was actually a curved vise with one side longer than the other. "I shrug my shoulder and the clamp closes." The tips met with an audible click. "Now I mail Amputee Alley all my right-handed gloves."

I decided we'd best get the war stories out of the way. If Tikima Robertson had been sent by some army shrink to have me open up, then we could check that off the to-do list. "How'd you lose the hand?"

"Shrapnel."

"In Iraq? I thought Marine women were kept out of combat."

"Oh, did I miss the memo about where the frontline

was?" She shook her head. "We were supposed to be in a secure area. I was riding with an AP reporter and we had the honor of driving by as one of the first car bombs detonated. The reporter was lucky. Only lost his laptop. You'd think he'd taken a round to the chest. I had to pull him screaming out of the vehicle." She looked at my leg. "Roadside bomb?"

"No. Rocket grenade at a checkpoint. Concussion knocked me out. Sunni insurgents in stolen Iraqi uniforms. Two of my buddies were killed."

Tikima nodded. She didn't ask any questions about how I was coping with the loss of my comrades or how I felt about becoming the proverbial one-legged man in an ass-kicking contest. I thought maybe she wasn't on shrink patrol after all.

"You know how I got here?" I asked.

"No. The only information the staff shared was that you're from Winston-Salem, your enlistment is up, and you're scheduled for release from rehab in a few weeks."

"I'm here because I talked to *The Washington Post* about the deplorable conditions at Walter Reed. And then I testified from a wheelchair on Capitol Hill."

She scowled. "I'm surprised you're not in Guam."

"Yeah, the administrators were all too anxious to have me disappear. Especially after I told them I wasn't interested in going through rehab to stay in an army that treats its wounded like curbside trash."

"I know," Tikima said. "I tried to get something done when I was there." She looked like she might cry at the memory.

"Well, some big asses got some big kicks. I'd hoped they'd send me to Salisbury about thirty minutes from where I grew up. The V.A. typed my name in the wrong place on the transfer form. Then Blackman got misspelled as Black Mtn and I wound up in Asheville because it's next to Black Mountain."

"Are you going back to Winston-Salem when you're released?"

"I don't know. My family's not there anymore. My parents were killed in a car wreck earlier this year and I have a brother in Birmingham who wants me to come there."

"Girlfriend?"

"I got the Dear John letter the second week I was in Walter Reed."

She leaned forward. "Stay here awhile. I'll help you find a place."

"And do what? Walk around the side of a mountain with the locals?"

"I'm a local. My family's been here for over a hundred years."

The door to the room opened and a nurse brought my roommate back from physical therapy. Old Mr. Carlisle was a World War Two vet in his eighties. His mind spun through the years like a revolving door and during our brief conversations he'd be storming the beach at Saipan one minute and walking with his late wife on Myrtle Beach the next.

Tikima got up and helped hold the wheelchair steady as the nurse assisted Mr. Carlisle back into bed. The nurse transferred his oxygen supply from his portable unit to the feed coming from the wall connector.

Then the nurse rolled the wheelchair to me. "Ready to work with your prosthesis?"

"What's the army giving him?" Tikima asked.

"A trans-tibial with good rotation. He can be on the golf course in a few months."

"As a caddy," I said. "My disability benefit wouldn't buy a bag of golf tees."

Tikima unsnapped her small purse and withdrew a business card. "Let's stay in touch. I might be able to find you gainful employment."

The embossed type read "Tikima Robertson—Consultant, Armitage Security Services."

"Need a night watchman?" I asked.

"I need someone with a brain. Unless you left that in Iraq along with your leg."

The nurse blushed, but Tikima's bluntness no longer bothered me.

"Then come see me." I patted the bag with the book. "And bring another Leonard. I'll be through this in two days."

Tikima laughed and turned to the nurse. "Work his ass off. Next time I'm here I want to see him tap dancing." She shrugged her shoulder and the gripping mechanism on her hook sounded like a castanet. With a flourish of clicks, she twirled out the door.

Two weeks passed and Tikima Robertson didn't return. I walked as many hours on my artificial leg as the rehab team allowed. The more adept I became the more I wanted to improve. I spent most of my days exploring the hospital halls or reading in the library where many of the donated books seemed to have been untouched. I wondered how Tikima had known I was a mystery buff and an Elmore Leonard fan in particular.

Tikima had come on a Saturday morning, and on the third Monday after her visit, the doctor in charge of my case told me I'd made all the recovery that was possible under their care. In other words, because of my hard work and commitment, I'd progressed enough that Uncle Sam would be cutting me loose at the end of the week. Adios and have a nice life.

The army had been my home since high school. My only immediate prospect was to go to Birmingham and transition for a few weeks with my older brother, his wife, and their three-month-old twin girls. The possibility of being a night watchman seemed infinitely preferable. I decided to contact Tikima, even though I'd hoped she would have made good on her promise to return. While Mr. Carlisle was in rehab, I phoned the number on Tikima's card.

A computerized voice announced Armitage Security Services and prompted me to direct-dial an extension or wait for a personnel menu. I quickly studied the card and found the three-digit number under Tikima's name. "This extension is no longer in service," came the automated reply. "You are being transferred to the operator."

"I'm calling for Tikima Robertson," I told the woman who answered.

I heard only silence and thought we'd been disconnected.

"Hello? My name is Sam Blackman. Tikima told me to call."

"Hold one moment please, Mr. Blackman."

After a few minutes of classical music, a strong baritone voice came on the line. "This is Nathan Armitage. How can I help you?"

"I'm trying to reach Tikima Robertson. She gave me her card and asked me to get in touch."

"Can you tell me the nature of your request?"

Just like a security firm to make you jump through hoops. "The nature of my request is to speak with Tikima. I'm a wounded vet in the Asheville V.A. hospital and she was kind enough to visit me. The name's Sam Blackman. Do you need my social security number to do a background check?"

I heard him take a deep breath. "Mr. Blackman, I'm sorry to tell you Tikima has died. I thought maybe you were one of her clients."

My mouth turned to dry cotton. I'd only met the woman for a few minutes, but I'd replayed the scene of her dancing out of my hospital room countless times. In Iraq, you understood soldiers went on patrol and didn't come back, but in Asheville, North Carolina?

"How?" I whispered.

His voice broke. "She was murdered, Mr. Blackman."

The word *murdered* rang in my ear. I sat staring at the door, seeing Tikima laugh and dance through it.

When I didn't respond, Armitage continued, "She'd been missing since June 2nd, that was a Saturday."

"The day she came to see me."

"What time?" Armitage asked.

"Around ten that morning."

"The police may want to speak to you. Can I give them your name?"

"Yes." I wound the phone cord into a ball with my free hand. "What happened?"

"We're not sure. Believe me, Mr. Blackman, we're pressing the police for action. Our company provides only protective security services for clients, we don't do investigative work. But Tikima was a friend and colleague to all of us. I've authorized a twenty-five-thousand-dollar reward for anyone providing information that can un-cover her murderer."

I'd worked enough cases with the military's Criminal Investigation Detachment to know the best leads come fast. If the police weren't even sure what happened, then the trail must be ice cold.

"You have to know something," I said.

"Only that Tikima's sister spoke with her that Satur-day afternoon. Tikima planned to pick her up for church the next day. She never showed up."

"What'd she do Saturday night?"

"Her sister said Tikima told her she was meeting somebody about work."

"A client?"

"None we know of."

"Where was her body found?"

Armitage hesitated. "Look, I don't know you, Mr. Blackman. You could be who you say you are or you could be involved somehow."

"Then just tell me what was in the paper. I'm clue-less. I'm in a hospital bed and I can't stomach reading the god-damned news."

"Some fishermen on the French Broad River found her body last Wednesday. She'd been weighed down with stones, but the current and the—" Armitage's voice wavered, "and the gases from the decomposition of her body brought her to the surface."

"Do they have a cause of death?"

"Hasn't been officially released but I've learned from the funeral home she died from a gunshot to the head."

What a cruel twist. Have your hand blown off in Iraq and then come home to be murdered. Tikima Robertson was someone who deserved better from life. "Have they held the memorial service?"

"Tomorrow morning at eleven."

"Where?"

"Mount Zion Missionary Baptist Church."

"I want the address."

"Mr. Blackman, you said you're in the hospital."

"I am. But somehow I'll get to the funeral tomorrow."

Armitage was quiet for a moment, and then said, "Can you be out front at ten-fifteen? I'll pick you up in a black Lexus."

"All right. And I'll be the one tap dancing on my new leg." I hung up and looked at the empty doorway. "Like I said, Tikima, no woman walks out on Sam Blackman."

TWO

AT EIGHT THE next morning, I looked over at Mr. Carlisle. He slept with a clear plastic oxygen tube dangling half out of his nostrils. Mr. Carlisle suffered from chronic respiratory problems—a condition created when a Japanese fuel tank exploded on Saipan and smothered him in black diesel smoke. He'd also spent a lifetime with cigarettes which, despite the tobacco lobby's claims to the contrary, continued the destruction of his lungs. He'd checked into the hospital a week after I arrived. Odds were he wouldn't be checking out.

During the six weeks of physical therapy since my transfer from Walter Reed, I'd seen Mr. Carlisle's daughter take him out every Sunday for dinner. She made sure he had something suitable to wear. The wardrobe that had come with me from Walter Reed consisted of military fatigues and a red Hawaiian shirt. Not the most appropriate way to show respect for the dead. My brother had moved my things out of our parents' home when the house had gone on the market, and he kept the few non-army clothes I owned waiting for me in Birmingham.

I slipped out of bed and grabbed the crutches leaning against the wall. With the stealth of a commando, I checked Mr. Carlisle's drawer for anything that might carry a decorum of dignity. He had several pairs of boxer shorts, black socks with elastic so frayed they

fell down around his ankles, two pairs of navy blue
slacks rolled up like miniature sleeping bags, and a
folded white shirt. I shook the shirt and the wrinkles
disappeared. The fabric contained so much polyester
it would melt under a hot lamp.

Mr. Carlisle stood a good six inches shorter than me
but he had at least an extra six inches around the waist.
I tossed my hospital gown back on the bed and tried
on his shirt. The length provided enough tail to tuck
in, but the sleeves stopped halfway down my forearm.
I turned back the cuffs. Casual but neat. I'd have to go
with my military pants. Thank God they weren't camo.
At least I wouldn't appear to have stopped at the church
on the way to a luau.

I sat on the edge of the bed and fit my artificial limb
into position. Such an odd feeling to look down and
see this impostor replacing part of my body. I knew
some men at Walter Reed who'd given their prosthesis
a name. I don't think this cold device and I could ever
be so intimate.

Mr. Carlisle coughed and shifted in bed. I kept my
back to him.

"Where you going, Sam?" he asked in a raspy voice.

"Thought I'd practice walking outside before it gets
too hot."

"Don't spill anything on my shirt." He rolled back
over.

I stopped at the nurses' station and said I was going
to the library. I carried the book Tikima had given me.
I asked the duty nurse to cancel my morning physical
therapy because I had a guest coming to talk about a
job possibility. All the nurses knew I'd been cleared for
release on Friday and they'd started cutting me slack,

like I was getting a few days of vacation before being dumped on the world.

The hospital had a truckload of forms being processed for my release. I'd had to give proof that my brother's house would be my next residence, and that I'd continue with follow-up physical examinations. The government must have been concerned I'd re-grow my leg and continue to collect disability. I didn't want to start another avalanche of paperwork to get permission to attend the funeral, so what the hospital didn't know was in everyone's best interest. Out and back in two hours, no stains on Mr. Carlisle's shirt, and no one the wiser.

I found a pen in the library and started to inscribe the Elmore book as a gift to the vets at the V.A. hospital from Tikima Robertson. Instead I wrote—From Tikima Robertson to Sam Blackman. June 2, 2007. Then it struck me I was holding the last gift she'd ever given.

Around ten I walked out the doors of the main entrance. I strolled along the driveway toward the front gate, pausing now and then to rest. The exertion of walking on uneven concrete taxed my stamina and my balance. Perhaps attending the funeral would be a mistake. What if there were a lot of stairs or Nathan Armitage couldn't park close to the church?

Before my doubt could overcome my resolve, a black Lexus turned into the hospital grounds. As it approached, I waved and stepped closer to the curb. Armitage eased the car over, reached across the passenger seat, and opened the door.

"Blackman?"

"I'm your man." I sat on the leather seat with my legs still outside. Armitage watched as I lifted the left one with both hands and swung it into the car. "Don't want to scratch your interior," I said.

"Don't worry about it. The car's leased." He stuck out his hand. "I'm privileged to meet you."

I gripped his hand firmly. The broad palm was tough and callused, not what I'd expect from a man who I thought sat behind a desk. Armitage wore a smartly tailored dark blue suit, white shirt, and impeccably knotted burgundy tie. His clean-shaven face had a golfer's tan with a thin band of white on his upper forehead where he probably wore a cap or visor. His short black hair had a dash of silver at the temples. I figured him for mid-forties.

"What's the book?" Armitage looked at the Elmore volume in my lap.

"In case you were running late. If I'm reading, hospital security doesn't think I just wandered out of my room."

He pulled the Lexus away from the curb. "How long have you been here?"

"A little over six weeks. Trying to get used to this damn tree stump."

"It's the feeling, isn't it? Like walking on one stilt but you're not sure when it's going to hit the ground or how high to lift it."

I couldn't help but glance at his feet.

He smiled. "No, I've got all my toes, but my best friend from the service lost both legs. First Gulf War. The one we fought the right way. He told me what it was like. Said the best thing about the artificial legs was they eased the phantom pains."

"I've noticed that too. Were you Army?"

"Marines. One of the things that bonded me to Tikima."

He shook his head. "I can't believe she's gone. We worked together nearly three years." Armitage turned onto Tunnel Road and headed into Asheville. "She was my top sales person. Her clients loved her."

"And you've got no idea who had a motive to kill her?"

"No. Like I said on the phone, we don't do investigative work. The police say the M.O. doesn't fit a random robbery gone bad, and no one has come forward to say they met with her that Saturday night. Whatever it was must have been personal."

"Boyfriend?"

"If she was seeing anyone, she didn't tell me. But something had been bothering her the last few months. She was preoccupied and moody. Still doing her job but without any zest. She'd even stopped visiting vets."

"I was surprised that my nurse didn't know Tikima, but she'd started at the hospital only a few weeks before I arrived."

Armitage took his eyes off the road a second to look at me. "That's why your call surprised me. Tikima didn't tell me she'd gone back to visiting."

"Maybe she'd worked out whatever was bothering her," I said.

Armitage raised his eyebrows. "I think her funeral's proof enough she hadn't." Again he turned to me. "What did she talk about, if you don't mind me asking?"

"She bluntly told me not to feel sorry for myself. Pissed me off at first, but she kept at me in a way that made me laugh. She said she'd come back."

"But she didn't. Anything else?"

I hesitated a moment. "Don't take this like I'm hitting you up for anything, but she said maybe she could get me a job if I decided to stay in Asheville. I thought she meant a night watchman or something. I guess your company provides those services."

"Among other things."

"Then she told me she wanted my brain, unless I'd left it in Iraq along with my leg."

Armitage snorted a laugh through his nose. "That's Tikima. What did you do in the service?"

"A Chief Warrant Officer with the Criminal Investigation Detachment. Army said they'd evaluate my situation. Maybe grant me a desk job. I told them no thanks."

Armitage nodded. "Maybe we can work something out."

Mt. Zion Missionary Baptist stood near the corner of South Spruce and Eagle streets a few blocks from the center of Asheville. I'd expected a little country church and was surprised by a gothic Victorian red brick sanctuary. Cars were lined up turning into the parking lot.

"When we're in front of the door, I'll stop and you can get out," Armitage said. "If you want to wait for me fine, but if you try the steps on your own, save me a seat."

I felt a little unsteady as I stepped up on the curb. Armitage drove on and I noticed his vanity plate—B C CURE. At first I thought he was advertising for the headache powder BC that's popular in the South, but then it hit me—Be Secure.

I made my way to the handrail that bordered the concrete stairs. Several people stepped aside when they noticed my wobbly gait. The steady stream of well-dressed mourners flowing into the sanctuary made me nervous that Armitage and I would find a pew. I gripped the rail and managed to climb to the doorway. Inside, an elderly black woman with a warm smile handed me a bulletin.

"I'll be on the back row," I said. "My friend, a white man in a blue suit and burgundy tie, will be looking for me."

"I'll keep an eye out," she said. "Thank you for being here."

Although it was only twenty minutes till eleven, the sanctuary was more than three-quarters full. Unlike my Presbyterian church back in Winston-Salem, this church filled from the front first. I sat on the aisle of the back pew where I felt more confident about being able to stand and get out.

The bulletin was a single sheet of paper folded in half to create four panels. On the front was the title "A CELE-BRATION OF HOMEGOING. TIKIMA ROBERTSON. 1972–2007." Inside, the order of worship listed a number of Bible readings interspaced between hymns. There was a eulogy to be delivered by the minister and something called Time of Remembrance. The music leaned toward spirituals with a theme of going home. I recognized *He'll Understand and Say Well Done* and *City Called Heaven,* but others were unfamiliar. I wondered if *Old Ship of Zion* had something to do with this church in particular. On the back panel were printed two short paragraphs: one of thanks from the family for the prayers and condolences which had been offered by the congregation and community and the other was directions to the cemetery. I hadn't thought about the funeral procession and wondered whether Armitage planned to attend the graveside service.

I'd been so intent on finding my seat that I hadn't paid attention to my surroundings. I looked up at gold chandeliers hanging from a ceiling of rich dark wood receding in layered thin slats that would cost a fortune today. Beautiful gold organ pipes framed the back of the chancel and the pulpit stood front and center. I leaned out of the pew to see down the aisle. On the floor in front of the pulpit sat a pewter and navy-colored casket. Across its bowed lid stretched an American flag.

Armitage nudged my shoulder, but instead of sliding over, I stepped into the aisle and let him in. When we were settled, I whispered, "Are you going to the graveside?"

"I hadn't planned on it."

I nodded in agreement. I wasn't ready to trust my leg trekking across open ground.

The congregation was predominantly black, but a significant number of white faces were in attendance. A few minutes before eleven, the organist began the prelude. Toward the end, the congregation stood as the family entered from a door beside the chancel. While we were still standing, the minister welcomed everyone and announced that the hymns for the service had been favorites of Tikima. She had specified them for her funeral before her deployment to Iraq. The irony of the situation was not lost on any of us.

I sang the songs as best I could. *Old Ship of Zion* turned out to be a spiritual about Jesus as captain of a ship rescuing souls from sin and sorrow. The minister's eulogy was directed to the family seated in front of him. He told of Tikima's lifelong growth in that congregation, her kindness, and her sacrifice in war, and that she and her family were no strangers to tragedy. But, as before, God's grace and strength would pull them through once again.

The "amens" began from the congregation. The minister led them from despair to hope and from death to life. He mentioned Tikima's work with the veterans at the V.A. hospital and how that was so like her to help others. The statement must have been a cue because the piano began playing while the minister said, "The greatest tribute we can pay Tikima is to continue her legacy by making this commitment—" He stopped and the congregation immediately broke into the song *If I Can Help Somebody, Then My Living Shall Not Be In Vain*. It was a powerful moment because I hadn't sensed it coming. I was part of the frozen chosen, not comfortable being spontaneous in church, or moving in the pews except to get in and out. But the lyrics and rhythm were contagious and even B C Cure Armitage swayed back and forth in time.

When the song was over and the congregation seated, an usher brought a microphone on a stand and set it beside the casket. The minister said Tikima's sister desired to set aside a few minutes for others to share memories of Tikima.

A few people rose immediately and made their way to the microphone. A Sunday school teacher who had taught Tikima, a basketball coach, a best friend who had known Tikima since kindergarten. The stories were personal and some of the speakers wept as they spoke.

As the Time of Remembrance continued, I became aware that no one had yet talked on behalf of the veterans Tikima had visited and even more aware that none of those waiting to speak was white.

I shifted uncomfortably in my seat. The line at the microphone had shrunk and no one else was getting up. Then I sensed someone standing beside me. I looked up to see the elderly woman who had handed me my bulletin.

"Would you like to say something," she whispered.

She phrased the sentence not as a question but as an approval.

I took a deep breath and stood. From the corner of my eye, I saw Armitage look at me like I'd lost my mind.

The last speaker was leaving the microphone as I walked down the aisle. My left leg seemed to hit harder with each step and a few times I had to grab the side of a pew to steady myself.

The minister gave a nod of reassurance and I turned to face the congregation.

"I'm Sam Blackman. One of the veterans Tikima visited in the V.A. hospital. I'm not supposed to be here because I haven't been discharged yet. But I'm not the first soldier the Army has lost track of."

A gentle ripple of laughter from the pews eased my tension.

"But I had to come, not because I knew Tikima for ten years or even ten months, but because I knew her for only ten minutes. That was long enough for her to make an impression upon me. An impression that for those ten minutes my health and my attitude were the most important things in her life. She challenged me. Well, *challenged* is not quite strong enough a word. She was a Marine and therefore didn't mince words. Her clear message to me was not to worry about what I've lost, but to work with what I've been given. I understand that and I'm trying. But I can't understand why someone like Tikima would be taken from us."

I paused and looked along the front rows where I

thought Tikima's family sat. Their tear-streaked faces nodded. "Unless it is to force us to pick up where she left off. And in that way we enlarge and multiply her spirit. We all become Tikimas."

I heard "amens" as I turned to the casket. I rested my hand on the flag. "I think she'd like that."

ARMITAGE AND I rode for a couple blocks in silence. Then he said, "That took guts to walk down that aisle."

"I probably looked like a peg-legged pirate."

"I'm not talking about your physical handicap. I meant what you said."

"Thank you. I hope I didn't look too foolish."

His knuckles whitened as he squeezed the steering wheel. "No. You made me look foolish. I should have been up there. Tikima had been my friend. You did what I didn't have the courage to do, and that embarrassed me."

He took a deep breath and smiled. "And thank you for doing it."

I didn't say anything because it wasn't about me.

When we pulled into the V.A. hospital driveway, Armitage asked, "When are you out of this place?"

"Friday."

"Where are you going?"

"My brother's in Birmingham."

"You're not staying in Asheville?"

"No."

"I can use you, Sam. Tikima was a good judge of character and so am I."

I picked up my Elmore book. "Thank you, but I need a little time to get my life in order."

He stopped the Lexus in front of the main entrance. "If you change your mind, you know how to reach me."

I shook his hand. "Thank you for the ride, Nathan."

NINE O'CLOCK THAT night I walked the halls, partly for practice, mostly because I couldn't sleep. I'd returned Mr. Carlisle's shirt to him and then crashed, not waking till supper time. Now I thought about the call I'd make to my brother, notifying him that I'd be coming Friday. The short, turbulent chapter of my Asheville life would be closed.

"Mr. Blackman." A nurse's aide hurried to me. "There's an after-hours call that's come into the desk for you. The woman says it's an emergency."

My pulse raced. My brother and his family were the only ones who would call about an emergency. I followed the aide as fast as I could.

"This is Sam Blackman."

"Mr. Blackman. Somebody broke into my sister Tikima's apartment while we were at the funeral."

The woman sounded close to hysterics.

"I'm sorry. Who is this?"

"Nakayla. Nakayla Robertson. I saw you at the funeral. Tikima told me about you. Whoever killed her came back when they knew no one was here."

"Nakayla, that happens a lot. Crooks read about a funeral and they rob the house during the service. Why do you think it's the same people?"

"Because they didn't take anything."

"Have you called the police?"

"Not yet. I wanted to talk to you."

The woman was making no sense.

"I don't see how I can help you," I said.

"Tikima thought you could help her. She left you a book."

"I know. I have it."

"An Elmore Leonard book?"

"Yes."

"Does it have a dust jacket?"

"No."

"*Up in Honey's Room*, right?"

"Yes. Why are you asking?"

"Because the dust jacket is in her apartment, but covering a different book. I think it was what they were looking for."

"I still don't see what that has to do with me."

"My sister was very organized. There's a Post-It note in the book with your name on it. I found it going through her apartment when she was missing, but I didn't know who you were till you spoke at the funeral."

"I asked Tikima to bring me another Elmore," I said. "She probably wrote herself a reminder."

"No, Mr. Blackman. The dust jacket isn't around another Elmore book. It's a ninety-year-old journal, and I think it got my sister murdered."

THREE

"A JOURNAL? WHOSE?" I asked.

"A boy. Henderson Youngblood. I have no idea who he is. Can we meet someplace? Maybe here?"

I looked around. The duty nurse had given me some space for what she thought was a family emergency, but she was watching to make sure I was holding up okay. "I don't have a car," I whispered. "And since I'm still a patient, I can't call a cab and walk out."

"Can I pick you up?"

"Sure. Anytime in the morning is fine."

"I mean tonight."

"It's after nine."

"I can be there by nine-thirty. Please help me, Mr. Blackman."

Help. *If I Can Help Somebody.* The song echoed in my head. What could I say?

Nakayla met me at the same spot where Armitage had stopped. Instead of a Lexus, she drove a green Hyundai subcompact.

Her features were lit only by the dash and the reflected lights of the hospital, but I could see Nakayla was a pretty woman. Thinner than Tikima, she had the same smooth skin and graceful neck. She wore her dark hair longer in relaxed curls. Somewhere since this morning's service she'd changed into blue jeans and a sleeveless pink blouse. The mountain air was warm enough that she didn't need a sweater.

"Thank you, Mr. Blackman," she said, as I closed the door.

"The name's Sam. Did you bring the book?"

"Yes. In the back seat. I thought we could grab some coffee while you examine it."

"Someplace close. I don't want to miss a bed check."

A few miles toward downtown Asheville we found an Applebee's. I followed Nakayla to a back booth. The waitress took our coffee order and I added a slice of apple pie and two forks.

When we were alone, Nakayla slid the book across the table. The dust jacket for *Up in Honey's Room* was too big for the volume it covered, but with a stack of other books no one would have noticed.

"Were there other books designated for people?"

"No. That was the only one."

"Then why mark it with my name?"

Tears formed in Nakayla's eyes. "In case something happened to her. That's all I can figure. She wanted you to get it."

"But she'd just met me."

Nakayla shook her head. "I think there's more to it. Tikima told me she'd picked up a book for a veteran who'd been transferred from Walter Reed. She said you had the right stuff."

"She told you this the Saturday after she saw me?"

"No. The day before."

"The day before? Are you sure?"

"Positive. We sometimes go to the Farmer's Market on Saturday morning, but she had to go to the V.A. hospital instead."

"How'd she know I liked Leonard? I didn't tell any-one."

"Tikima had a friend at Walter Reed from when she was hospitalized. The friend told Tikima you were coming and I guess she mentioned what you liked to read."

"And that's the right stuff?"

Nakayla lowered her eyes. "I thought she meant a guy she'd be interested in. You know, a good looking black man."

"And I'm neither."

Nakayla looked flustered. "No, I didn't mean—"

I laughed. "I'm just teasing."

I looked down at the book. If what Nakayla said was true, then Tikima had checked me out. But why? "You didn't tell the police about me?"

"I didn't have a name. And I didn't think about it. When Tikima went missing, I didn't see how a hospitalized vet had anything to do with her disappearance. I still don't."

I took a sip of coffee. "But then I spoke at the funeral."

She nodded. "And your name was the same one as on the Post-It. That's why I went back to her apartment tonight. I found it ransacked, and then I discovered the book wasn't what it appeared to be."

"And you haven't read it?"

"I called you right away. I was afraid they'd close the switchboard."

I picked up the book. "I guess I should read some of it." Underneath the cover, I found a leather-bound volume. The pages had yellowed, but the quality of the paper was good. The writing on the unlined sheets was in dark, blunt pencil. I flipped through the pages and saw that the entries filled about two-thirds of the book. Too many to read sitting in a restaurant.

"I'll start at the beginning, do a few pages, and see if I can understand why Tikima wanted me to have it. Then you can read it after you take me back and we'll talk tomorrow."

Nakayla cut a bite of the pie with her fork. She gave me Tikima's smile. "Don't spill anything on it."

"I'm careful. Just ask Mr. Carlisle."

The Journal of Henderson Youngblood

I was born in the year 1907, in the city of Asheville, of a good family, and given the Christian name Henderson, the surname of my mother's relatives in the neighboring county which also bears that name.

My father is Travis Scott Youngblood, a native of Asheville and Buncombe County, and the owner of Youngblood Funeral Services. My mother is Rachel Henderson Youngblood and I am an only child.

On Saturday, June 28, 1919, my teacher, Miss Nettles, gave me this leather-bound volume of blank parchment and the assignment to fill it with daily entries. She also presented me with a copy of a diary written by a man named Samuel Pepys. Actually it wasn't the whole diary. The title was "Selections from the Diary of Mr. Samuel Pepys Suitable for Young Readers." Mr. Pepys lived hundreds of years ago in London, England, and must have had little to do but scribble in his book, ride in his carriage, and go to bed.

Miss Nettles told me that I should be honest in what I write for what good is a man who would lie to himself. To that I would add what good is a man who would bore himself. Therefore, I prefer to label this volume not a daily diary but "The Journal of Henderson Youngblood," and though every word will be true and writ with my own hand, I will only record those events which will prove interesting enough for a second reading. Instead of Mr. Pepys, Mr. Robinson Crusoe shall be my inspiration, for his journal spoke of high adventure and dangerous encounters with cannibals. And I will try and recount what transpired in the words spoken by the participants, myself included, so that the reader may make of them what he will.

Although Miss Nettles might not approve, my first entry relates an event that occurred two months in the past. I think it merits inclusion since it is the reason Miss Nettles has given me these blank pages.

Friday, April 25th: I turned twelve and my mother packed a box of molasses cookies for me to share with my classmates. In our school, Miss Nettles teaches the room of 6th and 7th graders, and although I was recorded as a 6th grader, she had me read and write with the older children.

Our room totaled eighteen students, ten 6th graders and eight 7th graders. Some of the older boys had dropped out and gone to work, especially those whose brothers were serving in the Great War. There were only three 7th grade boys and all of them feared the armistice would hold and deny them their chance to battle the Hun. Father says we see enough death in this country without seeking opportunities for more on foreign soil.

My mother made enough cookies for each of us to have two, including Miss Nettles. The teachers don't make a big fuss over older birthdays like they do with the younger children, but Miss Nettles did select me to be the daily reader, and I picked a story from the Citizen newspaper on the possibility of the city building a memorial in Pack Square to Kiffin Rockwell. Mr. Rockwell was Asheville's most famous war hero, joining the French Foreign Legion before America even joined the conflict and becoming the first American to shoot down an enemy plane.

That night for supper my mother fixed roasted chicken and smashed potatoes. We had an apple pie made from the best of the fruit stored in the cellar from last fall's harvest. When the plates had been cleared from the table, my father brought out a long package wrapped in butcher's paper. My heart jumped because I knew it was the squirrel rifle he had promised to give me when I was old enough to clean and care for it myself. I expected it to be the one he had as a boy, but as I ripped away the wrapping, I saw fresh bluing on the barrel. I stared in amazement at a new Winchester bolt-action twenty-two.

"For me?" I stammered.

My father laughed. "If you take my gun, what am I supposed to hunt with? We'll sight it in tomorrow morning."

But around nine that night, Mr. Lucas Jefferson came by with word that his mother had passed and asked my father to tend to her burial preparation. Over my mother's objection, my father gave his blessing to my taking the Winchester into the woods alone.

Saturday, April 26th: I was up before the rooster behind Mr. Galloway's nearby farm crowed the sunrise. The chill in the April air meant my mother wouldn't let me out of the house without my corduroy jacket. She had already hung it on the back door latch, anticipating my early departure.

We live on the south side of Asheville, not too far from the village Mr. Vanderbilt built.

NOTE: That sentence sounds like a stutter, but that's what he did—Vanderbilt built his own village for the people who came to work on the big house he called Biltmore. That's a good name. By the time he died back in 1914, Mr. Vanderbilt built more than anybody else around these parts.

Mother says the south side of Asheville once had all the saloons, but the same year I was born, the town voted out the "demon rum" as she calls all whiskey. She says that was a good omen for me to be born in a town freed of the curse of drink. But I've heard my father tell Mr. Galloway that some people have died so pickled he was wasting embalming fluid on them. From drinking moonshine as folks call it, or white lightning. My father's warned me about walking up on somebody's corn squeezin's in the woods. Even with carrying my own gun, I know I've got to be careful.

I don't have a dog, though I'd sure like one. The motorcars are bad to run them down. But I do have a pony. Old Brownie had been my mother's since she was twelve. He's over twenty and gone gray enough that we ought to change his name, but he still gets around and likes to go trailing where the ground's not too steep. Brownie stays in the barn on Mr. Galloway's land. Mr. Galloway boards a few horses along with his milk cows. He's got the first good pasture land at the edge of town.

I left a note for my parents telling them I was riding Brownie into the forest by myself. I knew they wouldn't want me to have a gang of boys around my new rifle and I couldn't go firing off a gun in town anyway. Then I stuffed a couple of apples in my jacket pocket along with a box of shells, tucked the Winchester up on my shoulder like an infantryman, and marched the half mile to Mr. Galloway's.

He was in the barn, finishing his milking. He held my rifle as I saddled and bridled Brownie.

"This is quite a gun," he said. "And you're only eleven."

"Twelve yesterday, sir." I led Brownie out of his stall.

"I didn't give my Jamie his first gun till he was fourteen." Mr. Galloway patted the wooden stock with his big hand. "Should have done it sooner."

I didn't say anything. Mr. Galloway's son Jamie had died in France last year. The army said an artillery shell hit his trench and there wasn't enough of a body to send home for my father and Mr. Galloway to bury.

I swung up on Brownie and Mr. Galloway handed me the rifle.

"Where you headed?" he asked.

"Think I'll go out along the French Broad where the land's flatter and I can sight targets in the water."

He nodded. "Stay off the Biltmore Estate. The widow Vanderbilt's got the groundskeepers patrolling for poachers. Hate to see your pa have to come bail you out of the pokey." He laughed and slapped Brownie on the rump.

The pony jumped forward and then trotted into the morning light. We stayed along the pasture edge until we reached the trail to the Swannanoa. Brownie headed down the path without a guiding tug on the reins. We'd taken it every day last summer after I'd been given permission to fish the Swannanoa River alone. But today we'd ride farther away from any chance meeting with the other boys from school, to a spot upstream along the French Broad before it merged with the Swannanoa and flowed west of town.

Brownie struggled against me as I forced him onto the left fork off the trail to our fishing hole. Maybe he didn't like a path still hidden in shadows. Maybe he knew I was ignoring Mr. Galloway's warning and taking a shortcut across the Biltmore Estate.

We climbed a gentle ridge of white pines. A hawk shrieked overhead, followed by a chorus of crows. The black birds sounded their alarm until the hawk flew on to somewhere he could hunt in peace.

The white pines thinned and the crest of the ridge opened to laurel and scrub saplings. Timber clearing had left a patchwork of stumps, some with shoots sprouting from exposed roots. I knew I hadn't crossed onto the Vanderbilt property because old Mr. Vanderbilt was known for his forestry methods. Even though he'd been dead four years, no one cut timber on his land or the land his wife had sold to the government for Pisgah National Forest with-out planting seedlings afterward. My father told me Mr. Vanderbilt had hired a man whose only job was to manage the forest. That man must have worked hard. All I could see from the clearing were trees and more trees.

Brownie and I started down the other side of the ridge, entering a narrow trail marked by a freshly painted sign: PRIVATE PROPERTY—KEEP OUT! I'd be keeping out as soon as I could cross to the river, and I nudged Brownie with my heels to urge him forward.

The path brightened as more sunlight penetrated the new spring leaves of the hardwoods. We'd prob-ably followed the trail for thirty minutes when I saw mist suspended like a white band halfway up the tree trunks. The French Broad lay close by and the warming air lifted the fog in the shape of the wind-ing river itself.

The westerly breeze that carried the river's ghost toward us also brought a scent that stopped Brownie in his tracks. He whinnied and tossed back his head, his eyes rolling wide. I grabbed onto his mane with one hand and clutched my new rifle with the other.

"Easy, boy. Easy." My words had no effect on the pony.

Brownie reared back on his haunches so quickly I lost my grip and tumbled to the ground. He bolted over me, kicking my shoulder as he retreated up the ridge. I lay on my side and watched him disappear into the trees.

Then I heard a growl.

I rolled over and saw a large black bear appear

on the path no more than twenty yards away. He sat on his haunches, his back to me, and sniffed the breeze with loud, wet snorts. If he turned up the trail, he'd see me for sure. I reached for my rifle lying beside me. If the bear had encountered hunters before, maybe the sight of the gun would scare him off. If it didn't, the unloaded twenty-two would offer no defense.

He growled again, a gurgling menace of a sound, and he cocked his head so I could see his snout in profile. Foam lathered his jaws and an icy chill ran through me. I'd seen that foam on a mongrel dog shot down behind our house. Rabies.

I could have had a cannon and the rabid bear would still attack. My best hope lay in scurrying off the trail where I'd be out of sight in a second. I was downwind, and something on the breeze kept his attention. Even if he heard me, he might not follow. He hadn't connected Brownie's hoof beats with the right direction on the path.

I scrambled to my feet and tore through the underbrush, hoping to loop onto the trail beyond the bear's line of sight. The crackle of dry leaves sounded like firecrackers under my feet. From behind me, a growl rose sharply. I had no doubt the bear lumbered after me. Low branches whipped across my face and chest. I risked a glance over my shoulder and saw only trees behind me. Maybe I would make it.

Teeth crushed down on my ankle and pain surged up my leg like someone had slashed me with a fiery saber. I tumbled through the air and then felt something snatch me in mid-flight. I dropped to the ground so hard the air was knocked from my chest. Without breath, I couldn't even scream.

The right leg of my dungarees turned dark with blood. The teeth tearing into them weren't those of the bear, but a bear trap anchored by a chain looped around the base of an oak tree. I crawled back to put some slack in the chain. Beneath the blood shone the shiny steel, new and strong. I tried to squeeze the jaws apart, but I only made the pain worse.

A rustle from the underbrush caught my ear. The bear had followed me. I looked around for my rifle and found it lying on a pile of sticky, rotten apples. Bait. I had stumbled into the honey-laced lure meant for the bear.

I fumbled through my jacket pocket for the box of shells. They spilled out onto the leaves. I slid back the bolt and dropped a bullet into the chamber. One shot. I would get one shot.

The bear emerged and reared on his hind legs. I tried to kneel but my wounded leg collapsed under me. I flopped forward, bringing the rifle up with my elbow bracing the barrel. If he charged, I'd wait till the very last second before firing.

The wind shifted and the bear turned toward me. The smell of my fear must have hit his nose like a freight train. He growled louder, dropped to all fours, and came at me.

I aimed between his eyes and when I could hold off no longer, squeezed the trigger.

The roar of the gun startled me. The bear jerked in the air and sprawled to my right. A double echo of gunshots resounded through the hills.

"Don't touch him," a voice shouted.

I looked up the slope. A Negro wearing a brown canvas jacket and mud-stained pants slowly side-stepped through the trees. He kept a rifle that dwarfed my twenty-two pointed at the bear. "His spittle got the disease. Get it on you and you go crazy too."

He gave the motionless animal a wide berth till he stood at the head. In one motion, he shouldered the rifle and fired again. "That do him."

The man walked over and looked at my leg. "Gotta carry you to a doctor." He pulled a key from his pocket and opened a padlock linking two ends of the chain.

"Get my leg out," I cried.

"That leg bleed more when I free the trap. I want to have you where I can tie it off." He slipped the chain free of the trap. "I'll try not to hurt you, but you gonna have to go up on my shoulder." He squatted down and looked me in the eye. "What's your name, boy?"

"Henderson. Henderson Youngblood."

"The buryin' man's son?"

"Yes."

He grabbed me by the shoulders and lifted me up, careful to keep my weight off the leg. Even as careful as he was, the pain forced me to cry out.

"That's all right," he said. "You holler all you want. Don't have to prove nothing to me. That bear has a hole in his eye and it didn't come from my gun."

"But your shot knocked him over," I said. "Stopped him from giving me rabies."

"Maybe," he said. "We'll talk about that later."

He stood with me slung over his back like a sack of feed.

My head started spinning. "What's your name?" I mumbled.

"Elijah."

He took a first step. I don't remember the second one.

The next thing I heard was the gurgle of water. A cold wetness soaked my pants and I opened my eyes to see blue sky and the face of Elijah above me.

The intensity of the pain in my right leg made breathing difficult and I gasped for air.

"Lay easy," Elijah said. "The water will clean the wound and the chill numbs the pain."

I propped myself up on an elbow and looked around. We were on a flat mossy rock by a bold stream. Both of my feet dangled in the swift white water. "Where are we?"

"Never you mind. It's a place you ain't supposed to be, like where you were when that bear lit after you."

"Biltmore. But you ain't supposed to be here either."

He shook his head. "I work the grounds and I've been tracking that bear ever since he started killing the livestock."

The bear almost killed me, I thought. My twenty-two might have blinded one eye, but if the bear hadn't mauled me to death, his rabies would have got me for sure. Elijah had saved my life. The vision of the charging bear swept over me like a black cloud. Again I fainted.

When I came to, I heard my father's voice calling me. I found myself propped against Elijah on a mule. Then I saw my father and Mr. Galloway running across the timber clear cut at the Biltmore boundary.

Elijah dismounted and let my father take his place. Then he led the mule behind Mr. Galloway and told them the story. I buried my face in my father's shoulder and sobbed.

Sunday, April 27th: I woke up in the hospital. Mother and Father were beside the bed. Mother held my hand in both of hers. I could see tears on her cheeks. I couldn't feel my foot. I wrestled my hand free and lifted the starched sheet. My right leg ended in a ball of gauze and cotton. My foot and ankle were gone.

"May I get you anything else?" The waitress looked anxious and I realized she wanted us to leave. The restaurant was closing. I looked down at my full coffee cup and across the table at the empty pie plate in front of Nakayla. I had touched neither while reading the boy's journal. Nakayla hadn't interrupted me.

"No, we're finished," I said. "We'll be going."

When the waitress had retreated, Nakayla asked, "Did you find something?"

I slid the book back to her. "Yes. Tikima wanted me to have this journal because the boy writing it loses his foot. I guess she thought I'd find it inspirational." As I said the words, I felt disappointed that Tikima had given me some warm and fuzzy story for motivation. I'd expected more from her.

Nakayla bit down on her lower lip and then wiped

her eyes. "I'd hoped it would be something more. Something that would make sense of what happened."

"I know." I rubbed the aching stub of my leg. The world had stopped making sense for me too.

"MR. BLACKMAN."

A hand shook me awake. I must have been dreaming about Tikima because I thought she was shaking me again.

The duty nurse stood over me. "The woman who called last night. She's on the phone again."

I was awake enough to notice daylight coming through the blinds. "What time is it?"

"Nearly seven. My shift's over in a few minutes. Is it really an emergency?"

"Yes. Should I come out to the desk?"

"No. I can transfer her to the room phone." She wheeled the bedside table closer and left.

I snatched the receiver up in mid-ring. "Nakayla?" I whispered.

"Mr. Blackman, it makes sense. It makes sense." She was so excited she was nearly screaming.

"The journal?"

"Yes. Elijah was our great-great grandfather. In 1919, his body was found in the French Broad River. He'd been murdered."

FOUR

ALTHOUGH I DIDN'T know how I could help Nakayla, I couldn't dismiss the possibility that her sister had selected me for a specific reason. Around nine, I told the duty nurse I'd be working on my own for a few hours in rehab. Then, I slipped on my pants and Hawaiian shirt, and for the third time in two days, I made a break from the hospital.

Nakayla nearly ran over my good foot as she tried to save me from stepping down from the curb. I slid onto the seat and swung my prosthetic leg in without a problem.

"You're getting better," Nakayla said.

"In another twenty years, I might be able to walk on the damn thing."

Nakayla drove forward without comment and I realized my whining was petty self-indulgence to a woman who had just buried her sister. The psych docs in Walter Reed had warned me that my emotions would swing through extremes—that was normal. But the more insidious development would be letting those emotions harden into bitterness. Not only would that eat away at my spirit but it would also distance others from me.

"Now if they could put a retractable wheel on the bottom," I said, "like in those shoes the kids wear. You've heard the expression hell on wheels?"

Nakayla glanced over and saw what I meant to be a friendly grin.

"We could call you Scooter Man," she said. "Get you a red cape."

"I do have my Hawaiian shirt."

Nakayla cut her eyes to the gaudy pattern and then accelerated onto Tunnel Road. "Take my advice. Send it back to the Hawaiians."

I reached down, found the seat controls, and inched out a little more legroom.

Nakayla noticed my effort. "Sorry if you're cramped. I started to bring Tikima's Avalon but I'm not up to driving it yet."

My investigative instincts kicked in. "Where did they find her car?"

"What do you mean?"

"Was it abandoned near the river?"

"No. It was in her parking spot at the Kenilworth."

"The Kenilworth?"

Nakayla zipped the Hyundai up the ramp to I-40. "Her apartment building. Where we're going now."

"So someone picked her up."

"That's what the police think."

I heard the skepticism in her voice. "You don't agree?"

Nakayla glanced at the speedometer and set the cruise control. "Tikima told me she was going to meet someone, not that someone was picking her up."

I approached the other possibility as tactfully as I could. "Is there a chance she might have had someone up to her apartment? Someone she didn't want you to know about?"

Nakayla shook her head. "We were sisters. I knew

every man in her life—even the jerks—especially the jerks. She'd just broken up with a guy two weeks before and she wasn't seeing anyone."

"This guy she broke up with, is he a suspect?"

"I gave the police his name, but I doubt he's involved. He's married with two kids. When Tikima found out, she dumped him."

"How'd she find out?"

"I told her." Nakayla stared straight ahead. At first her smooth-skinned face showed no emotion, but after a few seconds, her dark eyes welled with tears. "She was my big sister. She looked out for me. After her injury, I tried to do the same for her." Nakayla turned to me. "My sister could be too trusting. I think she was about to put her trust in you."

I felt my face warm at what I took for a rebuke.

Nakayla saw the impact of her words and her eyes widened. "I didn't mean it that way." She shifted her gaze back to the interstate. "Just that she seemed ready to enlist your help when she hardly knew you."

"But you think she checked up on me?"

"Yes. And if she liked what she found out, she would have moved quickly."

"And if she didn't dig deep enough, she could make a mistake, like dating a married man."

Nakayla wiped her eyes with the back of her hand. "Something like that. But the words you said at her funeral prove to me she didn't misjudge you."

I felt my face flush again at the compliment. I stared out the side window at the ridges rimming Asheville and wondered if Nakayla could also be too trusting. What if Tikima had lied to her sister and hadn't broken off her relationship? My years as a warrant officer, especially working with military prosecutors, had shown me how often people will say what they know someone else wants to hear.

"You don't think it's possible that Tikima's plans could have changed after she talked to you? That her apartment could have been the meeting place?"

"She wouldn't have met a business prospect there. Usually they'd meet at the client's site or at a restaurant. Tikima would have called me again if her plans changed. I have a key to her apartment and sometimes I'd crash there to watch a video and stuff myself with popcorn."

"But you didn't that Saturday?"

"No. I had a date."

"So Tikima knew that."

"No."

No meant Tikima wouldn't have brought someone up to her apartment if she thought Nakayla might drop by. No also meant the sisters didn't tell each other everything.

Nakayla flipped on her turn signal and eased the car into the right-hand lane. A green exit sign read Biltmore Village one half mile. I sat quietly, not wanting the questions swirling in my head to come out as an interrogation.

"I had a working date, not a romantic one," Nakayla said. "I didn't discuss the specifics of my work with Tikima."

Working date? Who was I riding with? A hooker with a heart of gold?

Nakayla must have read my mind. "I'm an insurance investigator. I went out with a guy who'd filed a disability claim. We went clubbing and he was making moves his crooked chiropractor stated were impossible for a man enduring his alleged suffering and pain." Nakayla laughed. "He endured suffering and pain all right. I could see it on his face when he realized I'd snapped several shots with my cell phone of him contorting like a pretzel."

"You're a private detective?"

"No. I work for a company called the Investigative Alliance for Underwriters. We work exclusively for insurance companies. The Asheville office covers western North Carolina. Most of my time is spent on the phone interviewing neighbors and co-workers of people we believe to be filing fraudulent claims. Once in a while I work in the field."

My next question came without thinking. "Then why would Tikima come to me rather than you?"

Nakayla's answer was quick and short. "Whatever my sister was investigating, she must have thought it was too dangerous to involve me."

I said nothing. We both understood Tikima had been right.

The I-40 exit led onto Highway 25, the main road into Biltmore Village. In the left lane, traffic was backed up for several blocks, waiting to turn into the Biltmore Estate. I'd never been to America's largest private residence, but the proliferation of billboards throughout North Carolina made the exterior of the mammoth home as familiar as the Eiffel Tower. Henderson Youngblood's description of the surrounding landscape gave me a new connection, one that enticed me to walk on the property he had traversed eighty-eight years earlier.

Nakayla steered clear of the gridlocked tourists and we zipped through the village. The Biltmore mansion was not visible from the road, only the stream of cars disappearing into the forest through its massive gate. Perhaps that was the route Henderson Youngblood had taken on his pony.

A few miles farther, we turned right across from St. Joseph's Hospital and began climbing a winding road through an established neighborhood. Homes were eclectic in style—from ranches to two-story and even three-story structures built along the slope. I didn't see any apartment complexes other than an occasional duplex.

"Did Tikima live in an older residence?" I asked.

"You might say that." Nakayla swung the Hyundai along a looping road that circumscribed the top of a wooded knoll.

Suddenly the trees gave way to a grassy clearing and I was astonished to see a huge building towering above bordering pines. "Good God, is this her place? It's a grand hotel."

"Used to be. That's the Kenilworth Inn. Goes back to the 1880s. Then it caught fire and was rebuilt around 1913. It's on the National Historic Registry."

The stately old Tudor had to be five or six stories with wings rambling off a grand entrance marked by a high stone porte-cochere. Back in the day, hundreds of carriages must have unloaded at its doors.

"Hard to believe something like this still exists," I said. "And it's apartments?"

"Right now. A developer from the West Coast bought it. Saved it from being razed. Probably go condo someday, but Tikima liked to dream she was princess of the manor." Nakayla followed the road around a wide expanse of lawn. An American flag flapped atop a silver pole at the center of the arcing driveway.

"Princess of the manor," I repeated. "I can believe that."

"I called her queen of the asylum." Nakayla pulled into a parking space and yanked up the handbrake. "For most of its life, the Kenilworth Inn was a government hospital and mental institution." She opened her door, and then turned back to me. "I have a feeling you'll fit right in."

I stood and leaned against the car, setting my leg and taking a deep breath.

"Don't worry," Nakayla said. "I'll drop you at the front. You mentioned Tikima's car and I thought we ought to check it." She crossed behind her trunk and led me past a few vehicles to a silver Avalon. She reached in the pocket of her jeans for a key remote.

"Is that Tikima's key?"

"No. Her purse was never found. This is the spare from the apartment. I told you I thought about driving her car to pick you up." She double-clicked a button and the four doors unlocked.

"So the police didn't check it out," I said.

"They dusted for prints. The investigating officer theorized that Tikima might have been abducted as she started to get in the car. They looked for signs of a struggle, but found nothing."

We stood on black asphalt and I looked down at a collage of oil drips and pine sap. The hard surface showed no scrape marks or gouges. Any blood stains not washed away by rain would have been discovered by a halfway decent mobile crime lab.

"Can I look inside?" I asked.

Nakayla opened the driver's door. The interior was clean except for the expected litter of a few parking receipts and gum wrappers. The tan leather seats showed minimal signs of wear, but the gearshift in the console had undergone a change. A metal bolt had been attached to either end of the grip. It took me a second to understand this homemade modification had been done to accommodate Tikima's prosthesis. The pinchers could be anchored in the hole of each bolt, enabling Tikima to squeeze the release button and slide the gearshift into position. Clever, and I guessed a hell of a lot cheaper than a factory installation.

The unset handbrake between the seats showed a similar customization. A third bolt had been fastened to the button on the end and a small eyehook protruded from a wooden block taped midway down the lever.

I leaned in the car for a closer look. Scrapes on the parking brake's leather trim indicated Tikima had sometimes missed her makeshift device. I turned back to Nakayla. "You set your handbrake even though we're on level ground."

"Yes. Then you'll never forget it on steep ground. Mother forgot once and the car started rolling with Tikima and me inside. Tikima was ten and jumped in the front seat. She couldn't reach the brakes, but she steered the car past a tree and we crashed into a laurel thicket."

I moved clear of the door. "Then would Tikima have always set her parking brake?"

Nakayla stared into the car.

"Were you with the police when they dusted for prints?"

She seemed oblivious to my questions. "Tikima had

to have set the brake. She's the one who hounded me to do it before I even turned off the ignition."

I stepped closer and grabbed her arm. "Nakayla, were you here with the police?"

"No. I gave them the key. Why would they have released the brake?"

"I don't think they did. But you need to ask."

Nakayla searched my face for confirmation of what she must have suspected.

I nodded. "Yes. That's an explanation. Someone else parked her car." I edged between her and the vehicle. Since the police had found the doors locked, they probably concentrated their efforts on the exterior. They might not have even printed the interior.

Kneeling was difficult so I braced my right hand on the driver's seat and bent down to examine the floor mat. On the carpet to the left of the brake pedal, a smudge showed the imprint of a shoe. The dirt looked like dried sand laced with flecks of mica.

I pointed to the spot. "Could Tikima have left that footprint?"

Nakayla peered over my shoulder. "No. It's too big. And Tikima wore flats, high heels, or running shoes."

If we were looking at a clue, then I deduced a man had stepped in wet sand, gotten in the car, and rested his left foot long enough for the sand to dry into the carpet. The shape of the toe and the gap between the sole and heel suggested a dress shoe.

I walked to the rear tire. The tread and sidewalls were clean, but since Tikima's disappearance we'd had several heavy thunderstorms. I reached into the wheel well where the tire would have been protected from the rain and cupped my hand around its inner edge. Gritty particles clung to the rubber. I held my palm open to the sunlight. Mica sparkled amidst dirty brown sand.

Nakayla ran her delicate fingers over the grains. "The police botched it, didn't they?"

"I don't know. Maybe it's in their report."

She pulled her cell phone from her purse.

"Who are you calling?"

"The detective on Tikima's case." Nakayla punched in a number and gave me a hard look as she waited for an answer. "Lieutenant Roy Peters, please." After a brief pause, she said, "Nakayla Robertson. It's important." She turned to the open driver's door as if to be sure of her report. "Lieutenant, I'm standing by my sister's car and I believe there are some things you missed."

I wondered what the homicide detective must be thinking. At least Nakayla's voice was calm. She'd made the statement as a matter of fact.

"Tikima always set her handbrake, and unless one of your officers released it, then someone else parked her car." Nakayla listened for a moment. "No, Tikima wouldn't forget. And how do you explain a man's footprint on the floor carpet?"

Peters must have challenged the claim because Nakayla whirled around, her eyes locking on me like twin lasers. "I'm not imagining things. Chief Warrant Officer Sam Blackman found it. He's with the military police and he's done more in five minutes than the Asheville police did in five days."

My stomach knotted as Nakayla's temper boiled over. I didn't relish being on the bad side of some cop.

"Ask him yourself." She thrust out her arm, nearly hitting my face with the phone.

I touched the receiver like it was radioactive. "Sam Blackman."

"Since when does the military move in on a case without the courtesy of a call to the officer in charge?" Peters' words were clipped and curt.

"I'm not moving in on anybody."

"You got that right, buddy boy."

He got that wrong. I'm nobody's buddy boy. Peters was starting to piss me off. "I can't move in on someone who's not even there. You've left a hole in your investigation a car length wide. If you're more interested in covering your ass than in finding Tikima's killer, then fine. I'll hang up and let my commanding officer call your police chief. But remember, we telephoned you as soon as we found what you missed."

Nakayla gave me a thumbs up. I kept the phone to my ear hoping I wouldn't have to make good on my toothless threat.

Peters sighed. "Are you at the asylum?"

I remembered Nakayla's story about the history of the apartment building. "Yes."

"Stay by the car. I'll see you in twenty minutes."

I looked up at the sprawling complex. There I stood, on the lam from one hospital passing myself off as an investigator in a case I knew nothing about. The asylum. How appropriate. I had to be crazy.

FIVE

"TWENTY MINUTES?" NAKAYLA took back her cell phone, snapping it shut as an exclamation point to her question. "You and I aren't standing out in this hot sun for no twenty minutes."

"I'll be all right," I said.

"Get in the car," she ordered. "We'll wait in Tikima's apartment. I can see the parking lot from her window and you can read more of the journal."

She drove her Hyundai to the front entrance of the old hotel and then stood by the front door while I hobbled up the short flight of stairs. When I reached the landing, she punched a code in the electronic keypad and the door clicked open.

"Sit down inside. I'll be back in a moment."

I stepped into a shadow created not only by the lack of light but a shadow cast by the past. The lobby of the once grand hotel—hospital—mental institution looked barren and skeletal. The high ceiling and rich wood echoed the grandeur that had greeted the posh patrons of another age. Now scattered pieces of furniture made vain attempts to resemble areas of conversation. The back of the lobby appeared to be the original registration counter but sometime over the years it had been walled in as a separate room. A hallway divided it from a single elevator in the corner. To my right an open arch led into a lounge or reading room. Bookshelves held patches of aging paperbacks in a "take one—leave one" approach to a library.

A wooden bench to the left of the archway caught my eye. As I took unsteady steps toward it, the elevator opened and a blonde in a turquoise sports bra and black running shorts jogged out. She had the lean body of a runner and must have been jogging in place during the elevator's descent. With a nod of acknowledgment and a reflexive glance at my wobbling leg, she floated by me on legs that a thoroughbred might envy. Watching her sexy figure disappear into the bright sunlight, I thought how I'd never again be able to run stride for stride with a beautiful gazelle like her. Instead of descending in my own elevator of depression, I laughed out loud. Who was I kidding? I never had nor never would run with a woman like her. Regardless of the changes Iraq had wrought upon my body, the words *eye candy* or *trophy husband* just weren't part of my résumé.

The front door opened again and the lithe silhouette reappeared. Maybe I'd sold myself short. Miss Marathon knew a good thing when she saw it. The figure walked closer but remained dark. Nakayla winked at me.

"I see you met Jenny."

"What do you mean?"

"Cut the act and put your tongue back in your mouth. The good news is she lives down the hall from Tikima, the bad news is she has a girlfriend."

"Her loss."

"Yeah. And Jamie Foxx is picking me up for dinner." Nakayla walked past me and pushed the elevator button.

We stepped out on the fourth floor and the guise of a hospital replaced that of the grand hotel. Long narrow hallways spread out along three wings. Brown doors broke the white walls like a computer-generated repetition and I thought of the veterans who had lived and died behind them. These corridors held ghosts in search of both mind and body.

"We're all the way at the end," Nakayla said. "You'll get your exercise."

She unlocked the apartment door and I left the bare bones hospital behind. The first thing that caught my eye was the granite surface on the kitchen counters. They separated the open room into two areas—the compact, efficient kitchen and an L-shaped living/dining area that wrapped around it. To my left was a small leather sofa, a green upholstered reading chair with a stack of books beside it, and a sensibly sized flat-screen television sitting on a middle shelf in a stack of filled bookshelves. Farther in the room to the right, the dining space held a circular table with four hard-backed chairs. The top of the table was covered with files, notebooks, and envelopes. I noticed two books in the center: the disguised journal and a book about Thomas Wolfe. A hallway led down to what I expected to be a bath and bedroom.

The apartment was cozy with a mix of folk art from Africa and Appalachia. An intricately carved djembe drum sat in a corner by the bookshelf. Above it, a dulcimer hung on the wall. The place was more laid-back than I would have expected Tikima's home to be.

"You cleaned up the mess left by the burglars?" I asked.

Nakayla looked around the apartment as if seeing it for the first time. "I couldn't bear to see her things thrown about. They also dumped out all her drawers in the bedroom and pulled the mattress off the box springs."

I walked to the table and picked up the journal in Elmore Leonard's dust jacket. "And you think this is what they wanted?"

"Nothing else she has is new or unusual." Nakayla stepped behind the kitchen counter. "You want something to drink? Coffee? There's root beer in the fridge."

"Root beer sounds good. Haven't had it since I was a kid." I glanced over the files and note cards. "What about these papers?"

"Tikima had left them on the table. She'd spread out work from the office there. I didn't see anything to connect with the journal."

"Does she have a computer here?"

Nakayla bent over to retrieve a bottle of root beer from the refrigerator's inside door. "Back in the bedroom. I let the police go through it when she first disappeared. No unusual emails or websites." She set a brown bottle on the counter. "You want a glass with ice?"

"No. Just pop the cap." I thought for a second. "Did you check the computer after yesterday's break-in?"

"I didn't think about it. The computer was about the only thing left undisturbed." She slid the root beer across the counter.

"There's the possibility the ransacking of the apartment was a decoy," I said. "The real object could have been to delete something incriminating from the computer's hard drive."

Nakayla bit her lower lip. "Damn. I didn't even turn it on." She looked like she was about to cry.

"Probably nothing. I'll read the journal while you see if you notice anything different on her computer."

"Okay and I can watch for Peters from the bedroom window."

I nodded, and then took a gulp of the root beer. The taste was sweet and strong, the heavy carbonation burning my throat like a shot of whiskey. I took the bottle and the journal to Tikima's reading chair. Maybe I was doing exactly what she had done a short time before someone killed her.

Saturday, May 10th: I came home from the hospital two weeks after the attack by the bear. Father brought me in our hearse. The Model T had not been Father's first choice. He'd wanted to buy a new REO, a very fancy vehicle with designs carved into the wood panels and plush red velvet curtains drawn across the interior of the side windows. Heavy springs softened the ride, which Mother thought foolishness since the passenger couldn't feel anything. Father said those same family members who worried about the thickness of the cushions in the casket would be impressed.

But last fall while Father was still saving for the REO, he received a letter from a funeral home in Spartanburg, South Carolina, asking if he'd be interested in buying their hearse. The price was only two hundred dollars—far less than the REO. They were selling it because they were merging with a competitor— a marriage had united rivals into one happy funeral family. Mother insisted Father at least look at it, so we'd taken the train down the steep Saluda grade and been met at the depot by a strange looking contraption. A Sayers and Scovill horse-drawn hearse had been mounted to the chassis of a Model T. The cab of the car had been cut to leave only the driver and front passenger seats. The carved wood of the hearse's paneling had been fitted over the metal of the cab's roof and sides. The black enamel finish of the car blended with the color of the wood and at first glance the vehicle appeared to be of one piece.

The man from the Spartanburg funeral home said the craftsmanship of the woodwork couldn't be matched by the REO or any other motor coach. Then he kicked the tires and said how the Sayers and Scovill elegance was matched by Mr. Henry Ford's mechanical simplicity. The engine had been treated like a baby, and if we ever had a problem, any garage would know how to fix it.

All Mother could think about was the money we would save. We already had a Model-T passenger car so my father liked the idea of having backup parts handy. We bought the hearse on the spot and I rode in the back as we journeyed up the mountain through Tryon, Saluda, and Hendersonville. The ride was rough, the carriage top heavy causing the vehicle to sway as we went around the switchbacks lifting us above the flatlands of South Carolina. Through the wooden wall, I heard my father laugh and say we'd never be going but a few miles to the cemetery once we got home and mother was right, the passengers wouldn't complain.

But on the way home from the hospital Mother felt differently. I was the passenger. She laid a heavy winter quilt across the hearse's hardwood floor. She brought a down-filled pillow to support the bandaged stub of my leg, and she continually told my father to slow down and stay clear of the ruts.

I don't know who was happier when I limped into bed—me, Mother, or Father.

Sunday, May 11th: I slept till early afternoon and might have slept the entire day had Mother not come bursting into the room, throwing back the window sash so that my eyes filled with sunlight.

"Henderson, you must wake up." She bent over my bed, her face pale and her breath coming in short gasps.

"What's wrong?" I scooted to a seated position against the headboard and looked at the open door behind her.

"Mrs. Edith Vanderbilt. She's outside. She and Miss Cornelia. They've come straight from All Souls."

Mother scurried around my room, tidying as she moved. I'd never seen her so anxious. The ache in my leg was forgotten as my own panic swelled. I had been on the Vanderbilt land. Could they be angry? All Souls was the Episcopal church Mr. Vanderbilt had constructed in Biltmore Village. I knew Episcopalians prayed about trespasses in The Lord's Prayer. We were Presbyterians and prayed about debts. The Vanderbilts didn't have any debts and they didn't have any trespasses because they owned all the property they could possibly need.

"Your father's talking to them, giving me a little time to get you ready."

Even though the room was warm, a cold shudder ran through me. "Are they taking me to jail?"

Mother stopped in the middle of folding a handkerchief on my nightstand. Her worried expression changed into a smile. "Now whatever put that in your head?"

"I was on the Biltmore Estate. Mr. Galloway told me the Vanderbilts don't like trespassing."

"That colored man who found you—"

"Elijah."

Mother nodded. "Elijah told Mrs. Vanderbilt the bear chased you onto their land."

I had enough wits about me not to argue against Elijah's fib.

"Mrs. Vanderbilt insists on paying all your medical expenses since the bear trap had been set by one of her men."

"And she's coming to see me?"

"She wants to say hello and have Dr. Lynch take a look at your leg."

"Dr. Lynch?"

"Dr. James Madison Lynch, although everyone calls him Mike. He's the surgeon for the estate. He saved Miss Cornelia when she had appendicitis and all the other doctors were afraid to operate. I've heard Dr. Lynch say he was too new in Asheville to know any better."

"But Mr. Vanderbilt died of appendicitis." Even though I'd been only seven, I remembered how shocked everyone had been at Mr. Vanderbilt's death.

"That was in Washington, D.C. Folks round here say if Mr. George Vanderbilt had been tended by Dr. Lynch, he'd be alive today." Mother fluffed up the pillow behind me. "Now perk up and mind your manners."

She glided out the door and then I heard her say,

"Mrs. Vanderbilt, Miss Vanderbilt, please come in. Henderson was awake so it's no trouble."

Mother returned followed by a slender woman in a deep blue dress that had to be store bought—maybe even out of the Sears Roebuck catalogue. Her dark brown hair was pulled up under a cream colored hat with a mesh veil folded onto its narrow brim. She clutched a matching purse under her left arm and extended her right hand, palm up, more for me to lay my hand atop rather than grip.

"Pleased to make your acquaintance, Henderson." Her voice sounded pleasant and light, each word crystal clear and formed by book learning.

"Thank you, ma'am," I said, briefly meeting her eyes and then dropping my gaze to the bedspread so as not to rudely stare.

"And this is my daughter, Cornelia."

Mrs. Vanderbilt turned sideways and I saw the prettiest young woman step into my room. She seemed to float before me, her body adorned in light green fabric that shimmered like new spring grass in the sun. She had to be in her late teens, but not so much older that I couldn't dream of walking by her side and hearing of all the marvelous places she'd been and people she'd met.

"Henderson, my mother and I hope you are feeling better." She gave a nod of her head and the waves of her brown tresses rippled against her smooth porcelain neck.

"Henderson?" My mother's thinly masked admonition broke through. "They want to know how you are feeling."

"Much better, thank you." I looked at Mrs. Vanderbilt but couldn't keep my eyes from constantly returning to Miss Cornelia.

"That's good to hear," Mrs. Vanderbilt said. "But I'm not surprised. Elijah told me how brave you were."

I know pride is a sin, but I puffed my chest out a little.

Miss Cornelia stepped closer. "Elijah said you didn't even cry when he pulled your leg from the trap, and with the rabid bear lying right beside you."

Elijah had carried me to the stream before releasing the steel jaws, but Cornelia's eyes had widened as she spoke, and I thought the drama of Elijah's version shouldn't be corrected.

"Elijah was the one who was brave, Miss Cornelia. I hope to be able to thank him personally when I'm able to walk again." The lump in my throat came with unexpected suddenness. Walk again. Would that ever be possible? I could already hear the boys at school calling me Tiny Tim after Mr. Dickens' Christmas Carol.

"We want Dr. Lynch to take a look at your leg," Mrs. Vanderbilt said. "With so many of our young men coming home from the front with shattered limbs, he tells me progress is being made on artificial devices. We will do what we can to have you fitted with one."

According to Elijah's story, I didn't cry from the pain of the trap, but the kindness of Mrs. Vanderbilt and her daughter sent tears flowing down my cheeks.

Monday, June 30th: I have finished writing those entries that preceded Miss Nettles giving me this journal. I must report that the newspapers are filled with the story of the signing of the Treaty of Versailles. I did not know that this past Saturday, June 28, 1919, the very day Miss Nettles presented me this journal, would be of such worldwide significance. Perhaps it is an omen that my own writings will not be insignificant.

Today Dr. Lynch came to our house with what he called an extendable limb. The wooden leg is designed like a telescope. Dr. Lynch showed me how as I grow, the length of the leg can be adjusted. The wood is covered with leather, and more leather can be wrapped around it so that the thickness matches my real leg. Metal braces run on either side of my knee connecting the artificial limb to a sleeve that looks something like my mother's corset. I lace it around my thigh to keep the top of the leg snug against my stump. Dr. Lynch says that will be the worst part for awhile, because the wound is still tender and the pressure of putting my weight down will be painful. He told the truth. When I tried to take a step, my tender skin felt like it was on fire, and Dr. Lynch caught me as I fell.

"You're going to have to work hard," he said. "We'll take things slowly for the first few weeks. Once the wound has callused, you can concentrate on balance." He removed the leg and held it up. "I promise you that you'll have new bounce in your step. This limb came all the way from New York City. The foot is attached to springs, hinges, and rubber gaskets that enable the joint to mimic your ankle. Mrs. Vanderbilt gave strict instructions that I'm to monitor your progress and replace the limb whenever a mechanical improvement is developed or you outgrow it, even if you turn out to be seven feet tall."

My father came to the door of my room and informed Dr. Lynch that Elijah and a crew of four workmen had arrived. I left the leg on the bed and used my crutches to walk to the back door.

Dr. Lynch pointed to an area of the yard. "Flat and shady would be nice, don't you think, Henderson?"

"Nice for what?"

"To build parallel handrails. You'll need a safe place to practice on that leg. That's the way the veterans learn."

Within an hour, Elijah and the others had finished what looked like two fences about three feet apart, three feet high, and twenty feet long. Back in the bedroom, Dr. Lynch re-attached the leg, and he and my father carried me to one end of the chute. Without a word, Elijah left his men and stood at the other. He fixed his eyes on me and nodded.

I lifted my weight on each smooth bar and lurched from side to side. Every step was like walking on hot coals the way Miss Nettles said the snake charmers in India do. The twenty feet seemed like a mile.

When I got to the end, my body was drenched in sweat. Elijah caught me, and then hoisted me on his shoulders. Everyone clapped. The pain in my leg disappeared.

Friday, July 4th: The holiday has been special but not just for the fireworks and festivities. Mother packed a picnic lunch and she, Father, and I drove to Pack Square. Before my injury we would have caught the streetcar at the corner, but Father feared the swell of the passengers would be too much for me and my crutches. I'm not ready to attempt a public outing with my artificial leg, although I have been able to walk the length of the backyard chute without touching the handrails.

Father dropped Mother and me as close to the center of the square as possible and then went to park the car behind Mr. Wolfe's monuments. Mr. Wolfe and my father often work together serving burial needs for families. My father says Mr. Wolfe will probably have to give up the business since none of his children are following in his footsteps. His youngest son Tom is eighteen and studying at the University of North Carolina. Before he went away to school, Tom and I used to talk when I'd come with my father to look at monuments. Tom wants to write plays. Mr. Wolfe shakes his head and says there's more money to be made in writing epitaphs on tombstones. But writing stories seems to me to be a wonderful thing as even my journal gives me pleasure in putting words on paper.

Because we arrived at the square early, we claimed seats at the base of the monument to Governor Vance. It's a smaller version of the one in Washington, D.C., for President Washington.

Pack Square filled rapidly. The mood was jubilant, given the treaty signed in Paris only days ago. A banner proclaiming "Welcome Home" had been hoisted over the entrance to the courthouse. Although none of the soldiers in Europe at the signing of the treaty

could have returned this quickly, anticipation of vic-
torious homecomings was on everyone's mind.

In the square, veterans strolled in the uniforms
of their wars. I saw cars with the windshield sign
"Men in Service Welcome to Ride" unloading passengers at the edge of the square. I suspected some
of the soldiers were from the Kenilworth Inn—a
fancy hotel above Biltmore Village that was taken
over by the military and renamed "General Hospital 12." Men walked through the crowd in uniforms
from the Spanish-American War and there was a
scattering of blue and gray from the War Between
The States, or as Mr. Galloway calls it The War of
Northern Aggression. These elderly men may have
fought on different sides of the Mason-Dixon Line,
but they saluted each other in a union of pride that
their grandchildren had won The Great War.

Father found us before the band began to play
and the dignitaries further warmed the summer air
with their long-winded speeches. No matter. I enjoyed every minute.

We returned home late in the afternoon and discovered Elijah and his mule waiting at our back
door. He removed his leather hat from his head and
nodded to Mother and me. "Afternoon, Mrs. Youngblood. Henderson." He turned to my father. "May I
trouble you for a word?"

Father gave a quick look to my mother and something unspoken flowed between them.

"Mr. Elijah, would you like to come inside?"
Mother asked. "We have some sassafras in the ice
box that's nice and cool."

"No, ma'am. I'd best keep an eye on Junebug." Elijah cupped his hand over the muzzle of his mule. "But don't you stand out here in the sun on my account."

We were in the shade, but Mother understood Elijah had man talk on his mind. I wanted to hear what Elijah had to say so I fixed my eyes on him so hard that I saw nothing else.

My father said, "Henderson," in that way that meant I was to follow Mother into the house.

"The boy won't bother me none and what I got to ask won't pose no mind to one who's endured the likes he has."

Father said nothing, and I raised myself as high on my crutches as I could to be part of the man talk.

Elijah put his hat back on his head. "I need some burying help."

Now I did pull my eyes off Elijah because I had to see Father. Asheville had Griffins, a Negro funeral home just like they had Negro churches so that everybody kept to their own kind. I'd never seen a burying done any other way.

Father pursed his lips at the very idea. "What kind of help?"

"My uncle Hannable passed over in Cincinnati. He'd gone there from East St. Louis." Elijah added that comment as if it meant something special.

Father nodded.

"He's coming by train to Biltmore Village, but I'd like to carry him the rest of the way so his kinfolk can pay their respects."

"Carry him where?" Father asked.

"The family plot north of Gainesville."

Father's mouth dropped open. "Gainesville, Georgia?"

"Yes, sir. That's why I need motorized transport. Too far for Junebug and a wagon, and Griffins don't have no vehicle much better." He licked his lips and I saw sweat running down his temples. "I've done asked about a Gainesville funeral home coming up here since it's a two-way trip no matter how you skin it."

"A white funeral home?" Father asked.

"No Negro funeral home down there has a motor hearse either." Elijah set his lips tight across his teeth and when he spoke again, his mouth hardly moved. "The Gainesville funeral home told me they didn't want no nigger business." Elijah's eyes dropped to the ground. "We could let out early before sunrise. No one would have to know."

Father's face turned red and I thought he can't get angry at Elijah. What else is the poor man supposed to do? And we owed him. I owed him.

"If we leave before sunrise it'll be because we want an early start on the journey," Father said, "not because of the color of your uncle's skin."

Elijah's face relaxed. "I'll be paying you, Mr. Youngblood. This ain't no charity case."

Father cut his eyes to me and to the shortened leg of my pants tied in a knot where my shinbone used to be. "Don't worry about it."

Elijah took a step forward. "I'm sincere about that. We're doing business here. You'll be put out enough. We'll need to go by way of Greenville and I figure we'll stop in Liberty where my sister's people can feed us and pay their respects. Ain't no other place you and me can eat together."

My father took a deep breath. I knew he'd made up his mind.

"When's the coffin arriving?" he asked.

"Tonight."

"Anything else has to be done?"

"No. The undertaker in Cincinnati did everything. Some folk I know will help load the coffin at the depot and we'll bring it here whenever you tell us."

The next day was Saturday and I knew my father didn't want to travel on the Lord's Day.

Elijah must have figured that too. "We could load up tonight and set off early in the morning. If the weather holds, we could be back before nightfall. You tell me what chores you were planning to do tomorrow and I'll see that they're done."

Father shook his head as if it were the craziest thing he'd ever heard. "All right. You can put the body in the hearse. But that train out of Cincinnati is always late so if you need to stay over use the sleeping porch on the side. We'd better head out around four. It'll be a good sixteen hours, round trip."

"Thank you, Mr. Youngblood." Elijah buried his hand in his pocket and pulled out a wadded red bandana. He unknotted a leather thong tying the four corners together. A roll of greenbacks lay in the center of his palm.

My father shook his head again. "You can pay me something when we get back."

"No, sir. You'll need to fill that hearse with gasoline tonight and a couple extra cans in case we run dry before the stations open." Elijah smiled. "Unless you got that Ford engine tuned for moonshine."

Father laughed and took a couple bills. I laughed too. Mountaineers were always telling revenuers their corn squeezin's were for fuel, not drinking, even though most of them didn't have automobiles.

"What'll you do with your mule?" Father asked.

"I'll see if Mr. Galloway will keep her. If not, one of the men who helps load the coffin can take her tonight." Elijah stuffed his money back in his pocket without retying the bandana and then held out his hand. Father shook it.

I didn't ask if I could go with them. That way Father couldn't tell me no. I wasn't keen on sleeping in the hearse with a dead man, but I figured after the coffin was loaded, no one would look to make sure the occupant hadn't left. By the time Father discovered I was a stowaway, we'd be down the mountain and too far along our way.

Saturday, July 5th: I heard the clock in the parlor strike two. Elijah and his helpers had loaded the coffin in the hearse a little after midnight because the Cincinnati train had been late as Father predicted. For nearly two hours I lay on my bed unable to sleep and with the clock chimes still echoing through the house, I slipped from beneath the sheet fully dressed. By the light of the half moon shining through my window, I wrote a note for Mother telling her I'd gone to Georgia. I didn't want her to worry. Then I affixed my artificial leg, grabbed the pillowcase I'd stuffed with a change of clothes and a heel of bread from the pie safe, and used my crutches to ease out the kitchen door.

In the distance, I heard a dog howl. Close by, I heard the steady snores of Elijah coming from around the corner of the house. He had accepted Father's offer to sleep on the side porch and I took comfort that if the dog didn't wake him, my climb into the back of the hearse probably wouldn't either.

The double doors were latched but unlocked. I realized the problem immediately. Getting into the hearse would be easy, but how could I secure the doors once I was inside? No one built a hearse expecting the rider to get out.

The locking mechanism was a bolt that dropped into a clasp rather than slid into place. I lifted it free and opened the doors. A thin layer of clouds had shrouded the moon and in the dim light, I saw a rough pine coffin strapped down to the floorboards. Elijah's uncle must have been a good-sized man because the coffin seemed larger than standard and the hearse was weighted down several inches. With little play in the springs, I knew the bumps and jolts of the rough roads would jar me every mile of the journey.

I laid my crutches along the left side of the coffin and tossed my pillowcase on the right. I fished my folding knife out of my pocket and then pulled myself inside. The hinges were stiff enough that when the first door closed it stayed shut. I adjusted the drop bolt on the other door so that it hung at an angle over the edge. Then I opened my knife until the blade was perpendicular to the handle, turning it into a hook. I snagged the bolt in the crook of the knife and pulled the door closed. I slipped the blade down the narrow seam until the bolt caught in the clasp. In the blackness, I felt like I was inside a coffin with a coffin. I re-pocketed my knife, crawled back to my pillow case, and lay down. Within a few minutes, I fell asleep.

The squeak of the car door woke me. I nearly cried out before I realized where I was. Father said, "Turn her over," and I heard the crank and then the engine coughed to life. Another sound filled the air: heavy rain pounding on the wooden roof of the hearse. The clouds that had veiled the moon must have been a gathering storm. Going down the mountain in a torrential downpour was an invitation to disaster. If Father missed a turn or hit a washout, the hearse would become my coffin.

Elijah climbed in beside my father. The Model T backfired once in protest and then lurched forward. I was on my way.

Without a clock I could only watch the thin gap between the doors for any—

Nakayla called from the bedroom, "Peters just pulled up. We'd better get down there before he touches anything."

I marked my place in the journal with the inside flap of the dust jacket as Nakayla came down the hall. "This kid had quite a vocabulary. Hard to believe he's only twelve. Shows how bad our education system has gotten in ninety years."

"I thought so too," she said. "How far did you get?"

"The hearse just started down the mountain."

"You can finish it after our little chat with the law."
She opened the door.

"Wait," I said. "Get a bottle of root beer."

"You still thirsty?"

"No. An attitude adjustment for Peters. How can a
man stayed pissed off if you hand him a root beer?"

Nakayla smiled. "I can tell you're a cheap date."

SIX

"STAY HERE. I'LL get the car." Nakayla started down the front steps of the Kenilworth.

"No. I'll walk."

She turned around. "Are you sure?"

"Yes. I've got you to lean on, don't I?"

Her perfect teeth sparkled in the sunlight. "Of course. But I suspect you're a pretty independent guy, Chief Warrant Officer Blackman."

Nakayla understood me. I didn't want the police detective to see her go for her car and then chauffeur me across the parking lot. We began walking, Nakayla holding back to match my pace.

"And don't tell Peters about the journal," I said. "He'll take it in as evidence."

"He'll need to know sometime."

"Not till after I've finished reading it. And I want to look at the files on the table. Your sister had them out for a reason."

"Maybe some of the files are missing," Nakayla said. "I plan to give Armitage a list."

"Maybe. But whoever broke in pulled books off the shelves even though the files were in plain sight. I think your first instinct was right. They wanted the journal."

Detective Peters had parked his unmarked Crown Vic behind Tikima's Avalon. He was bending over the rear tire, probably collecting a specimen of the sandy soil I'd discovered. We were about thirty yards away when he stood up. He must have been six feet tall and thin as a bayonet blade. He was at least fifteen years older than me but his hair didn't have a hint of gray. It was the same sandy-brown color as my own, and with the weight I'd lost in the hospital, I could have passed as his younger brother. He wore a lightweight blue suit and white shirt with a paler blue tie knotted around the unbuttoned shirt collar. Peters could have been a Public Defender or a Clerk of Court—he had the off-the-sale-rack wardrobe that met the minimum standards—except the heavy black shoes branded him as a cop. You can tell a lot about a person from their shoes, and Peters was looking at mine.

I saw his expression change. He'd arrived pissed off, ready to put me in my place. As I lumbered toward him like an arthritic bear, he looked momentarily confused, then pissed off again. Except now he was pissed that he couldn't chomp down on me. Picking on cripples hadn't made for promotions since Nazi Germany. I had a leg up on him and I saw no reason not to kick him with it.

I extended my hand carrying the root beer. "Here, Officer Peters. I thought the mountains were supposed to be cool."

He took a sip and relaxed. "Pretty good. Thanks." He leaned back against the Avalon, then remembered it was evidence and rocked forward on the balls of his feet.

"We can sit on the lawn." Nakayla pointed to a group of Adirondack chairs clustered on the parking lot's grass perimeter.

"I'd like to get off this leg," I said.

"Sounds good to me." Peters gestured for us to lead the way. "Mind if I ask how it happened?"

"I was in the wrong place at the wrong time. Iraq was the wrong place and the wrong time was any and all the time."

We settled in the chairs and I stretched my leg. The tender stump tingled as weight came off it. The doctors had been right about one thing. Wearing the prosthesis cut down on phantom pains. It replaced them with real ones.

Peters took a gulp of the root beer and set the bottle on the wide wooden arm of the chair. "So, what's the military angle on this case? I thought Tikima had been discharged."

"I'm not authorized to comment on what may or may not be the military's interest."

"But you are a Chief Warrant Officer, aren't you?"

"Yes. Most recently with the Criminal Investigation Detachment in Baghdad." I looked over at the Avalon. "I'm more familiar with cars that blow up."

Peters shot a glance at my leg and I let him think a car bomb had injured me. I hadn't lied to him about my past or said that I was officially investigating Tikima's murder. I hoped to get as much information as I could before I had to come completely clean.

Peters shook his head. "Sorry if I came across the wrong way. We shouldn't have missed the footprint and the sand on the inside of the tire. If those two soil samples match, then we'll know a man drove the car some time recently. Unless the specimen is unique, it'll be hard to determine from where."

I nodded. "Maybe. But I saw a lot of sand in Iraq. That was wet sand that clung to the tire and coated the sole of a shoe. Wet sand that might have come from the edge of a river."

From the corner of my eye, I saw Nakayla tense. Since her sister's body had been found in the French Broad, the off-road sand might have come from the site of the killing, or at least the spot where her body was dumped. "Did you check access points upstream?"

"Yes. There are a few places where kayaks and canoes put in."

"What about the fishermen who discovered the body?"

"They'd come on the river about a quarter mile upstream. They had a johnboat on a trailer and needed a spot large enough to unload."

I clasped my hands behind my head and took a deep breath of the fragrant air. "So our killer may have needed a space at least as big."

"Why?" Nakayla asked.

"Unless he lives here at the Kenilworth, he had to have an accomplice follow with a second car. Both vehicles might have been at the river." I turned back to Peters. "Any way to tell how far Tikima's body could have drifted?" I knew these questions were painful to ask in front of Nakayla, but I had no choice.

"Given the weights, I don't believe too far. The site where the fishermen launched would be the limit."

"Why?" I asked.

"Above that the French Broad flows through the Biltmore Estate. No public access and Biltmore has tight security. We'll run tests on the soil at all the access points below Biltmore." He took another drink of root beer and smiled. "I'll let you know what we find."

"Are you going to flatbed the car into police headquarters?"

"Yes."

"And recheck for prints?"

Peters frowned. "We went over it thoroughly the first time."

"Somebody missed the footprint."

He shrugged. "You know how it is. You get focused on fingerprints and miss things that aren't fingerprints."

I just stared at him. It was a lame excuse for botching a forensics investigation and he knew it.

He cleared his throat. "Look. The case file shows the team dusted everywhere, even behind the rearview mirror and we both know most crooks forget to wipe that clean."

"And did they find something there?"

"Yes, but too smudged to be of use."

"Right hand or left?"

"Right, I think. That's the hand you usually use to adjust a rearview mirror."

"Not Tikima Robertson," I said. "Discernible fingerprints or not, that should have attracted somebody's attention."

Detective Peters' face bloomed scarlet. He got out of the chair like it was wired to a thousand-volt generator.

"Where are you going?" I asked.

"To get that flatbed wrecker here. Then my team's crawling over that Avalon with tweezers and a toothpick. I can guaran-damn-tee you if there's anything there, we'll find it."

Nakayla and I watched him hustle to his car.

"You think they screw up all their investigations this way?" she asked.

"I don't know. They thought the car hadn't been moved so they just gave it a quick once over. You started things rolling with the handbrake."

"You noticed it." She rubbed her palms back and forth on her thighs with nervous energy. "I'm glad we've held back the journal."

"I'll finish reading it this afternoon, and then we can decide what to do with it." I looked at Peters' empty chair. A yellow jacket hovered over the open root beer bottle, drawn to the sticky syrup drying on its lip. I'd tried to be sweet to Peters but that didn't mean I still wouldn't get stung. "Did the police go through those files on Tikima's table?"

"No. Peters got a list of Tikima's clients from Armitage at the office."

"Did Tikima usually bring work home?"

"Yes. Particularly new prospects. Her job was to sell them a package of services."

"And are those new prospect files on the table?"

Nakayla's smooth forehead wrinkled. "I don't remember them all. I saw Senior Sanctuaries, a company that runs several rest homes in the area. They've been a client for a number of years. And the Biltmore Company."

"Biltmore Company?"

"Yes. It owns and operates the estate, plus all the side ventures like the winery and hotel."

"Armitage provides them security?"

"No. They've got their own team. Tikima and Armitage did some consulting for them."

Nothing unusual there. But Peters had just mentioned the French Broad flowed through the estate, and from the boy's journal I knew Tikima's great-great grandfather had worked for the Vanderbilts. "When Peters leaves, let's go through those files. Maybe we'll find a connection." I brought up a mental image of the dining table. The folders had been scattered with a book in the center. "Was your sister a fan of Thomas Wolfe?"

"Not that she ever mentioned."

"And that book was with the files?"

"I moved it around some, but yes I found it on the table."

Having a book on Thomas Wolfe in Asheville was no surprise, but I wondered why Tikima didn't leave it by her reading chair rather than with the files and journal. Like the Biltmore Estate and the Vanderbilts, Thomas Wolfe was mentioned in the journal. But what any of that had to do with Tikima's murder in June 2007 was beyond me.

We sat quietly for a few more minutes while Peters talked on his two-way. I couldn't hear what he was saying, but his wild arm gestures indicated something was keeping him riled up. When he hung the mike back on the transceiver, he walked toward us with a face even redder than when he left. I was afraid blood could come squirting out his ears.

He stopped behind his chair and gripped the back so hard the vibration toppled the root beer bottle to the ground. Yellow jackets would be all over the spill within minutes.

"What's wrong?" I asked. "Won't they send a tow truck?"

"What's wrong?" Peters' voice held a steely edge. "I'll tell you what's wrong. Our dispatcher told me she's had two calls about you."

"About me?" I suspected someone had blown the whistle on my little game.

"Nathan Armitage called in a report saying you saw Tikima Robertson the day she disappeared."

"Good. He said he would."

"Why the hell didn't you mention it to me?"

"We haven't finished talking yet. It was next on my list."

Peters' eyes narrowed to slits. "And who assigned you this case?"

I figured if Armitage had phoned in my name he'd also told the police about my circumstances. "I never said I was assigned by anyone. My interest is personal."

"Personal." Peters looked back and forth from Nakayla to me, trying to read how personal it might be. "The dispatcher also said we received a call from the V.A. hospital's security department. A patient named Sam Blackman is missing. He hasn't been discharged and is supposed to be confined to the hospital grounds. Now whether that means you're AWOL or not isn't my concern, but I'm taking you back right now and you're going to tell me everything you know about Tikima Robertson."

I leaned forward in the deep chair and used the armrests to hoist myself up. "Walter Reed was all too glad to get rid of me. I didn't know I'd become such a cherished commodity here."

"Don't flatter yourself. From what I understand your brother's raising holy hell, accusing the military of abducting you." Peters stepped toward me like he was taking me into custody.

My brother. Had Stanley called and then gone ballistic when the staff couldn't find me? I reached out and took Nakayla's hand. "Let me get this sorted out and we'll finish our talk tonight. I'm confident Detective Peters will make headway with these new clues."

Peters wasn't buying my conciliatory act. He stepped

between us, grabbed my elbow, and steered me to the Crown Vic. As we drove away, I saw Nakayla pick up the root beer bottle and walk toward the huge apartment building without so much as a glance over her shoulder.

SEVEN

On the way to the hospital, Peters grilled me about Tikima's visit. I held nothing back because there was precious little to be held back. But I didn't tell him what had occurred since her visit: the discovery of the journal and my suspicion that Tikima had sought me out because of my investigative skills. Peters also wanted to know my plans after my discharge. When I told him I'd be going to Birmingham, he seemed torn between relief that I'd be out of his hair and concern that a potential witness would be leaving town.

As we turned onto the hospital grounds, Peters said, "If you're not being discharged till Friday, I want you to write up a statement about Tikima's visit and any speculation you might have as to why she chose to see you when this place is full of vets."

"I forgot to mention she said Armitage Security Services could have a place for me."

Peters stopped the car at the entrance to the ambulatory wing. "She knew your background?"

"Evidently."

Peters opened his door, and then stayed in his seat. "One thing I'm not clear on. Why did Nakayla take you to Tikima's apartment if she hadn't noticed the handbrake yet?"

The question stopped me for a second. Nakayla and I hadn't worked out our story. I'd come for the journal, but I didn't want Peters to know that. I decided to share my suspicions about Tikima's motive for visiting me. "I had the same question you did. Why did Tikima choose me? So I asked Nakayla how Tikima found out about me. She said her sister had a friend at Walter Reed who told her I was being transferred. I thought if I could discover who that friend was I could make contact and maybe learn what prompted Tikima's interest. I went to the apartment to look for a possible lead. A name in an address book or a Rolodex that I'd recognize."

"And did you?"

"I didn't have time."

Peters cocked his head. "Didn't have time? What were you doing in the apartment while waiting for me?"

"Discussing the implications that someone drove Tikima's car. That sidetracked everything."

I doubted Peters believed me, but he had no other choice.

"Have Nakayla show the names to you here," he said. "Then I'll want to see them." He hopped out and was around to my side of the car before I could stand. "I'm going to deliver you to hospital security and tell them you're not to leave your room unattended."

I stood and gripped the open door for support. "Come on, Detective. How am I supposed to compose a statement sitting in bed while the guy beside me is gasping for breath? I give you my word I'm not going anywhere. I've only got one more day."

"Sam!"

The shout from the hospital entrance came before Peters could reply.

I was shocked to see Stanley hurrying toward us. He wore red plaid pants and a solid red golf shirt. My older brother is shorter and stockier than I am, and he looked like a giant fire hydrant moving along the sidewalk.

"Stanley. What are you doing here?"

He glanced past me and saw the electronic equipment in the unmarked police car. "Are you under arrest?" He turned his wide eyes to Peters.

"No, he's not," Peters said. "He's been helping me with an investigation."

Stanley frowned at me. "I thought you were through with that nonsense."

"That nonsense is the brutal murder of a young woman." Peters leaned forward and towered over my brother.

Stanley backed up, lifting his open palms as if to surrender. "I'm sorry. I was just so worried. The hospital didn't know where Sam was. And with all the trouble he stirred up for the government—" His plea trailed off to a whimper.

I extended my hand to Peters. "Thanks for the ride. You'll get your statement." He'd been a decent guy in front of Stanley and I wanted him to know I appreciated it.

"And Tikima's contact at Walter Reed," Peters added. "We'll talk before you leave."

Stanley and I watched the police car pull away.

"Jesus, Sam. How'd you get involved in a murder?"

"She was a vet I met here." I started toward the hospital entrance, not wanting to go into the story any further.

"Sam, you're walking pretty good. Ashley and I were wondering if we needed to put some handicapped stuff in the house."

"Handicapped stuff?" I entered through the automatic doors stride for stride with Stanley.

"Yeah, a walker, special toilet seat. Whatever the doctor says you need."

Before I could answer, two of the hospital's security team approached us.

"Officer Blackman?" The younger, bulkier man stepped closer. He looked like he could bench press both Stanley and me without any trouble.

"Yes," I said.

"We're to escort you to your room. Dr. Anderson wants to examine you since you've been off the premises." He addressed me like I was a kindergartner who had strayed out of the playground.

"I'm fine," I snapped. "I just walked from the curb. I've been helping Detective Peters." I stepped past the young man flexing his biceps to his companion who looked like a retired cop. "Tikima Robertson's murder."

The older security guard clicked his tongue against the roof of his mouth. "She was a pistol, Tikima was. I'd bet my pension she put up one hell of a fight." He glanced at his partner. "But you've still got to see Dr. Anderson."

"I will. Just give me a few minutes with my brother. He's got to drive back to Birmingham."

Stanley started to speak but I silenced him with a glare.

"We'll use the library if that's all right. Five minutes. Come on, Stanley."

Before either of the guards could object, I set off down the hallway with my bewildered brother in tow. As I hoped, the library was empty. I pointed my brother to a chair and closed the door behind us.

"I'm not being released till Friday. Why are you here two days early?"

Stanley pulled his chair closer to the table as I sat across from him. My brother the banker looked like he was interviewing me for a loan. "Ashley and I thought there were things I'd need to go over with your doctor. We've been reading information online about amputees and the adjustment problems. There's limb shrinkage and psychological stages—"

"And that's why I've been in the god-damned hospitals for four months. I don't intend to become a burden to you and your family."

Stanley reared back and I realized I'd shouted at him.

"I'm sorry. I appreciate your concern, but I don't plan to be at your house for more than a couple weeks. And there's nothing for you to do here except pick me up on Friday. I thought I made that clear over the phone."

Stanley shifted uncomfortably and stared down at the back of his pudgy fingers. "I'll be here Friday, but I'm driving to Winston-Salem this afternoon. There are some issues with Mom and Dad's estate."

"Issues? What kinds of issues?"

"Walt Misenheimer said Galaxy Movers is making a settlement offer tomorrow."

Walt Misenheimer had been a good friend of my parents. With my consent, Stanley had retained him to file a lawsuit against the company that killed our parents. The driver of the Galaxy moving van had failed his drug test, but instead of immediately terminating him, Galaxy had given him a long haul on short turn-around. When the amphetamines burned out, he crossed the median of Highway 52 and slammed head-on into my parents' Buick. They were returning home from their Saturday afternoon run to Walmart. Their lives were lost because Galaxy failed to enforce their own zero-tolerance drug policy. That's how I saw the case.

"Walt said never take the first offer," I said. "Especially when the last thing Galaxy wants is for this to go before a jury."

"That's why I want to be there in person. Make them look me in the eye when they put a price on Mom's and Dad's lives."

"Why didn't you drive straight to Winston-Salem?" I asked. Stanley's fastest route would have been through Atlanta and Charlotte. "You could have picked me up on the way back."

My older brother cleared his throat like a professor beginning a lecture. "I thought we'd have more leverage with Galaxy if I had your power of attorney. You know, make a counter offer that they immediately accept or we take them to court."

Something in Stanley's voice took me back to our childhood when he would try to convince me to spend my birthday money on a toy he wanted.

"Did Walt suggest that?"

"No. I just thought I'd be prepared." He forced a grin. "Walt did say he wanted Galaxy to know you would be a wounded vet appearing in court."

That sounded like a lawyer. Parade me and Stanley's twin babies in front of the jury.

"If I give you power of attorney, won't it have to be notarized?"

Stanley's forced grin slid into a sly smile. "Already done. A notary at the bank understands your situation and completed the paperwork. All you need to do is sign."

I didn't like Stanley springing this request on me, not that an earlier discussion would have made any difference. When our parents were killed, I was in the air between Iraq and Walter Reed with a field dressed wound still raw from triage where saving my leg had been a distant second priority to saving my life. Stanley had borne the brunt of burying our parents and I still felt some guilt about it.

"All right."

Stanley visibly relaxed. "I'll get the papers from the car."

"But I want you to call me before you agree to anything."

"Sure, Sammy." He scurried out of the library leaving me wondering what was really going on.

AFTER THE REQUIRED physical examination by Dr. Anderson proved I'd not been damaged by my unauthorized adventure, I received permission to return to the library. I wrote down my conversation with Tikima for Detective Peters and included my appearance at her funeral. I figured Nathan Armitage had mentioned it in his report and my omission would only make Peters more suspicious of me.

I was giving my statement a final reading when Nakayla entered. She carried a large paper shopping bag in one hand and a thermos in the other.

"Glad to see you're here and not in jail," she said.

"Not much difference. Although I'm sure I'd look cuter in an orange jumpsuit." I waved her to the chair Stanley had occupied several hours earlier. "Did you bring me some reading material?"

"Yes. You can finish the journal. I also brought the

Armitage Security files Tikima had in the apartment."
She handed me the journal and set the stack of files
between us. Then she laid the Thomas Wolfe biography alongside it.

"Why'd you bring this?" I asked.

"Because it was with the other things. And I noticed
Tikima had written the words *Ted Mitchell*, that's the
author's name, and a phone number on the first page."

"Who's the phone number?"

"I assume Ted Mitchell. He lives here and works at
the Wolfe Memorial."

"What about the friend at Walter Reed? Did you find
that number?"

Nakayla nodded. "I called every 202 area code in
her address book until I struck gold. Maria Costello."

The name didn't sound familiar. "Is she a nurse?"

"Works Physical Therapy. She said everyone calls
her Cookie."

I laughed as I remembered the rotund, dark-haired
woman in PT who was always smiling no matter how
much I complained. "Cookie. Never knew her real
name. We called her that because she would reward you
with a chocolate chip cookie if you completed everything in your therapy session. If you didn't, she ate it."

"Cookie and Tikima had stayed in touch. You evidently made an impression on her."

"Because I always got Cookie's cookie."

Nakayla spread her fingers on the top of the table
as she got to the heart of her story. "When you were
transferred to Black Mountain, Cookie told Tikima that
she had a live one coming. Both had been upset by the
conditions at Walter Reed and Cookie told Tikima you
were being exiled away from the media."

"A little late. The bedpan had hit the fan by then."

"Tikima had wanted to talk to you, but Cookie said my sister really got interested when she learned you had been in the Criminal Investigation Detachment."

"Did Cookie say why?"

Nakayla leaned closer. "She said it was personal. That justice was long overdue and she needed someone to help who wasn't part of Asheville's history."

"History?" I looked at the journal and then the Thomas Wolfe biography. "We've got plenty of history. Wish I knew what to do with it."

Nakayla pointed to the journal. "For starters, read it."

I flipped through the yellowed pages and found where I'd left off. The date was Saturday, July 5, 1919. Henderson had just sneaked inside the hearse. The kid sure told a good story.

EIGHT

ELIJAH CLIMBED IN beside my father. The Model T back-fired once in protest and then lurched forward. I was on my way.

Without a clock I could only watch the thin gap between the doors for any sign of daylight.

If Elijah and my father spoke to each other, their words were too low for me to hear over the sound of the engine and pounding rain. At times the jolts from the bumpy road knocked the breath from my lungs, but the scariest moments happened when the rear end would fishtail, the tires sloshing as the dirt roads turned to mud. I wasn't afraid that the hearse would slide into a ditch. I was afraid the hearse would slide off the mountain. We were on the same road we had taken from Spartanburg when Father purchased the hearse, a snaking, narrow way that in places had been carved out of the mountainside.

For several hours, I lay in terror with only the single thickness of pine boards between me and a dead man. The storm clouds must have been thick because the road had leveled before even a hint of gray marked the seam between the doors. I breathed easier knowing we were in the flatlands and the danger of tumbling into a ravine had passed.

The downpour continued and the Model T crawled along through what must have been a blinding torrent. At this speed, we would be lucky to make Georgia by nightfall let alone return home by Sunday. As the morning light brightened, the air in the hearse grew warm and heavy. My leg began to hurt. I slipped the support strap off my shoulder and pulled my phthisic stump clear of the socket. The pain eased. I lay back down and the rocking of the floorboards softened to a gentle sway. Somewhere outside of Greenville I fell asleep.

A door slammed and I awoke with a start. The hearse wasn't moving. Sunlight streamed through the slit between the doors. I heard Father's voice and then Elijah calling out to someone. In less than a minute, three other people spoke, but they were too far away for me to understand the words. Then I heard the chattering of children.

The inside of the hearse had become as hot as an oven and I was afraid Father would go off to discuss burial arrangements. My parents had warned me about playing in empty boxcars in the Asheville freight yard. Children had accidentally been locked in and died of the heat. I scrabbled around and crawled to the rear doors. Propping myself on my good knee, I pounded my fists against the mahogany planks. Outside a woman screamed.

This was not the way I'd wanted to reveal myself to Father.

The doors swung open and daylight burst in like an exploding Fourth of July rocket. I flung my forearm over my eyes and squinted against the brilliance. Black silhouettes backed away, some running, some stumbling. They must have thought I'd crawled out of the coffin.

One figure remained, and as my eyes adjusted, I saw Father scowling at me.

"What do you think you're doing?" he asked.

My mouth went dry. I looked beyond him to Elijah who drew closer. He stared at me and then at the coffin as if I might have damaged it somehow. Behind him, a few Negro men and women froze, the panic in their faces replaced by curiosity. A girl of no more than four peeked around the faded floral skirt of a bone thin woman who must have been her mother.

Father slapped his hand hard against the floorboard. "I asked you a question, Henderson."

I didn't want to be disciplined by my father in front of these people. I didn't have a convenient lie so I grabbed at a convenient truth. "You never said I couldn't come. I didn't want Mr. Elijah to have to ride in the back."

The color rose in his face and I realized I had insulted him. My father wasn't like so many others in town who called Elijah and his people niggers or made them give way on the sidewalk. He would have made me ride in the back just like I did when we brought the hearse up the mountain from Spartanburg.

"I'm sorry," I sobbed. "I didn't want to be left behind." Blinded by tears, I swept my hand around, clutched my artificial leg, and lifted it over my head. "Left behind with this."

"You could have asked me," Father said. I heard the hurt in his voice.

All my posturing vanished and I let the leg fall against the coffin with a loud clatter. My chest heaved and I buried my face in my hands. Father let me cry.

After a few minutes, he said, "And I could have asked you."

I raised my head. Father reached out his hands to help me down.

No one spoke while I leaned against the hearse and attached my leg. The sun shone directly overhead, pulling steam out of the soaked ground. Sweat rolled into my eyes.

My father leaned in the hearse. "I'll get your crutches."

"Too wet. They'll sink."

We were parked about fifty feet from the main road, and if there had ever been gravel on this driveway, it had long ago been beaten beneath the surface.

"Where are we going?" I asked.

"In for lunch," Elijah replied. "This here's my cousin Bessie's on my mother's side."

Father took my arm and we walked around the hearse. About twenty yards away stood a small one-story farmhouse. A buckboard wagon had been unhitched in front. In its bed, bushel baskets were filled with peaches and I guessed Bessie's family was either taking them to market or selling them to passing cars. In the shade underneath the wagon, chickens and guinea hens pecked at worms and grubs driven up by the rain.

As we walked, the others fell in behind us like Father and I were leading a parade. Beyond the house, I spied a well and three outbuildings—a barn with doors open on either end to let air pass through, a shed with a tin roof that sheltered a smithy, and an outhouse set farthest from the well. Its door opened and an older woman came out still arranging her dress.

"There's Bessie," Elijah said. "These are her children and grandchildren. Bessie's man fell under a hay mower a couple years back. Her kinfolk are trying to get her to move north where they can get good jobs. Can't say as I disagree. Ain't no future in sharecropping."

As the woman came closer, she fixed her sharp eyes on me and then glanced at Elijah.

"One more for lunch," Elijah said. "This is Mr. Youngblood's son Henderson."

"Nice to meet you, ma'am," I said.

She smiled. "A well-spoken lad." She turned to my father. "Thank you kindly for bringing Uncle Hannable so we can pay our respects."

Then I noticed that everyone including the four-year-old were in their Sunday-go-to-meeting clothes. "Are we in Georgia?"

"Liberty, South Carolina," Father said. "The deceased is to be buried in a family plot in Georgia."

I remembered Elijah saying that yesterday and how this was the only place we could eat together because of what they call the Jim Crow laws.

"I was left a little piece of land that was the old homestead," Elijah said. "Mail the tax money in every year. It's overgrown now because the ground's hilly and doesn't take easily to a plow. But when I quit working for Mrs. Vanderbilt, I aim to set that right."

Father helped me up the two plank steps to the front porch. As we walked by the wagon, the pungent odor of ripe peaches hung in the air. Miss Bessie must have seen me eyeing them.

"We'll give you a gunny sack of those peaches to take with you. Folks in Georgia make a big to-do over their peaches, but to me there's nothing better than a South Carolina peach."

She opened the screen door and nodded for Father and me to enter. "Everything's just about ready. There's a wellspring in the kitchen if you'd like a cool drink or to splash some fresh water on your face."

I noticed no one else but Miss Bessie, Father, and I had come up on the porch. I entered the house first. The front room was small and a single table stood in the center with one chair facing away from the window and placed before a plain white china plate and dull utensils.

"We brought the kitchen table out here so it won't be so hot. I'll get another plate for the boy."

Father caught the woman's arm as she passed. "Isn't anyone else eating with us? Elijah?"

Miss Bessie turned and looked as proper as any school mistress including Miss Nettles. "You are my guests. The others will eat outside after you've been served." She pulled a second chair from a corner of the room and set it on the near side to Father's.

I looked over my shoulder and saw the younger woman with the child now standing in front of the screen door. The youngster pressed her face against the mesh, bowing it in until it wrapped around her features like a metal veil. Here we were at the only place on our journey where coloreds and whites could eat together and we weren't eating together.

Father and I sat and Miss Bessie brought another set of utensils. She picked up Father's plate. "I'll carry the food hot from the kitchen. I hope you don't mind having your Sunday dinner on Saturday."

"We're honored by your thoughtfulness," Father said.

As soon as Miss Bessie disappeared, I asked, "Why are we here by ourselves? Shouldn't you insist we all eat together rather than make them wait outside?"

Father smiled and shook his head. "The point is that because we can all eat together, they are offering this privilege on their terms. I wouldn't take Elijah's money and he understands that. But to not take a man's hospitality is something else. Remember that, Henderson, and show your appreciation by cleaning your plate."

Having had no breakfast and smelling the tantalizing aromas of fried chicken and cornbread would make that an easy obligation.

"But I'll insist there be no second helpings until everyone else has eaten," Father said.

"Yes, sir. How much longer till we reach the burial site?"

Father pulled his silver pocket watch from his trousers. "Now that the weather's cleared we'll make better time. I reckon between four and five o'clock. We'll have a couple of hours of daylight. We've probably got to dig the grave."

"There's nobody at the cemetery to do that?"

"There's no cemetery. It's a family plot and Elijah's the only member who's going to be there. He said he'll take a shovel and pickax from here. I'll help as much as he'll let me."

Miss Bessie returned with two plates heaped high with a thigh and drumstick each, snap beans, mashed potatoes, and cornbread soaked with butter. "You want sweet milk or sweet peach tea?" she asked.

Father looked at me to answer first.

"What's peach tea?"

"Sun-brewed tea with peach juice squeezed in. Mighty delicious."

"That's what I'll have, please."

"Make that two, please," Father said.

"Eat slowly," Miss Bessie said. "I want you to save room for dessert." She rested her hand lightly on my shoulder. "Guess what that's gonna be."

"Peach pie?"

She laughed and patted my head. "You've got a smart boy, Mr. Youngblood. A smart boy."

I ate my fill, careful not to wolf down large bites, which would have raised my mother's eyebrows had she been there.

Before dessert, Father slid back his chair and loosened his belt a notch. "If I had extra money, I'd open up a diner for Bessie in Asheville. That woman knows how to cook."

Miss Bessie came into the room with two slices of steaming peach pie. From the smile on her face, I knew she'd heard Father's compliment.

As we prepared to leave, Elijah laid a shovel and pickax in the narrower space between the coffin and side of the hearse. "I'll ride back here," he said. "Henderson's done taken the rough road."

"No," I said. "I'm more comfortable where I can stretch out my leg." Truth be told, sitting in the passenger seat would have been much better than bouncing on the floor.

"Let's keep the doors open so Henderson has more air," Father said. "We can tie them against the sides." He crawled in the hearse searching for extra rope and then looked at the coffin. "Elijah, did you use them all?"

"Yes, sir. With the rain, I didn't want the load shifting on some slippery curve."

For the first time I took a good look at the coffin. Four lengths of rope stretched across its width and were tied to the recessed eyehooks in the heavy plank flooring.

"We won't need the middle two," Father said. "Henderson, squeeze up on the other side and untie the ends."

I wormed my way over the shovel and pickax where I could attack the knots. While I was undoing the second one, I noticed one of the nails in the coffin lid was bent over and smashed into the wood. Hammer claw marks scratched the grain around several others. The Cincinnati undertaker needed better craftsmanship. Father would never have done such a poor job.

We stopped at a general store in the next town of Westminster for gasoline. The owner filled the tank and the two spare cans Father stored under the front seat. Then we followed him inside to pay at the register. Elijah bought me a handful of penny candy.

"We'll be coming back through tonight," Father told the man. "What time do you close?"

The old fellow stroked his scrawny beard and then hooked his thumbs in the suspenders of his bib overhauls. "I lock the pumps at five o'clock. Won't open up till seven Monday morning, tomorrow being the Lord's Day and all."

"Anybody else open later?" Father asked.

"Nope. Not in Westminster. Might be somebody back in Easley, but I don't know for sure." He risked a quick glance at the hearse and whispered, "You got a body out there?"

"Yes. Bound for Gainesville."

The man shook his head. "Even if you and your boy just unload it, you won't make it back to Easley in time."

I knew the boy he meant was Elijah, not me.

The man shifted his wad of tobacco from one cheek to the other. "Course, I reckon I could let you pay in advance."

"Pay in advance?" Father asked.

"Yep. I got a storage shed out back and could leave a couple cans filled. Nobody would bother them."

"But I won't know how much I need."

"There's that." The old man leaned across the counter. "I figure two five-gallon cans ought to do it. At two bits a gallon that would come to two-fifty."

Father thought about it.

"You can trust me," the man said. "Give me the money and the gas will be there."

"I don't think she'll take ten gallons."

The man shrugged. "Suit yourself."

Elijah looked at my father and then the man behind the counter. "Sir, how about we buy five gallons in advance. You leave the extra can and we'll pay for any more we use."

"You can trust me," Father added, giving back the storeowner his own words.

The man's sallow face colored. "Ain't that I don't trust you. What if somebody else takes the gasoline?"

"Then you're saying you'd rather me lose all my money?"

Father and Elijah had snared the man in his own words. He was either saying he couldn't trust my father or he'd lied when he said no one would bother the cans.

Elijah jingled the coins in his pocket. "Mr. Youngblood, what if I paid this gentleman an extra nickel a gallon for his kindness. That way he'd have a dollar fifty instead of a dollar and a quarter. And I'd pay the extra nickel on any more gas we took from the second can, since it might be hard to measure it out proper."

The storeowner eyed Elijah as if seeing him for the first time. It must have dawned on him that Elijah had paid for my candy and he had even more money to spend. "That'll probably be all right." He spit a stream of brown juice into a cup by the cash register. Then he chuckled. "Shoot fire, if I can't trust an undertaker, who can I trust? You'd be the last man to let me down." Then he laughed his head off with a high-pitched giggle.

Father joined in, even though he'd heard that joke a thousand times. Elijah gave me a wink as he slid his coins across the counter.

We drove from Westminster to Toccoa, Georgia, and on through Cornelia and Baldwin. I'd never been to Georgia before and it didn't look any different than South Carolina. As I bit into one of Miss Bessie's peaches, I wondered if she'd been teasing me about them.

The closer we came to Gainesville the more hills we encountered. A couple times I had to grab onto the coffin's ropes to keep from sliding. Elijah gave my father directions that became more descriptive— left at the split willow or right at the mossy rock. The last leg of the journey whittled down to not much more than a trail across a scruffy pasture. The only sign of civilization was a stone chimney, the relic of a cabin either burned or rotted down to the ground. Through the open hearse, I watched it grow smaller.

Then the hearse stopped and Father cut the engine. Out of the sudden stillness rose the gurgling of water. We were near a stream.

I grabbed my crutches for aid on the uneven terrain and found Father and Elijah standing in front of the hearse. Ahead, a small square of ground had been marked by a picket fence, long reduced to broken, faded slats. Four boulders, flattened and chiseled on one side, rose above the weeds. The headstones weren't like the finely carved and polished monuments that Mr. Wolfe provided for my father's customers, but out in this wild, unkempt place, they seemed appropriate. In the lower corner of the family plot, a mound of turned earth at least a yard high showed where Elijah's Uncle Hannable would be buried. Beyond the far side of the fence, the land dropped off and I knew the stream ran at the bottom of the slope. Cattle must have grazed here at one time, roaming outside the graveyard's perimeter and drinking freely from the water below.

I hobbled closer and looked over the fence down into the empty pit. "Mr. Elijah, who dug the grave?"

"Some of my cousin Bessie's people came after I wired them about Hannable."

I edged nearer to the rickety gate alongside the open hole. From the pile of dirt sprouted seedlings of broom straw and rabbit tobacco. Evidently, the mound had sat there some time and I wondered how long the body had been in Cincinnati. The coffin maker lacked carpentry skills but the embalming procedure must have been first rate. I'd smelled not a whiff of decomposition.

As if reading my mind, Elijah said, "Uncle Hannable languished for awhile. We knew his time was drawing nigh."

Father unhitched the gate and stepped past the grave. "Are these your parents?" He knelt down to examine one of the hand-hewn stones.

"Yes. And my grandparents on my father's side. Old Mr. McAlway owned this property and he'd owned my grandparents before the war. They were house servants in Atlanta and when Mr. McAlway had to give them their freedom, he gave them a piece of land so as they'd keep an eye on his hunting property. Mr. McAlway had planted grain here to lure in the quail so it was easy to convert it to farm pasture."

Mr. Elijah walked over to the far stone. "We picked this spot to Granddaddy's liking. He'd fish down in that stream. Taught me to catch trout. The gravesites are high enough to be clear of spring floods, and nobody bothers them back here."

My father stood up and looked around. Overhead

a hawk shrieked as it soared toward a copse of pines. "Are you the last of the line?"

"I've got a son in Chicago. Too far for him to help me. He told me he wants to come to Asheville when he's earned enough money. But he doesn't feel much connection to this place."

"Your wife in Asheville?" Father asked.

"Sarah died in Chicago in 1902 when our boy was 17. I'd been down here working for Mr. Olmsted and I'd go north every winter when the ground froze up. I'd first worked for Mr. Olmsted when he was doing the Chicago World's Fair. When he learned I was from around these parts, he wanted me to help with the Vanderbilt commission. That was in 1893." Elijah shook his head. "Mr. Olmsted could look at a piece of land and see every plant, tree, and stream he would put there, whether it was one acre or a hundred thousand acres."

"He put in streams?" Father asked.

"Diverted them. We changed the channel for the stream going into the Vanderbilt estate. Mr. Olmsted wanted the carriage road to go alongside it and put that natural feeling into the guests so they knew they were leaving the city behind."

My father stood and moved to another stone. "Your parents came here with them?"

"No. Only after granddaddy died. I was twelve when they came to work the land. I spent five years here with no other company except nature and the school books my momma got from the county. She was stricter than any teacher would have been."

"And then you moved to Chicago?" Father asked.

"I wanted to go someplace I could use my education. I met my wife in 1883 and we had a good life. But when Mr. Olmsted brought me back to the mountains, it was like my soul being rejoined to my body." He took a deep breath. "Well, we'd best get that coffin in the ground. I want to find a stone for the head. Then I'll be back someday to set a proper marker."

Father positioned the hearse as close to the grave as possible. He and Elijah used the ropes to lower the coffin into the ground. The hole wasn't as deep as some I'd seen.

Elijah shoveled the dirt on top of the lid with quick rhythmic strokes. In a short time, the grave was filled. He patted the earth into a rounded crest with the flat of the blade and then grabbed the pickax. "I'll find a stone and then we can be on our way. Always good rocks in the stream."

"Let me help you," Father said, and he followed Elijah down the slope.

I sat beside a headstone, not wanting to be disrespectful by squatting on a grave. I brushed away a thin layer of moss. Crude letters had been notched into the rock: Annabelle Robertson—born 1823, died 1881. She would have been Elijah's grandmother. Born a slave and died a free woman on her own piece of land. Without standing, I crawled to a second marker. Obadiah Robertson—born 1844, died 1902. Elijah's father, also a slave.

I wondered how old Elijah was. The far grave must have been his grandfather's. Elijah said his parents came here when his grandfather died. Elijah had been twelve. The same age as me. I read the stone. Malachi Robertson—born 1819, died 1875.

Malachi, Obadiah, Elijah. A family of prophets. Elijah would have been born a slave in 1863. Even I could see that held no claim on his life. A slave was something somebody else made you, not who you really were. Mr. Elijah was wise. He had helped move streams. He had gotten the gasoline for our return home. He had saved my life.

Sunday, July 6th: I spent most of the day writing the entry for yesterday's journey to Elijah's property. Our return trip was uneventful and not worth recording, other than we got home at four in the morning and father excused me from attending church. Mr. Elijah slept on our porch again until a respectful hour when he could retrieve his mule from Mr. Galloway.

Mother fixed breakfast for all of us before she and my father left for the Sunday service. I was told to go back to bed, but I sat on the porch with Elijah and listened to his stories about the building of the Vanderbilt mansion. He spoke reverently of Mr. Olmsted, like we were having our own church service except Mr. Olmsted was the creator.

"As smart as that man was," Elijah said, "he'd listen to my ideas. I liked geology, how the shape of the land comes from what's under it. 'Build your house upon a rock,' the Good Book says. So I wanted to know where the best rock lay, and where the seams were if you had to split and move it. How the water would flow and what the streams can tell us about their source. The great flood back in 1916 should have come as no surprise. Earthen dams can't hold the runoff from these mountains."

Almost three years ago, July 16th, Biltmore Village and the west side of Asheville had nearly been wiped out when two hurricanes moved through the mountains in less than a week. Two lakes burst upstream and the French Broad and Swannanoa turned deadly. I knew families whose farms had been destroyed and children drowned.

Mr. Elijah took his leave. The hour wasn't quite eleven, but a decent enough time to call on Mr. Galloway.

I went back to bed and fell asleep. A noise at my open window awakened me. Mr. Elijah stood outside with his mule.

"Sorry to disturb you, Henderson. Mr. Galloway must have been at church, but I left him some money for his troubles. I couldn't find Junebug's pack, so I'd appreciate it if you or your father would ask about it if you see Mr. Galloway first."

I promised to tell Father and said I'd be checking on my pony Brownie at the stable tomorrow.

Then Mr. Elijah said a strange thing. "It might be best if you and your father didn't tell anyone where we went yesterday. Let that be our secret. Someday maybe I can reward you for your help if you come visit me in Georgia."

"You're moving?" I asked.

"I think the Lord is leading me there, Henderson. The time may be soon." He doffed his leather hat and turned away.

Wednesday, July 9th: This evening Dr. Lynch came banging on our door during supper. He apologized to Mother for interrupting and then asked to speak to Father outside. Mother and I waited in the kitchen where she put on a pot of fresh coffee. The aroma had filled the room when Father returned. His face was gray as wood ash. Dr. Lynch followed.

"Would you like coffee?" Mother asked.

"Thank you, but no," Dr. Lynch said. He looked to my father.

"I'm afraid I have some bad news," Father said. "Dr. Lynch came to tell me that Elijah Robertson was pulled from the French Broad River this afternoon. He's dead."

My stomach knotted up. In my mind I saw Elijah at my window with Junebug. "No," I blurted out. "That can't be. He was too smart. He knew the river better than anybody."

Dr. Lynch stepped forward. "Son, it's hard for any of us to believe." Again, he looked to my father, but my father only nodded.

"Elijah didn't drown," Dr. Lynch said. "He had been beaten."

Mother gasped and collapsed on a chair at the table. Father came to her side. The air in the kitchen got heavy, almost smothering me. Tears blurred Dr. Lynch's kind face and I felt his hand on my shoulder.

"I've reported the circumstances of his death to the sheriff and Asheville police chief. More importantly, I've told Mrs. Vanderbilt. She will make sure they look into it. She's the one who asked me to fetch your father so we can prepare for the burial at Mt. Zion."

I wiped my eyes. "Mr. Elijah wanted to go to Georgia. He told me."

"Georgia?" Dr. Lynch turned to my father. "Is this true?"

"Yes. He has property there, but he's very active at Mt. Zion, and maybe that would be—"

"No," I interrupted. "He told me himself. The Lord was calling him. He should be buried there."

"I'll talk to Mrs. Vanderbilt," Dr. Lynch said. "She offered to take care of expenses, but she thought he'd be interred in Asheville."

"Elijah has a son," Father said. "If Mrs. Vanderbilt has a way to reach him, then he can make the decision."

Mother lifted her face from her hands. "We have our son because of Elijah. For God's sake, take the man where he wanted to be."

I knew Mother's words touched Father's heart. If Elijah's son consented, we'd again make the trip to the graveyard by the stream.

And I remembered Elijah's words: Tell no one where we went. I had just broken that promise.

Vocabulary and style getting away from him. Ask Harry about the mule.

"What does this mean?" I swung the journal around and pointed to the words written at an angle across the bottom of the page. "Vocabulary and style getting away from him. Ask Harry about the mule."

Nakayla only glanced at them. "I don't know. Seemed odd to me when I read it."

I flipped through the remaining pages of the journal, but they were all blank. "Did Henderson stop and then somebody else wrote a criticism? And who's Harry?"

"Was that Mr. Galloway? He had the mule."

"I don't think so." I searched the front of the journal. "Only Galloway's son Jamie is named. The one who was killed in France." I closed the leather cover, convinced of what we had to do next. "Detective Peters needs to know what we've got. If Mrs. Vanderbilt pressed for an investigation, there might be a file still in existence."

Nakayla shook her head. "Get real. A file on a black man's murder from nearly ninety years ago? Even the Vanderbilts didn't have that kind of clout. There are pictures from those days of the uniformed police and robed Klan attending a public funeral as mourners. You think Elijah Robertson mattered to them?"

"Tikima matters today. Maybe Peters can make the connection."

"You were the one who didn't want to lose control of the journal," she said.

"When I thought it could help us, and before I met Peters. The handbrake on Tikima's car humbled him enough that he's focused on the case." I reached for the folders that had been on Tikima's dining room table. "Anything come to light from these?"

"No. I've listed the companies on top."

On a sheet of yellow legal paper, Nakayla had printed six names: Senior Sanctuaries, The Biltmore Company, U.S. Forestry Service—Pisgah National Forest, Gold for the Taking, Woolworth Walk, and The Thomas Wolfe Memorial.

"Interesting that the Wolfe Memorial and this biography of Wolfe were together," I said.

"The memorial's more of a museum. They're a client, as are the rest of the companies. The author, Ted

Mitchell, works at the memorial." Nakayla turned over the book and pointed to a phone number handwritten on the white label with the barcode and price. "This is Tikima's writing. The phone number isn't for the memorial. I cross-checked through my computer and it's Ted Mitchell's home."

"Did you call it?"

"No. I wanted to wait until we decided what questions to ask him."

I opened the file marked Wolfe Memorial. Several documents on Armitage Security Services letterhead outlined an installation proposal for equipment and monitoring. There was a list of employees with job descriptions and access requirements. Ted Mitchell's name had been circled. The last stapled section was an executed contract between the memorial and Armitage. Tikima's signature appeared on the line as the Armitage Security Services Representative.

"Tikima was interested in Ted Mitchell," I said. "I hope she didn't just borrow the book from him."

"Wolfe's mentioned in the journal. Maybe Tikima was looking for facts to support the journal's story."

I set the file aside and re-examined the book. *THOMAS WOLFE—An Illustrated Biography*. Ted Mitchell was credited as the editor. The pages were filled with illustrations, photographs, and photocopies of Wolfe's manuscripts. I studied an excerpt from *Look Homeward, Angel*. The page was written in longhand. Suddenly, one little word jumped out at me. I held the place and grabbed the journal. The very first sentence confirmed my suspicion.

"Come here," I told Nakayla. "Look at this."

She walked around the table and leaned over my shoulder.

I pointed to the top sentence of Wolfe's handwriting. "See the word *of*, how he writes it as one character with the *o* just hinted at. The same all through this page." I moved my finger over to the first sentence of Henderson Youngblood's journal. "And here."

I was born in the year 1907, in the city of Asheville, of a good family, and given the Christian name Henderson, the surname of my mother's relatives in the neighboring county which also bears that name.

I touched the three handwritten "ofs."

Nakayla's finger brushed my own, as if she had to feel it herself. "They're the same. The handwriting's identical."

"Yes. Henderson Youngblood didn't write this journal. Thomas Wolfe did."

NINE

"WE NEED TO talk with this Mitchell guy as soon as possible," I said. "Tikima might have gotten information from him that put her in danger."

Nakayla pulled her cell phone from her purse and punched in the number Tikima had written. After a few seconds, she said, "His answering machine. Should I leave a message?"

"Yes. Tell him you're Tikima's sister and you need to speak to him."

The beep sounded from the receiver. "Mr. Mitchell, I'm Tikima Robertson's sister, Nakayla. She left me some information you might find interesting. Please call me." Nakayla gave her cell number and flipped the phone closed.

"If he works at the Wolfe Memorial, maybe he's there now." I looked through the file and passed Nakayla the number.

Whoever answered told Nakayla that Ted Mitchell was off and would return Friday. She should call back then.

"Maybe he's out of town," Nakayla suggested.

"Maybe. But see him first thing Friday morning."

Nakayla's brown eyes widened. "Won't you come with me?"

"I'm supposed to go to Birmingham. Stanley will be anxious to get back."

"I'm not sure what to ask Mr. Mitchell and he might be the key to everything. We could go by as soon as you're discharged. We'd delay your brother no more than an hour."

Nakayla's plea drove straight to my heart. "All right. I can hold Stanley up an hour or so. I'll try to get out of here early." I patted the journal. "We know your great-great grandfather was murdered. I hope Mitchell can help us separate more facts from fiction."

Nakayla rested her hand on the journal next to mine. "I'd like to know who gave Tikima this. We're a family who's always been proud of our heritage. This wouldn't have been kept a secret."

"Maybe she told Mitchell where she got it." I slid the journal away. "Let's see what we can learn from the rest of the files."

Nakayla pulled her chair around to my side of the table.

"Did Tikima ever talk about any of these clients?" I asked.

Nakayla tapped the Biltmore Company file. "She had a season pass to the estate. She said it was her only perk."

"How many times can you see a house?"

"A house whose interior takes up four acres? Quite a few times. But the gardens and winery were her favorites. We'd go there to picnic and pretend the estate belonged to us." Nakayla looked me in the eye. "It does in a way. Starting with Elijah, our family helped build it. Free men and honest labor. We can still see the work they left behind."

I sorted through the Biltmore documents while Nakayla explained them.

"Tikima negotiated an annual contract that included a review of their security procedures and a rate should Armitage provide extra personnel."

I skimmed the five-page contract. "Were they having crime problems?"

"No, but at peak seasons like Christmas and the summer, Armitage supplies supplemental guards. They usually work the service entrances and other points where they don't have to interact with visitors."

"Why?"

"Biltmore stresses guest satisfaction. All employees are trained to make visitors feel welcomed and give them information about the estate. Tikima's security people just don't know enough to be able to do that."

"How many guards does Armitage carry on its payroll?"

"About two hundred."

I whistled. "That's a lot of employees?"

"But when you figure many of the clients have round-the-clock needs, the manpower required mounts up."

"So, a number of Armitage guards would know the back roads and entrances to the Biltmore Estate?"

"I guess so. None of them work there permanently. They rotate in and out. What are you thinking?"

"I'm just wondering if Tikima asked any of the Armitage guards to look out for something, not only at Biltmore but with any of these clients." I waved my hand over the files.

Nakayla looked doubtful. "You mean she took someone into her confidence?"

"Not necessarily. More like made a special request or asked a question that might sound out of the ordinary."

"Do you think all of the guards need to be interviewed?"

I shook my head. "But ask Armitage if the police spoke with any of the guards at these sites. He'll make the connection and probably speak to them himself." I didn't tell Nakayla I intended to mention the guards to Peters after he got the files. Since Tikima's body had been discovered downstream from the Biltmore Estate, I couldn't assume Armitage guards weren't involved. Better to have simultaneous internal and external investigations going on in case Tikima had uncovered wrongdoing in her own company.

"Maybe Tikima asked something of the wrong guard," Nakayla said.

Her brain and mine were in lockstep. I smiled, impressed that her grief hadn't clouded her thinking. "At this point, you're smart not to rule anything out." I grabbed the next folder. "Gold for the Taking. There's an enticing phrase."

"A mine-it-yourself tourist attraction. You buy a bucket of dirt to sift in a water sluice. You keep what you find."

I opened the file. A few photographs of the site were taped to the inside flap. A big sign on a hillside glittered with gold letters—GOLD FOR THE TAKING—and had a cartoon of a prospector lifting a nugget the size of his fist. There was a photo of a gift shop and another of kids lined up at what looked like a feeding trough. The papers in the file included quotes for security hardware and overnight guards. "Does the company need security for what they pick from the ground or what they pick from the tourists' pockets?"

"A little of both," Nakayla said. "They salt the buckets with semi-precious gemstones and fool's gold. But at least they're honest about it. You can also buy buckets of native dirt if you're a purist."

"Anybody ever find anything?"

"Yes. A few years ago an eight-year-old girl found an emerald estimated to be worth over twenty-five thousand dollars. It was in all the papers."

"I bet the sluice was hopping the next day."

"For a few weeks." Nakayla pointed to the picture of the gift shop. "They have a display case in there of some of the gemstones that have been discovered. Tikima installed the security system."

"Do they buy the gems back?"

"No. These are examples of what the family's unearthed over the years." Nakayla pointed to the signatures on the contract. "Phil and Judy Ledbetter. They own over a hundred acres and have reserved the most promising areas for commercial mining. Every few years you'll hear of some huge emerald or sapphire they've discovered. The tourists don't set foot on those sites."

"Is this near the Biltmore Estate?"

"No connection. Gold for the Taking is over ten miles outside of Asheville in the other direction, closer to Black Mountain and this hospital."

I set the file aside. The next folder was labeled Woolworth Walk. "What's this?"

"A place downtown. It used to be a Woolworth Five and Dime, but now people rent booths. All sorts of arts and crafts."

"Like a studio?"

"No. Like an arts department store. Painters, woodworkers, sculptures, and jewelry designers sell their creations. Tikima dealt with the building owners when they installed a security system."

A paperclip held a note card to the inside of the folder. Tikima had written two names: Herman Duringer and Malcolm Grant. I flipped to the last page of the contract. The signature read Andy Culpepper. "Did the building change hands?"

Nakayla studied the names. "Not that I know of. The store's not a big client. Tikima rarely mentioned it."

The next file proved to be the thickest one. The U.S. Forestry Department—Pisgah National Forest. Most of the papers were government contracts, bids, and completed application forms to be an approved Federal vendor.

"Don't tell me Armitage supplies freelance rangers," I said.

"Hardly. The National Park Service has some gift shops and exhibits that use security and surveillance systems. Tikima liked working with the rangers. I think if she ever thought of changing jobs, she would have become a park ranger. She loved being outside."

Like most government documents, the paperwork in the file was dense and unreadable. Another note card was clipped to the back of the folder. James Taylor—Cradle of Forestry.

"You think this is James Taylor, the singer?" I asked.

Nakayla laughed. "No. If Tikima met that James Taylor, she would have told me."

"Maybe it's a song. Cradle of Forestry. Like Sweet Baby James."

Nakayla laughed harder. "The Cradle of Forestry is an historic site in Pisgah. It's where George Vanderbilt established the first school for forestry in this country."

"Okay." I closed the folder. "Now that you know I nearly failed North Carolina history, let's move on." The last file bore the title Senior Sanctuaries. "Sounds like places for old birds," I said.

"In a way. The company owns several retirement communities in the area."

The paperwork was almost as thick as the Forestry documents, but clipped together in packets representing different operations. Names like Restful Ridge and River's End seemed more appropriate for cemeteries and I guess in fact they were the next to the last stop. I thought of a marketing brochure my parents had received for a mausoleum. My dad had called it a post-retirement condominium.

Of the six communities in the file, only one had a note attached in Tikima's handwriting. Golden Oaks. Her note read "find out who he talked to."

I showed the paper to Nakayla. "Any idea what this means?"

"No. Tikima was always jotting herself notes. You saw that in the apartment." Nakayla flipped through the Golden Oaks papers. "Looks like they were building a new wing and she gave them a quote on security hardware. Maybe she wanted to know if there were any other bids."

"The estimate is dated two months ago. Would she keep the file at home that long?"

Nakayla looked at the folders spread across the table. "I hadn't seen any of these files in her apartment. She must have brought them home a day or two before she disappeared."

The quote sheet was addressed to Sandra Pollock, Director of Operations at Golden Oaks.

"Odd that the note says 'find out who he talked to' when Sandra is a woman. Mention that to Peters."

"Okay." Nakayla didn't sound very enthused.

"Peters will do all right. Just stay on him."

"You don't get it, do you?"

Since I had no idea what I was supposed to get, I could only stare at her.

"I'm an annoyance to Peters. I can read it in his eyes. Maybe because I'm a woman, maybe because I'm a black woman. He'll humor me and then go on about business as usual. But with you he's competitive. The way you nailed him on Tikima's car. If he solves this case, it'll be because of you pushing him."

I didn't believe she had pegged Peters correctly, not after the way he had barked at Stanley. But Nakayla hadn't seen that fire in Peters' eyes. For her, Peters had already dismissed the case as unsolvable, not worth any particular effort. Given the way Elijah's murder must have been handled, I couldn't blame her for being skeptical.

"Look. I'm going to Birmingham but I'm not disappearing off the face of the earth. Keep me posted on what develops and I'll dog Peters long distance until he's afraid to answer his phone."

A smile burst across Nakayla's face. "Would you?"

"Sure. I'll even get a cell phone and make Peters one of my free-call buddies."

She squeezed my hand as a thank you. Then she kissed my cheek. I remembered how tough it can be to bear your grief alone and wondered how many family members Nakayla had sharing her sorrow. I'd gotten the word about my parents' deaths as I lay in a hospital ward. The nurses sent a chaplain to talk to me, but I only wanted to speak to Stanley. I wanted family. Our phone conversation was one of the few times we hadn't ended up arguing. Still, I'd been left with words I'd wished I'd spoken to my father. They haunt me because how can you be reconciled to a dead man?

I cleared my throat. "Tell me about your family. Do you keep up with Bessie's side?"

"Bessie?" She looked at the journal. "Yes, there was a Bessie. In our family lore she migrated north and she's someone who did disappear off the face of the earth. But my great grandfather Amos came down from Chicago when Elijah was killed."

"Amos?"

"Yes. He worked at the Biltmore Estate, married, and had a son named Harrison. I guess they'd used up all the prophet names by then. Grandpa Harrison died ten years ago. My father had been his only child. His name was Clyde. For three generations, only one child, a son, had been born in each marriage."

"Until you and Tikima," I said.

"Yes, but Tikima tried to be a son. Our father had been a Marine in Vietnam. She enlisted as soon as she turned eighteen. Daddy was very proud. For awhile."

I turned toward her in my chair, sensing the story was heading in another direction.

"Our mother died of breast cancer at the age of forty-five. She'd been everything to Daddy. Tikima was stationed overseas, and I was a teenager and totally into myself." Nakayla sniffled and wiped her eyes. "He went into depression and six months later killed himself. I'd been out all night. As I snuck in the next morning, I found him on the kitchen floor. No note. An empty Jim Beam bottle on the table and a pistol by his hand."

Nakayla's tears fell freely and she made no effort to wipe them away. "Grandpa Harrison died shortly after that. His heart just quit." She looked up at me. "It must be a terrible thing to bury your child."

I thought of the countless Iraqi women I'd seen wailing in the funeral processions for their sons and daughters. And the stateside burials of my fellow soldiers with mothers and fathers crying and clinging to each other. Grief for a lost child knows no borders of language or geography.

"So, the other people on the front pew at the funeral, they weren't family?"

"No," Nakayla said. "Close friends and church people who'd seen Tikima and me grow up. But no blood family." She bit her lower lip and stared at the wall.

"I'm the end of the line," she whispered. "The last of the Robertsons."

TEN

AT EIGHT THE next morning, I stopped by Dr. Anderson's office in hopes of catching him before he started his rounds. Anderson had final say on my release and I wanted to be first on his next day's schedule. Fridays were especially hectic with discharges and weekend passes, so a morning release could drag on into the afternoon.

His assistant was away from her desk. I knocked on his door under the Private sign. Anderson opened it quickly. His craggy face frowned as he saw me as yet another unexpected problem.

Anderson was career army, a no-nonsense medical man whose displeasure could extend to the brass above him as well as the veterans in his care. He played no favorites and suffered no fools.

"Blackman, what is it?"

"Sorry to bother you, sir. I have a favor to ask."

Anderson rubbed a hand through his close-cropped gray hair and looked around his messy office. "You'll have to ask it standing. There's no place to sit."

"This won't take long. You know I'm being released tomorrow."

He grunted. "As if you haven't already been out of the hospital enough."

"I'm sorry about that too. But my ride to Birmingham needs to leave first thing in the morning and I was hoping—"

"Hoping you could have an early discharge," he said, finishing my sentence.

"Yes, sir."

Anderson sighed. "I suppose so. Be sure and get your supplies from Hinnant this afternoon."

"My supplies?"

He glared at me from under his bushy eyebrows. "Right. If you'd been here when you were supposed to be yesterday, you'd have been given an appointment. The Hinnant people are up from Charlotte."

I knew Hinnant constructed the prosthetics for many of the vets. They'd fitted me for my permanent leg upon my transfer from Walter Reed and had shown me how to use the socks and liners needed as the swelling went down and my stump became better conditioned.

"Don't I just order from them?" I asked.

Anderson's expression softened. The old doctor seemed amused by my confusion. "Yes. But I want them to check you out one more time, especially since you're leaving the state. And I want to make sure the second leg fits properly."

"What second leg?"

"You're entitled to two. Sometimes the bean counters in Washington discourage us from ordering them. I didn't want to say anything until I knew the request had cleared and I'd gotten the model I wanted."

Crusty Dr. Anderson had evidently gone to bat for me. "Thank you." I offered my hand and he gripped it firmly. "Did you get me the one with racing stripes?"

"Better than that." He glanced down at my prosthesis. "What you've been working with is fine for everyday use. If you land a desk job or walk on smooth sidewalks, you'll find it more comfortable." He winked. "But you're a young, active guy. Hinnant's fitted the second leg with a foot model called Venture, designed for more rugged activities. Uneven terrain, running, why a guy in Florida is a champion surfer. Hinnant will check you out on it, and I've ordered a supply of multiple ply socks, liners, and gels. You'll continue to have some atrophy and shrinkage in that left limb, and even the humidity will affect how well the socket fits on some days."

I'd learned the paraphernalia required could fill a small suitcase. I had several liners with attachment pins that fit over my stump for locking into the prosthesis' socket. A team of horses couldn't pull the leg free. But fit was crucial and special socks went over the liner to ensure I wasn't rubbing tissue that was never meant to bear body weight. Adding and removing socks of different ply thickness was key and adjustments were constantly being made as conditions changed.

"I appreciate what you've done for me," I said. "When I need another checkup, I'd like to come back here and see you."

Anderson clapped me on the back. He'd never been so "touchy-feely" before. "If I've not been put out to pasture. But I'll be in Asheville either way so look me up." He lifted a clipboard off his desk. "I'll schedule you to see Hinnant's people at two this afternoon. After that, I'll make sure everything's ready for your discharge."

I turned to go.

"Blackman. After I saw you yesterday, I heard you'd slipped out to look into Tikima Robertson's murder."

I stopped and faced him. "Yes, sir. Tikima had visited me. Her sister thought maybe I could help some-how."

"Did you?"

"Let's just say I might have gotten the police back on track."

Anderson nodded. "Tikima was a good soldier. I served with her father in Vietnam. I'd like nothing more than to see her killer brought to justice."

I WENT TO the library to review my statement for Peters. A fresh look on a fresh day helped me make sure the report was as clear and concise as I could make it. I planned to have Nakayla deliver it to the detective along with the journal and the Armitage files as soon as we met with Ted Mitchell at the Wolfe Memorial. I thought about going with her to the police station, but Stanley would be itching to leave and after his brief run-in with Peters yesterday, another encounter might only set a combative tone for our drive to Birmingham.

I folded my statement and stuck it in the journal. As I rose from the table, Carol, one of the physical therapists, entered.

"There you are." She handed me a scrap of paper. "You had a phone call and when you weren't in your room, the guy said he couldn't hold."

I looked at a string of numbers scrawled in pencil.

"Did he leave a name?"

"No, just asked that you call as soon as you could."

I studied the digits. "They're too many to be a phone number."

Carol laughed. "Shhh. It's a 336 area code. Long distance. I gave you the access sequence so you can dial directly out of the hospital. Let the VA pick up your tab."

336. The area code in Winston-Salem where Stanley was meeting with the lawyers for Galaxy Movers.

"Thanks," I said. "Was Mr. Carlisle in the room?"

"Yes. Look, if it's personal, you can use my phone. I've got a session starting in five minutes in the gym."

Carol closed the door to her small office, leaving me with one of the rarest possessions you can find in a hospital—privacy. I scooted closer to her desk, lifted a pen from several stocked in a coffee mug and tore a sheet of paper from a notepad with the unpronounceable name of some pharmaceutical product stamped across the top. A glance at the pen showed me it was courtesy of another drug company. Eliminate promotional pens and pads and prescription drug prices would probably be cut in half.

A good seven or eight rings sounded before a voice answered. "Sam?"

"Yes."

"It's Walt. I've stepped outside our conference room and can't talk long."

Walt Misenheimer. My first thought was Stanley had screwed up the power of attorney. It served him right for playing loose with the notarization.

"What's wrong?"

Walt's words dropped to a whisper. "They're offering four hundred thousand dollars."

"Four hundred thousand?" The amount was larger than any check I'd ever seen, but Walt said the number like he'd been handed a wad of used Kleenex.

"Yeah. I mean that's about what I'd expect for a first offer."

"What'd Stanley think?"

"He wants to take it. I know he has your power of

attorney, but I couldn't in good conscience accept that without talking to you."

Stanley the banker certainly knew the value of a dollar. I was surprised he'd go against Walt's advice.

"I know things have gotten tight for him," Walt continued, "and the sale of your parents' home doesn't close for another two months." He paused and I heard his muffled words, "Just another minute." Then his raspy whisper returned. "Christ, I still think he let the house go too cheap."

Stanley was executor of our parents' estate. Papers had been sent for me to sign in the hospital, but I'd been too pre-occupied with getting my life back to pay much attention.

"I'm afraid he's making decisions he'll regret later," Walt said. "When he's back on his feet."

"I'm not following you. I know there must have been unexpected expenses with the twins."

"He didn't tell you about the bank?"

"He told me he might be transferred because of the merger."

Walt sighed in my ear. "Sam, he was laid off over six months ago. I know he's got creditors hounding him, but accepting this settlement is a big mistake. And God knows what kind of medical expenses you could be facing long term."

My brother was out of a job? I'd seen the pictures of his big house with the swimming pool. His wife Ashley never met a designer dress she didn't like. Premature twins and medical bills. His half of the settlement, even after legal fees, could solve a lot of immediate problems. And if I lived with them, I'd be bringing my disability income to the happy party. Instead of feeling sympathy for Stanley, I felt manipulated. When was he going to tell me? After I didn't see him go to work for a week?

"What kind of money should we be talking about?" I asked.

"Five times that," Walt said. "Maybe even ten times. I'd say between two and four million."

"And Stanley knows that?"

"Yes, but he's afraid Galaxy will drag this thing out in court. That's always a possibility. But Galaxy knowingly put a drug abuser behind the wheel of a moving van. That's not right." Walt's voice choked. "Your parents were my friends for over forty years and I admit this is personal for me. I want the bastards to pay. But even setting aside my own feelings, I can't advise you to take this offer. Since you're named as a co-plaintive, I can stop Stanley if you'll rescind your power of attorney."

Suddenly Carol's office shrank to the size of a closet. I felt claustrophobic as Walt's words closed in on me. I needed to walk because I think better when I walk. Except now I had to think even about walking. I stood up shakily, stretching the phone cord to its limit. "Do I have to send you something in writing?"

"No. I recognize your voice. And I originally placed the call."

"Stanley's going to be furious with you."

Walt chuckled. "Not half as much as with you. So, what do you want me to do?"

"I'm revoking Stanley's power of attorney and I'm settling for nothing less than five million dollars."

"Good for you." Walt paused. "This can get messy, especially where Stanley's concerned. Try not to have things escalate to where you're suing each other. Nobody wins those legal fights."

"Don't worry. I'm going to be very objective and dispassionate. Because you're right. I have to worry about my future."

THE TWO O'CLOCK meeting with Hinnant Prosthetics lasted nearly an hour. Kale Hinnant watched me walk and then had me remove the leg, socks, and liner. He checked for redness or irritation and told me to keep everything as dry and clean as I could. Even a wrinkle in a sock rubbing against my stump could create a problem. Then he had me try the second leg. There was a different feeling that was hard to describe. Sort of like the suspension in a car that's been adjusted to handle rougher roads.

"Walk some trails with it," Hinnant said. "Get accustomed to the way the foot responds on different terrain and at different gaits."

"What about shoes?"

"Excellent question. Are you planning on wearing any cleats?"

"Not unless I get invited to try out for the Carolina Panthers."

Hinnant laughed. "Believe me, they could use the help." He picked up the prosthesis and examined the foot. "If you're not wearing anything other than a standard athletic or walking shoe, then this dynamic setup should be fine. But if the Panthers call—"

"You'll be the first to know." I shook his hand and carried my extra leg and supplies to my room.

Stanley stood outside my door. He made no move to greet me, but his face grew redder with each step I took. I stopped directly in front of him, my arms filled so that I couldn't make a point of not shaking his hand.

Through clenched teeth, he said, "We need to talk."

"No, we needed to talk. But you didn't tell me a god-damned thing. Just had me sign the paper to give away what should have been a fair and just settlement."

"Five million dollars?" His voice yipped like a frantic dog's. "You think they'll shell out that kind of dough? We're talking years to collect a tenth of that."

"I don't give a damn about the money!" A part of my brain tried to reel back my emotions, but I thought, so much for being objective and dispassionate. "You lied to me, Stanley. That's what hurts."

Stanley's red face drained pale. He glanced up and down the hall. A nurse came out of a patient room to see what was wrong. I waved her away.

"I didn't lie," Stanley protested.

"A lie of omission is still a lie. Those sons of bitches killed our parents and you're letting them off easy because you've got your ass in a financial sling, and you weren't man enough to tell me."

"I thought you had enough problems of your own and God knows it's all about you." His lower lip quivered and suddenly he was on the verge of tears. "Killed our parents? Where were you when Mom and Dad needed you? You who defied Dad and skipped college. You who left me to take all the crap—'work hard at the bank, Stanley, join the Rotary, Stanley, you and Ashley come to lunch at the club on Sunday, Stanley.' God, I was never so happy as when I got transferred to Birmingham where I could breathe on my own."

I stepped closer to him. "Don't lay your spineless life on me. If you ran to Birmingham because you couldn't

stand up to Dad, that's not my fault. A little more courage and maybe you wouldn't have gotten fired. Ever
think about that. A little more backbone and maybe
your wife wouldn't spend you into the ground." I knew
as I spoke I was hitting below the belt but there was too
much anger boiling out for me to stop.

Stanley's face went calm and he stared at me for
a few seconds without saying anything. Then a cold
smile creased his lips. The transformation caught me
off guard, as if he knew he held a trump card and I'd
overplayed my hand.

"And you haven't run away, little brother? Joining
the army wasn't running away? Well, what has your
running gotten you?" He looked at the leg in my arms
and then down to the metal pylon visible beneath my
shorts. "I only lost my job."

Stanley spun around and walked off. I watched him
go, my anger turning to fear, not that I'd lost a brother
or that I now had no place to go. I was afraid that Stanley had spoken the truth.

ELEVEN

As Nakayla walked through the cafeteria toward me, several patients turned their heads from their hospital trays, stopped chewing, and eyed her appreciatively. She wore a light green pantsuit with a cream silk scarf loosely knotted around her neck. She moved gracefully, and I felt a tingle of desire that warned me more than my leg was healing.

I got up from the small corner table I'd commandeered and offered my hand.

Nakayla slid her slender fingers around mine and squeezed. "Are you all right?" Her eyes studied my face while her grip tightened.

"No. Not really. Let's get something to eat and I'll tell you."

I'd called her at work after Stanley left because she was the only person I could confide in. I'd asked if she would meet me for dinner, the hospital cafeteria being the one and only choice.

We each took a pre-packaged tossed salad and a cup of coffee. My food sat untouched as I told her about my parents, my argument with Stanley, and that I wouldn't be going to Birmingham. She didn't interrupt, but a few minutes into my story, she set down her fork and gave me her undivided attention.

I finished saying, "So, I guess I'll go back to Winston-Salem to be close to the case. At least I'll have my honorable discharge and my disability income, and I've saved some money over the years. There wasn't much to buy in Iraq. I'll probably stay here for a few days till I can arrange transportation. I know this is the height of tourist season, but can you recommend a motel?"

For a few seconds, Nakayla said nothing. She looked away, and then locked her piercing eyes on mine. "The first thing you're going to do is make peace with your brother."

"What? I'm not going to beg him to take me in?"

"I'm not asking you to. I think going to Birmingham would be a mistake." Her eyes moistened. "But I thank God Tikima and I were close. We'd had our share of arguments—some real catfights—because we were both strong-headed and I was the rebellious little sister. But I couldn't bear it if my last words with her had been spoken in anger."

"I'm not apologizing for what I did."

"Then why are you upset? I could see it in your face halfway across the cafeteria."

"He tried to trick me."

"And you stopped him. If this were a business deal, you'd be happy."

I slapped the table, sloshing coffee out of both cups. "It's not a business deal, it's my parents' deaths we're talking about."

"Right. Your family. Like your brother. I'm not saying you didn't do the right thing, but did you say the right thing? If Stanley were killed in a car wreck driving home tonight, would you have any regrets about the words you spoke?"

Nakayla's question cut to the heart of the matter. I thought about how I'd called Stanley spineless and painted his wife Ashley as a selfish socialite wannabe. What did I know about their life together, a life that now included twin girls and no income? And although Nakayla was projecting onto me her own fears, the woman had just lost her sister, and that raw wound, as real as the one that cost me my leg, must have hurt so much that she didn't want anyone else to go through it.

"I did say some things I regret," I confessed. "They had nothing to do with the legal case."

"Then I think you need to make peace over that. I'm not suggesting you back down on what you think is the right course of action for your lawsuit."

"Some time will have to pass."

"No. Time will only complicate matters. If you say where you were wrong you're also clarifying where you think you're right."

I shook my head. "I don't trust myself."

"Then write a letter. Do it tonight. We'll mail it in the morning. You can call in a few days."

"And if he won't talk to me?"

Nakayla smiled. "Then he'll have to live with the consequences, not you."

"And in the meantime?"

She licked her lips, suddenly nervous. "I have a proposition for you. You can stay at Tikima's."

For a second, my mind flashed on the apartment as a potential crime scene—the disguised journal and files on the table and the break-in while mourners attended Tikima's funeral. To be living there, sleeping in the bed of a murdered woman, hadn't been in my realm of possibilities.

"I don't know," I said. "Are you comfortable with all of her personal belongings in it?"

"You're welcome to anything that fits you." Nakayla's bittersweet smile wasn't without warmth. "We Robertsons are very practical. The rent's paid through the end of the month, you're helping to find Tikima's killer, and you need a place to stay."

The only objection I could raise would be my discomfort at being in the home of a homicide victim, but I sensed that response would be hurtful to Nakayla, depersonalizing her sister into some kind of macabre specter.

I shrugged. "Okay. If you're sure."

Nakayla seemed relieved. "Good. I'll straighten up tonight. What time can you leave in the morning?"

"As soon as the administration office opens. Probably no later than eight-thirty."

"I'll be here." She stood.

I got up and steadied myself against the table. "I'd like to run by Walmart and pick up something other than a Hawaiian shirt."

"We'll do that second."

"What's first?"

"We mail your letter to your brother."

THE THOMAS WOLFE MEMORIAL VISITOR CENTER was a light blue building on Market Street between Woodfin and Walnut. The shop in the lobby offered all of Wolfe's novels, a variety of Wolfe biographies including Ted Mitchell's, and a collection of pictorial books of historic Asheville, most of them concentrating on the late 1800s and early 1900s. A reception desk with a cash register was on the left wall. The woman behind it greeted us pleasantly. Her nameplate read Susan.

I let Nakayla do the talking while I stood beside her,

confident in my new golf shirt and beltless slacks only thirty minutes off the Walmart rack.

"We're here to see Mr. Mitchell," Nakayla said.

Susan looked confused. "You have an appointment with Ted Mitchell?"

"No. But I was told he'd be here this morning so we took a chance."

Ted Mitchell hadn't returned Nakayla's voicemail, and we suspected he'd been out of town and might be driving straight to work.

"Ted's leading the first tour. He won't be free till after eleven."

"Has the tour started?" Nakayla asked.

"No. I'll be calling everyone to the rear doors in about ten minutes."

Everyone at the moment seemed to be a retired couple browsing the books and two young men listening to recordings of Wolfe family members on old-fashioned telephones across the lobby.

Nakayla set her handbag on the counter. "We'll take two tickets."

I reached for my wallet. "Let me get them."

Susan looked from me to Nakayla.

"Okay, big-spender," Nakayla said.

I pinched one of the crisp twenties fresh from the ATM.

"That'll be two dollars, sir."

"Two dollars?"

Susan winked at Nakayla. "They're a dollar each."

"I can't buy a cup of coffee for a dollar."

"That's why we don't sell coffee."

I felt guilty with my eighteen dollars in change and dropped a five in a donation box. During the wait, Nakayla and I looked through several books of old photographs. Was I peering into the world of Henderson Youngblood or the world created by Thomas Wolfe?

The announcement came that the tour was beginning.

"What are we touring?" I asked.

Nakayla pointed through the lobby's rear windows to a two-story yellow house next door. "Wolfe's mother ran a boarding house. You'll see what it was like when Wolfe lived there."

Ted Mitchell proved to be a middle-aged man with dark-rimmed glasses and salt and pepper hair. He introduced himself and encouraged us to ask questions. The older woman warned she was a retired English teacher and would be giving us a test at the end of the tour. Her husband laughed and assured us she wasn't kidding.

With the group at ease, Ted passed out cards to each of us. "I want you to imagine you've just arrived at the train station and a young boy handed you this card. The year is in the early 1900s and the boy is Thomas Wolfe, whose mother often sent him to find boarders."

The card read "Old Kentucky Home Just Off The Car Line No Sick People Rates Reasonable Mrs. Julia E. Wolfe, Proprietress." The phone number had only three digits.

"Now ladies and gentlemen," Ted Mitchell said, "follow me as we walk back through the years and enter Thomas Wolfe's childhood."

I held back, letting the faster walkers go first. Nakayla strolled beside me, her handbag containing the journal tucked under her arm.

Our group sat for a few minutes in rockers on the wide porch, breathing the mountain air and listening

to Mitchell explain the history of the house. The name
Old Kentucky Home came from an owner who pre-
dated the Wolfes and had moved from Kentucky. Even
though we were in Asheville, somehow the name fit.

The interior was a maze of halls and rooms. White-
washed walls, dark trim and wide plank floors conveyed
the feel of a bygone era. I had trouble navigating some
of the stairs and Ted Mitchell would patiently wait for
me to catch up before sharing his stories, often pointing
to a portrait, piano, or fireplace to illustrate his point.

In one of the bedrooms, Mitchell mentioned Wolfe
had stayed there when he returned for a few months in
1937, eight years after the publication of *Look Homeward, Angel*, which had so scandalized Asheville. By
then Wolfe's novels had made him a celebrity and the
town was anxious to wrap itself in his fame. Mitchell
pointed to a table where he said Wolfe had written the
story "Return" during his visit. A little over a year later,
Wolfe would be dead.

The tour moved on but I lingered by the table, studying the piece of paper with Wolfe's handwriting left
there as an example of the author's presence.

Nakayla stepped beside me. "What do you think?"

I was tempted to pick the small sheet up, but I didn't
want to violate Mitchell's request that we not touch anything. "I don't see the telltale 'of' in these few sentences,
but the large, bold style of the letters is the same."

"You're still comfortable showing him the journal?"

I took her arm and led her after the others. "Yes.
Otherwise everything comes to a dead end."

The tour ended back in the adjacent building. Mitchell encouraged us to see a short film on Thomas Wolfe
that would be starting soon in the auditorium. After the

others had thanked him and moved through the double doors to find seats, Nakayla spoke up.

"Mr. Mitchell, do you have a few minutes?"

He looked past us to the auditorium. "You'll miss part of the movie."

"My name is Nakayla Robertson. I left you a voice-mail on your home machine asking to speak with you."

"I'm sorry. I've been out of town and returned last night to find lightning had fried the answering machine and my TV." He glanced at me, not sure why the two of us would be tracking him down at home.

"This is my friend Sam Blackman. Mr. Mitchell, my sister was Tikima Robertson."

Mitchell stepped back. Our names had meant nothing but Tikima's clearly jolted him. "She was your sister?"

Nakayla nodded.

"I read about her in the paper."

"Did you talk to her?"

"Yes. On the phone. We were supposed to meet, but she never showed up."

"When was this?" I asked.

"A couple weeks ago. I think a Monday when the Memorial was closed."

I retraced the dates from Tikima's Saturday visit. "June 4th?"

"That sounds about right. I can check my calendar to be sure."

"What did she want to talk about?" I asked.

"She said she might have a Wolfe manuscript. Of course, I was interested." He looked at Nakayla and shook his head. "But then she never came."

"I have what she wanted to show you," Nakayla said.

Mitchell's eyes brightened. "You do?" He looked

around the lobby. Several people browsed the books, waiting for the next tour. "Let's go to the staff break room. I have about twenty minutes."

We followed him through a door marked Staff Only. The room was more like a hall with a refrigerator at the end and a stainless-steel double sink on the left. Mitchell motioned us to take seats around a small table.

I was hoping Nakayla would just hand him the journal and not prompt him with any clues as to why we thought Thomas Wolfe wrote it. She must have read my mind. She opened her bag and pulled out the journal. She had wrapped it in tan chamois. Without saying a word, she slid the bundle across the table.

Mitchell eyed it for a few seconds and then unwrapped it so the volume rested in the center of the soft leather. "May I?" he asked.

Nakayla nodded.

He opened the cover. As he read down the first page, his eyes widened. "The penmanship bears a strong resemblance and it's written with a pencil like Wolfe used, but there's an artificiality to the language that's not Wolfe."

"What if he were trying to write like a twelve-year-old boy trying to write like Robinson Crusoe?" I asked.

"The voice," Mitchell said. "Yes, that would affect the vocabulary and sentence structure. You're sure this isn't authentic, that a Henderson Youngblood didn't write it?"

"We're not sure," Nakayla said. "We found the journal alongside your biography of Wolfe in Tikima's apartment. Then the entries break off with a few strange sentences."

Mitchell flipped through the pages carefully till he

came to the end of the writing. He read aloud, "Vocabulary and style getting away from him. Ask Harry about the mule."

"We don't know who Harry is," I said.

Mitchell turned back a few pages and read for a couple minutes. He mouthed a word or two as they made an impression.

"We don't know why Tikima thought Wolfe might have written it," I said. "But we saw the handwriting similarity between the journal and examples of Wolfe's manuscripts in your book." I mentioned the unique style of the word *of* and our feeling that the language grew more adult as the story progressed.

Mitchell pursed his lips. "If it is Wolfe, I could see him getting immersed in the narrative and losing the boy's perspective, especially in a first draft. Can I keep this awhile?"

Nakayla looked at me.

I shook my head. "Sorry. We're going to turn it over to the police. There might be a connection with Tikima's death."

The blood drained from his face. "Really?"

"Maybe. The police will have to make that determination."

Mitchell turned a few more pages, almost caressing them. Then his eyes froze. He whispered a strange word that I couldn't make out.

"What's that?" I asked.

He turned the journal around and pointed. I read phthisic.

"Yes," I said. "That stopped me too. I don't even know how to pronounce it let alone know what it means."

"Tiz'ik," he said. "Phthisic is most commonly used as a medical term. It means shrunken, atrophied." He turned the journal so he could read it. "'My leg began to hurt. I slipped the support strap off my shoulder and pulled my phthisic stump clear of the socket. The pain eased.'"

"Pretty sophisticated for a twelve-year-old," I said.

Mitchell nodded. "Pretty sophisticated for anybody. Anybody except Thomas Wolfe. He liked medical terms. Phthisic appears on the second page of the first chapter of *Look Homeward, Angel*. He uses it to describe the feet of a carved stone angel. If Wolfe didn't write this, then someone went to the trouble to copy his handwriting and vocabulary."

"How much could this be worth?" I asked.

"To scholarship or to collectors?"

"To whoever would pay the most."

Mitchell closed the book and rubbed his fingers over the leather. "Hard to say. It's not part of a known Wolfe work and it's too incomplete to have any publishing value. As talented as Wolfe was, he's not enjoying the stature of Hemingway or Faulkner."

"Let me put it this way," I said. "Is the journal worth killing someone?"

"I wouldn't think so."

This was the answer I expected. If the journal was worth a fortune, Tikima could have brought it to someone like Mitchell without involving me. Let the literary world know of its existence and sell it on the open market. But Tikima wasn't seeking to find the journal's highest bidder; she was launching an investigation based upon it.

I was ready to move to the question I believed to be

crucial. "If Wolfe wrote this, then it's fiction. But in the journal one of the characters, Elijah Robertson, is murdered. Elijah Robertson was the name of the great-great grandfather of Tikima and Nakayla, and he was actually murdered on the dates given in Wolfe's story."

Ted Mitchell got up from the table, went to a storage cabinet, and returned with a copy of his biography of Wolfe. "Thomas Wolfe's fiction was experienced fact set in the context of fiction. That was the big row created by *Look Homeward, Angel*. There were people in Asheville who annotated their copies with the real names, and many of the thinly disguised characters were not depicted in a complimentary way."

Mitchell opened his biography to a page near the middle and pointed to a photocopy of typescript. We could see the word *Julia* scratched out and *Eliza* handwritten over it.

"Julia was Wolfe's mother," Mitchell explained. "The mother in *Look Homeward, Angel* was Eliza. You can see he didn't bother to change the name until after someone had typed his longhand pages. Asheville became Altamont, other place names were barely changed if at all." He took back the biography and rewrapped the journal in the chamois. "I'd say if Wolfe did write this, odds are every event is rooted in something he experienced or something someone told him happened."

"And people were upset by what he wrote in *Look Homeward, Angel*?" I asked.

"Like I said during the tour, he didn't return to Asheville for eight years."

Nakayla took the journal from Mitchell and then hesitated. "Maybe Mr. Mitchell should read it. Tell us what he knows to have happened in Wolfe's life."

My gut instinct sent a sharp warning. "I'm more concerned about what may happen in Mr. Mitchell's life. The less he knows about the journal the better." I turned to Mitchell. "My advice is for you to say nothing about our conversation or the existence of this volume. If the police bring it to you, then say what you want at that point. But I'm not going to mention your name to them."

"Why not?" Mitchell asked.

"Two people tied to the journal have already been murdered. I don't want you to be the third."

"WHERE DID TIKIMA get the journal?" Nakayla asked the question as we walked to her car in the Wolfe Memorial parking lot. "That's what the police are going to ask."

I'd been mulling the question myself. With Mitchell's analysis that Wolfe likely wrote it and that the events described probably happened, the source of the journal would be the best lead for understanding its meaning. But we had no idea where to begin other than the files Tikima had taken from the Armitage office. We. What was I thinking? This wasn't my case. I'd followed my curiosity about an eighty-eight-year-old journal hidden in an Elmore Leonard dust jacket with my name posted on it. Now I knew the journal might not be that old, was probably a mixture of fact and fiction, and most importantly a problem for the Asheville police, not for former military criminal investigator Sam Blackman.

"So, what do we do next?" Nakayla asked.

"We take this to the police. All of it. You'll say you found the journal last night, but without my name on it. That's a tangent Peters would fixate on that will waste time. We'll show him the Wolfe handwriting connection and your family link to Elijah. If he contacts Ted Mitchell, well, we'll say we didn't want to involve Mitchell in something that might be a wild goose chase."

Nakayla stopped at the driver's door and spoke over the roof of the Hyundai. "Why not tell him we talked to Mitchell?"

"Because I don't know why Tikima didn't go to the police in the first place. Instead, she planned to talk to me. Maybe she heard exaggerated compliments from Cookie at Walter Reed, maybe my notoriety from the congressional hearings attracted her interest, or maybe she just felt more comfortable talking to a fellow military officer."

"You say Tikima didn't trust the police, and so you don't trust the police, but you're handing them the investigation?" She shook her head. "You're giving up."

"It's not about me!"

The frustration in my voice hit her like a slap. Her cocoa skin darkened. "No. I guess it's not." She yanked open the door and got in.

I hesitated, angry at myself for snapping at Nakayla and unsure how to make amends. I'd spoken without thinking, saying I couldn't be sure of the police while telling Nakayla to depend on them to solve her sister's murder.

And it was about me. I'd been a good warrant officer, specializing in obtaining evidence and using investigative procedures to support the military prosecutors. As a new civilian here in Asheville, I wouldn't have access to forensic labs or data bases. I'd be playing detective, a cartoon version hobbling around without the authority to conduct searches or interrogate anyone. A prescription for failure.

The psychologist at Walter Reed had warned me of

the stages amputees go through. Depression and feel-ings of inadequacy will commonly occur. But the flip-side of that emotional journey is the compulsion to overachieve, to prove to the world and yourself that you are every bit the man you were before a part of you had been severed from your body and soul. Finding the way between those two extremes would be an ongoing challenge. I needed to find that way now.

I opened the passenger door and leaned in. "Is there a Kinko's nearby?"

"Yes," she said coolly.

I maneuvered into the seat and turned to face her. "Before we see Detective Peters, let's copy the journal and the files. As far as we know, the journal belonged to Tikima and should eventually be returned to you. The files will go back to Armitage. But with our own copies we can work parallel, staying clear of the police while learning what we can." I thought about the time that might take. "Today's June 22nd. You've got the apartment for a little over a week?"

"Tikima's now on month to month. As executor of her estate, I'll keep paying the rent."

"No. I can't accept that."

"Why not? I'm going to hire you. This is part of your expenses."

"I'm not a licensed investigator. If you insist on pay-ing me, then I'm leaving for Winston-Salem. But if I'm your friend, helping as I can with little expectation of success, then I'll work day and night."

Nakayla looked away. I heard her swallow. When she faced me, tears sparkled in the corners of her eyes.

She held out her hand. "You've got a deal, Mr. Blackman."

"No. You mean you've got a deal, Sam."

TWELVE

THE ASHEVILLE POLICE DEPARTMENT was located on Pack Square in the center of the city. As Nakayla maneuvered her Hyundai through a construction detour, I noticed the square was getting a major facelift. Orange barricades and plastic mesh fencing cordoned off streets and sidewalks.

"What are they doing here?" I asked.

"Creating a new square. There'll be an amphitheatre at one end and an overall layout to encourage pedestrian traffic."

To me it didn't look like the pedestrians needed any encouragement. The sidewalks and outdoor cafés were filled with people.

"The town seems to be jumping," I said.

"Coming into its own again. Back in the 1960s when many cities spent money on urban renewal, Asheville was too poor to raze its old buildings. All it could manage was to minimize the disrepair. Now that same architecture is a treasure to be renovated, not replaced. People are appreciating what had been the glamour of the early 1900s, a style no one can afford to build today."

The police station didn't exude the art-deco or gothic design of yesteryear. The functionality of 21st century law enforcement trumped aesthetics, and though nice enough, the municipal building housing the police and fire departments could have been found in countless cities across the nation. In the police station lobby, we asked for Detective Peters at an information window more appropriate for a bank teller.

In less than five minutes, Peters stepped through double doors and signaled us to follow him. He actually smiled when he saw the files under my arm. He led us into a small conference room and we sat at a round table that dispelled the interrogative atmosphere where the officer sits on one side and the suspect on the other.

I passed him my handwritten statement. "Here's the report of my conversation with Tikima on Saturday, June 2nd. I've also included a summary of my attendance at her funeral last Tuesday and the discrepancies of the handbrake, footprint, and sand particles discovered at her car on Wednesday."

Peters slid the sheets to the side without looking at them. He pointed to the folders. "What's that?"

"These are the files from Armitage Securities that my sister had in her apartment," Nakayla said. "You told me you wanted them."

He nodded and I handed them over. We went through them one by one with Nakayla giving Peters the same background information she'd told me. I mentioned the connection between the Biltmore Estate, the French Broad River, and the Armitage guards.

"You think there might have been internal work troubles at Armitage?" Peters asked.

"Just an observation," I said. "I don't know enough about anything to venture an opinion. But, you told me Tikima's body was found downstream of the Biltmore Estate."

"Does Nathan Armitage know about these files?"

"Not yet," I said. "Nakayla made a list that we're going to give him."

"Don't." His sharp tone was an order, not a request. "I'll be speaking to Nathan personally."

"And you want to hit him cold with these companies. Read his reactions."

Peters smiled. "I forgot you played the game."

I doubted Peters forgot much of anything. "The game," I said. "I'm only a spectator of this one, but I'd like to follow the score."

"From Birmingham?"

"From Asheville. I've decided to hang around a little longer. Do some legwork."

Peters didn't miss the double meaning. "If you're going to practice walking, I advise you to stay clear of places where you'll get under somebody else's feet. My partner's on vacation, but I don't need a new one."

"I'm just a tourist," I said, knowing all of the places in the folders except Golden Oaks were tourist attractions.

"Where are you staying?" Peters asked.

"The Kenilworth. Tikima Robertson's apartment."

Peters looked to Nakayla for confirmation.

"I'll give you the phone number," she said. "So you can reach Sam."

Peters slid back his chair. "Okay. So maybe you can buy me a cup of coffee now and then."

I lifted my hand like a policeman halting traffic. "Maybe you'd like a cup now and then we'll show you what we've saved for last."

Peters stopped halfway up from his chair. Nakayla took the chamois-wrapped journal from her purse and set it on the table. Peters eased into his seat and leaned forward. He waited for the story.

Nakayla described its discovery in the Elmore Leonard dust jacket, omitting my name on the Post-It note and saying she'd found it only the previous night. She summarized the content, setting the hook with the murder of Elijah. Then she pulled out the Wolfe biography and I showed Peters the handwriting similarity. A feral look came across his razor-thin face and I knew Tikima's case had suddenly jumped up several notches in importance. Every cop likes the bonus of solving a cold case and Elijah's eighty-eight-year-old murder was positively frigid.

He picked up the journal and thumbed through it. "You say the dates Wolfe uses are the actual dates that match your great-great grandfather's murder?"

"Yes, or they're near enough. I know he was buried in Georgia, though none of us had ever been to the grave."

"And you think this is what the burglars were after when they broke into your sister's apartment the day of the funeral?"

"Yes. Nothing else was taken."

Peters drummed his long fingers on the journal. "Why didn't you report the break-in?"

"Because I thought nothing was taken. I'd rather the police focus on finding a killer, not a burglar."

Peters looked at me. I shrugged, trying to appear sympathetic to the detective's predicament. The burglary scene was now three days old.

"How many people have been in the apartment since then?" he asked.

"Just Sam and me," Nakayla said.

"Then I'll want it dusted. And I'll want both of you printed for reference. Maybe Tikima has prints on file from her military service." Peters turned to me. "But as you pointed out the other day, any right-handed prints will have been made by someone else."

Peters stood, taking the journal and files with him. "I'll want to review these before talking to Nathan Armitage, and I'll have the crime lab at the apartment as soon as I can. I'll need you there to let them in."

"It's Sam's apartment now," Nakayla said.

Peters shook his head. "Whatever."

PETERS HAD US printed before we left the police station and we'd then gone straight to the Kenilworth, careful to leave our copies of the journal and Armitage files locked in the Hyundai's trunk. The mobile crime lab arrived a little after one and sent us scurrying to escape the powder, brushes, and lifting tape that would sweep through the apartment.

With a bottle of root beer each, Nakayla and I sought refuge in the shade of the side yard and the comfort of the Adirondack chairs. We watched tenants and visitors slow their cars as they looped around the expansive lawn and saw the police vehicle parked alongside the stone porte-cochere.

"I guess I'll be well scrutinized by my neighbors for the next few days," I said. "I'd hoped to live here unnoticed."

"The building's big enough that you'll soon be indistinguishable from the lobby furniture. Tikima said the place offered the anonymity of a New York City residential hotel in the setting of a mountain cabin."

"Your sister lived in New York?"

Nakayla laughed. "Only in her mind. She'd visit friends in Manhattan at least once a year. She liked the theatre."

I remembered the brief encounter in my hospital room. "She could be quite dramatic, I bet."

"When she wanted to be. But in a crisis, there was nobody calmer."

We sat in silence for a few minutes. I suspected Nakayla shared my thoughts. What had Tikima's final crisis been like? Had she seen her assailant or the 38 caliber pistol the medical examiner claimed to be the murder weapon?

Nakayla sighed and took a sip of her drink. "We'll need to get some groceries after the police leave."

"I'll be all right."

"With what? Grazing on the lawn? I cleaned out the refrigerator last night. You don't have any wheels and it's a pretty far hike to Ingles."

"Okay. A few groceries. Guess I'd better rent a car tomorrow."

She glanced at my prosthesis. "Are you cleared to drive?"

"Not a stick shift in the Indy 500, but an automatic transmission should be no problem."

"I'm hanging with you tomorrow and Sunday for sure. Let's wait till Monday. No sense paying more than you have to."

I tipped my bottle of root beer to her. "The practical Robertsons."

"Damn straight. And Monday we'll have the make, model, and tag number of your rental so the resident manager can add it to her file. I forgot to tell you she gave her blessing for you to sub-rent under the terms of Tikima's lease." Nakayla toasted her bottle to me. "You're now an official tenant."

I raised my bottle to the old building. "Don't you mean I'm now an inmate in the asylum?"

"That goes without saying. Anybody sane wouldn't get involved in this case." She took a deep breath. "Thank you, Sam."

"Well, I might be crazy, but we'll need to approach this investigation logically. And I'd like to stay clear of Peters for as long as we can."

Nakayla set her bottle on the armrest and folded her fingers under her chin. "Then let's go back to the beginning."

"When's that?"

"When Frederick Law Olmsted enticed Elijah Robertson to leave Chicago and help him create his landscape masterpiece. I think tomorrow we should pay a house call on George Washington Vanderbilt."

"I can guarantee he won't be home."

Nakayla gave me a sly smile. "Maybe. But with over a million visitors traipsing through George's bedroom each year, I can guarantee that we'll escape detection by Detective Peters."

I shook my head. "Not in my experience. We're more likely to meet George Vanderbilt coming out of his bathroom wearing only a toothbrush."

THIRTEEN

"THOSE ARE THE smallest golden arches I've ever seen." I pointed to a wooden sign where the McDonald's logo had been carved into a background of rusty red. The roughly four-by-five-foot sign stood beside the entrance to the fast-food restaurant whose understated exterior made it unique among the thousands of McDonald's franchises I'd seen in my life.

Nakayla eased her car forward as traffic trickled through the main intersection in Biltmore Village. "There're even marble counters in the restrooms. The town's restrictions dictate all buildings comply with architectural standards compatible with those used when Vanderbilt constructed All Souls Church and other village property."

"So what's their burger called, the Big George?"

Nakayla slipped through the yellow light and we approached a mammoth brick archway towering over our lane. "No. Since McDonald's swallowed the building code, the public gets to swallow the Big Mac."

We passed underneath the arch of Biltmore as one in the procession of cars slowly flowing beside a rippling stream. The lush vegetation of the landscape contained a variety of plants: tall hardwoods and pines, islands of rhododendron and ferns dotting a sea of moss and wildflowers, and patches of bamboo that appeared and disappeared like Chinese screens masking the sparkling whitewater. The morning sun, high enough to clear the mountain ridges, sent shafts of light through the leafy canopy. The richness of gold and green made me feel like I was traveling through an Old Master's painting.

"Is this the entrance that your great-great grandfather helped build?"

"Yes. The stream was diverted at several places to accompany the road. Before Vanderbilt bought the land, loggers and farmers had clear-cut and decimated the forest. Everything you see now was specifically planted by Olmsted. Hundreds of thousands of plants were grown in the Biltmore nursery or transplanted from elsewhere."

"It doesn't look landscaped."

Nakayla laughed. "That's the point, Sam. To show off Mother Nature at her natural best."

The scenic lane continued for several miles before crossing into a valley of open pastures. We reached a crossroads where a security officer waved some of the cars straight ahead and others up a left-hand lane to a large brick and stucco building.

"Passholders can just enter," Nakayla said, "but I need to get you a guest ticket."

She parked the car and we went into the Visitor Center. I followed her past a scale-model displaying the locations of the house, winery, hotel, and stables. Then we hit a crowd of people vying for the shortest line in front of at least ten ticket windows.

"Quite a business," I said.

"This is nothing. Sometimes you have to buy a timed admission. You can only enter the house on the quarter hour stated on your ticket."

"How much is it?"

Nakayla waved her hand dismissively. "I'll get a dis-count with my pass. You can buy me lunch."

We waited about ten minutes until the woman be-hind the window said, "Next please," and we stepped forward. Nakayla showed her pass and asked for a guest ticket and two audio tours. Nakayla handed her a credit card as the woman rang up the total. I owed Nakayla a very nice lunch.

When we returned to the car, Nakayla said, "Let's tour the house first. That takes a couple hours. We'll use the audio headsets because you'll get a crash course in Biltmore history that way."

The road meandered between woods and pasture for a few more miles until a parking attendant waved us into a lot. All I saw were trees bordering it.

"Where's the house?" I asked.

"We'll take a shuttle."

"You don't think I can walk?" An edge crept into my voice.

Nakayla opened her door. "I wasn't thinking about you. The road is so steep that I prefer to use the shuttle. I'll meet you at the entrance, Daniel Boone."

Chagrined, I followed her to the pickup point.

The shuttle bus held around twenty-five and the ride was long enough to prove Nakayla correct. We drove through another gate, immediately turned right, and before me lay the largest house I'd ever seen.

A long esplanade stretched more than several foot-ball fields in front of it. The house ran perpendicular, and its central entrance aligned with a wide circular fountain spouting in the middle of the manicured lawn. Alongside the grand doorway rose a spiral of windows that must have enclosed a huge stairway ascending four or five stories to the roof. The exterior of the house appeared to be grayish yellow stone with ornate carvings around the windows and eaves. The steep roof had a bluish tinge broken by countless chimneys. Behind the house and blending with the roof lay a wall of the Blue Ridge Mountains, hazy in the summer's morning air. I was struck that I saw no other manmade edifice between this French castle and the Appalachians.

As we rode along the esplanade, Nakayla said, "What do you think?"

"I think I'd hate to heat this place."

As we entered the grand foyer, an attendant handed us each a brochure, took our audio tour tickets, and directed us to a cart where headsets and players were being distributed. A quick lesson showed me how to follow the room map on the brochure and dial up the accompanying narration. Nakayla and I proceeded to the first room, the Winter Garden, and I began a journey into a world of art and luxury that was overwhelming. Occasionally, Nakayla and I would exchange a few words, but most of the time, I was mesmerized by what I saw and heard. I wasn't alone. Often I stepped around people frozen in the rooms and halls, their eyes focused on some painting or piece of furniture, their hands clutching their audio devices, and their mouths hanging open.

One woman in the enormous banquet hall stood like a traffic cop, her arm pointing here and there. I realized she was reenacting what the narrator was saying, repeating his words to herself. Her finger went to the carvings over the mantel above the huge fireplace, swung to the flags of the original thirteen colonies displayed along the length of the walls, and then swept to the loft opposite the fireplace where a pipe organ was playing. A man who had to be her husband stepped beside her, pulled one of the earpieces off her head, and said above the notes of the pipe organ, "Winnie, they built the house faster than you're taking the tour." She nodded, put the earpiece in place, and started pointing again.

Two things made a strong impression on me. The chess set and table owned by Napoleon Bonaparte was fascinating enough, but when the narrator said the table had held Napoleon's heart for three days before his burial, I really took a closer look. The music room, finished later than other rooms on the first floor, caught my attention because the narrator said priceless art from the National Gallery in Washington, D.C., had been stored there during World War II. An enemy bomber certainly would have had trouble navigating through the mountains in search of a target.

Off the music room, Nakayla and I stepped onto a wide stone terrace. The view of the mountains was spectacular.

"See the tallest peak to the left." Nakayla pointed out the distant summit. "That's Mt. Pisgah, the heart of Pisgah National Forest."

"Nice to have a national forest next door," I said.

She turned to me. "George Vanderbilt owned that mountain. When he stepped out on this terrace, he wasn't looking next door."

"Impressive. So he gave it to the government?"

"His wife Edith sold the land after his death to the U.S. Department of Agriculture. She knew protection of the forest would have been her husband's goal anyway, and she chose the best way to make that happen."

We walked back inside, and I noticed from the brochure that our tour continued on the second floor. As I'd thought, a wide, suspended staircase rose just off the main foyer. I stood in the middle of the spiral, looking up at an ornate wrought-iron chandelier held in place by a single bolt in the ceiling four stories above my head. Not only did I get dizzy, I got nervous thinking about all the weight that could come crashing down on me. I saw the multitude of tourists going up the stone steps that had no underneath support but simply stuck out at right angles from the wall. Yet, these architectural designs that defied gravity paled in comparison to the effort it would take me climb the staircase.

Nakayla watched from the foot of the banister. Her smile was warm and understanding.

"Is there an elevator?" I asked.

"Yes. Mind if I tag along?"

The rest of the tour covered a series of bedrooms, servant quarters, salons, and sitting rooms. Then we took the elevator to the basement. The windowless stone hallway led us to a strange open space called the Halloween Room. The story goes that one Halloween the Vanderbilts threw a party and everybody came down to this basement room to draw on the walls. The floor to ceiling canvas must have brought out the child in everyone, for the drawings were plentiful and some were actually quite good. Many appeared to represent some narrative story that might have developed on the spot. Sort of like cave paintings by the rich and famous.

Although the walls were interesting, attention soon became focused on the old photographs displayed in cases interspersed through the room. They documented the clearing of the property and construction of the house until its opening on Christmas, 1895. Nakayla motioned me over to one photograph. The caption identified George Vanderbilt and Frederick Olmsted standing on a dirt road in front of a crew of what must have been nearly fifty men. Black men and white men not separated by race. The workers wore rugged clothes and shoes. Some looked uncomfortable posing for the camera.

"Tikima and I always stop here," Nakayla said. "We wondered which of the men is our Elijah."

"You don't have a family picture?"

"No. I suspect Elijah didn't have money for such things. Besides, any photographs would have been taken in Chicago with his wife, and he must have left them there."

I stepped closer to the picture, peering into the faces of the black men, trying to read some sign that would show me who was Olmsted's favorite, the one whose body would be found over twenty-five years later floating in the French Broad River. Tikima had stood where I did, asking the same question, and heading for the same fate.

"WANT ANOTHER GLASS of wine?" I opened the leather-bound list and scanned the Biltmore Estate whites. "Maybe a Sauvignon Blanc?"

"No. The Pinot Grigio was fine." Nakayla took the last bite of her shrimp salad and dabbed the corners of her mouth with her napkin. "The quality of the label has certainly improved over the past few years."

Nakayla and I had eaten at the bistro right beside the winery and selected our entrees based upon the wine we wanted to drink. I'd polished off two beef medallions, grateful for anything not prepared by a hospital.

I drained the last of my Merlot and caught the eye of our waitress. "I'm no connoisseur," I told Nakayla, "but I could get into sampling the entire list. Do my part to support the local economy."

The waitress appeared at my right elbow. "Would you care for dessert?"

I winked at Nakayla. "You've still got my lunch money to burn. Try something."

Nakayla shook her head. "I'm too full. There's ice cream down at the stable. We can walk there later. Tikima and I always took a calorie-filled trip down memory lane."

"Because of the stable?"

"No. The ice cream. When we had good report cards, our parents would treat us to the Biltmore Dairy Bar. It used to be in the village right outside the estate."

"If a good report card was the requirement, I'd have never been in the place."

The waitress returned with the check, I left a generous tip, and Nakayla and I walked to the end of the winery parking lot. A flat expanse of pasture lay before us. A river ran along its far border with a thick wall of trees lining the opposite shore.

"What's that?" I asked.

"The French Broad. Farther downstream it merges with the Swannanoa."

Farther downstream was where Tikima's body had been found. On this side of the river, the pasture seemed to go right to the water's edge. Easy enough to access with a four-wheel-drive vehicle. There were probably service roads a regular car could navigate. Nakayla had driven her car from the shuttle parking lot to the winery. I wanted to get closer to the river.

"The stables are down to the right," she said. "It's not a bad walk."

"Let's drive. But not to the stables. We need to find a way to the river."

"You're looking for the place where they—" She couldn't finish the sentence.

"Right now I'm just looking. I'd like to see how fast the current flows and whether there are some sandy banks that could match the traces on Tikima's Avalon."

"All right." She started for the car. "We'll backtrack toward the house. I think I saw a service road on our way here."

The sign EMPLOYEES ONLY by the single lane blacktop served as encouragement, not a deterrent. The smooth pavement led across the field and must have been a farm road for getting agricultural equipment to various sections of the cultivated bottom land. Not being a farmer, I had no idea if the plants around me were for people, livestock, or soil retention. No one seemed to be working the field, probably because it was Saturday.

"So, this really is a working farm," I said.

"Yes." Nakayla slowed the Hyundai as the asphalt suddenly turned to gravel. "Friends have asked me why I like to come here. How can I stand to be around such obscene wealth?"

"What do you tell them?"

"That the Biltmore House is both a national treasure and a business. George Vanderbilt always saw it as a working estate. His grandson Bill Cecil and the younger generation have never taken any federal money so I'm not watching my tax dollars at work."

I looked out over the field and saw the winery in the distance. "I've seen enough of my tax dollars at work, thank you. This would be an improvement."

The road arced right and brought us to within twenty yards of the river. Looking ahead, I could see we wouldn't get any closer.

"Stop the car. I want to walk to the bank."

Nakayla parked in the middle of the road. I got out and stepped carefully over the uneven ground. The strip of land between the river and the road was uncultivated, but the wild grass didn't grow higher than my ankle. The terrain sloped down to the water's edge where the vegetation changed to reeds. Between the stalks, the ground became cracked mud rather than loose soil. Some of the reeds were bent, pointing downstream.

"What do you think?" Nakayla asked.

I kneeled down on my good leg and grabbed a fistful of dirt. "This isn't what we found in the car." I opened my hand for her to see. "It's sediment from high water, not sand that's been pounded into grains by the constant turbulence of the current."

"Isn't it all from the river?"

"Yes, but heavy rains erode dirt from the hills, turning the water muddy. Flashfloods raise the level and as the river recedes, the soil is left to dry." I got to my feet and pointed to the fields. "That's one reason the bottom land is so fertile."

"Tikima wasn't killed along this section?"

I shrugged. "The only speculation I'll make is Tikima's car had to be elsewhere. It could have been here at some point that Saturday night, but the footprint on the carpet was sand from a different location."

I sidestepped down the slope to the bank. The river flowed dark and slow, unbroken by the whitewater I'd seen on the stream along the entrance to the estate. Trees grew on the opposite bank, their tangled roots exposed where the current stripped the earth beneath them. Dragonflies darted around me. A water snake glided by, barely creating a ripple in its wake. Looking upstream and downstream, I saw no break in the shoreline, no sandy beach where Tikima's killers would have dumped her body.

The evidence of the recent river rising made me wonder if the police had taken a swifter current into account when determining how far Tikima's body could have traveled. I remembered we'd had several gully-washer thunderstorms over the past few weeks. I'd ask Peters.

"Someone's coming." Nakayla grabbed my hand and pulled me toward the car. "What should we tell them?"

A white pickup sped down the dirt road. The vehicle slowed as the driver saw us walking toward the Hyundai.

"Wait for them to ask us questions," I said, and gave a friendly wave to our visitor.

The driver's door bore the Biltmore Estate logo. The truck stopped directly behind Nakayla's car. The window rolled down.

"Can I help you?" A man who looked to be in his early forties asked the question without the ever-present smile of the other employees. The Biltmore security insignia on his sleeve made clear he expected an answer.

I kept walking closer so I wouldn't have to shout. "We just wanted to see the river. Any put-ins along here? We'd like to bring our kayaks next time." I eased up to where I could read his nameplate. Jake Matthews.

He rubbed two fingers across his black mustache as he eyed Nakayla and me carefully. "Kayaking? You'd best go upstream to the Bent Creek section. Take 191 a couple miles and you can't miss it. Right across from the North Carolina Arboretum and beneath the Blue Ridge Parkway."

"Thanks. This is a pretty spot."

He nodded. "Yep, but it's not open to guests. You need to turn around and drive back to the public road."

"Certainly, Officer Matthews." I turned to Nakayla, remembering the name written in Tikima's file. "At least we won't have to get Luther to bail us out."

She hesitated a second and then picked up the cue. "You'd never hear the end of it."

Jake leaned his head farther out the window. "Y'all know Luther?"

"Yes," I said, "but it's been awhile since we've spoken. He probably gets weekends off now."

Jake laughed. "He wishes. Weekends we need everybody here, even the boss."

"I suppose you've still got the Armitage guys covering the back entrances."

"Yeah. If we can keep them awake."

"Do you suppose Luther would mind if we dropped by to say hello?"

Jake grinned. "No. I'm headed back to the office now. You can follow me."

Nakayla made a Y-turn on the narrow road while Jake swung his truck in a circle over the grass.

"What are you going to do when this guy takes us to Luther Rawlings?" Nakayla asked.

"I'll say 'Hello, good to see you again.' He'll hesitate, not sure of when we met and I'll let him off the hook by re-introducing myself and you."

"Okay," Nakayla said skeptically.

"Then you'll say that Tikima was your sister and she spoke highly of him. I'll take it from there."

With our script firmly in hand, we trailed the pickup to a building beyond the ticket center. A number of company vehicles ranging from golf carts to heavy-duty pickups were in the lot. Jake pointed out his window to a visitors spot and parked a couple spaces away. He took us through the front entrance and down a hall to an open door at the end. He knocked on the jamb and stepped into the office.

"Brought some friends to see you, Luther." Jake winked at me like he'd planned the whole thing.

A beefy man pushing retirement looked up from the paperwork on his desk. His florid face was rough as sandpaper and his stony expression hinted at a personality to match.

I stepped forward, my hand extended. "Luther, good to see you again."

Without the slightest hesitation, the head of security pushed his rolling chair away from his desk. "Who the hell are you?"

Not exactly the response I'd been expecting. "Sam Blackman." I dropped my hand to my side. "We met through Tikima Robertson. This is her sister Nakayla."

"Mr. Rawlings," Nakayla said, sensing we'd better jump back on more formal ground.

"Tikima Robertson," Luther repeated.

"Yes, sir. My sister."

Jake Matthews rubbed his mustache, not sure what was happening.

Luther stood, and I thought he'd never stop rising. The man must have been six-and-a-half-feet tall. In his uniform, he looked like a battalion crunched into one person.

"Thanks, Jake," he said. "I'll catch up with my old friends Sam and Nakayla for a few minutes. You can close the door."

His colleague backed away. "Nice to meet you folks."

"Likewise," I said.

No one said anything until the door clicked shut and Jake's footsteps faded away.

"Odd," Luther said. "I rarely forget a face, especially one connected to a gimp leg."

I felt my face color.

"We've never met, have we." His words were a statement, not a question.

"No," I said.

"Good. So let's start over. Who are you? Reporters?"

"We're who we said we were, except for knowing you. I'm Sam Blackman and I was discharged from the V.A. hospital yesterday. Nakayla is Tikima's sister."

Luther scratched his face with a broad hand while he thought things over. "So what do you want?" He motioned us to take the two chairs opposite his desk and then he sat down.

I decided to get right to the point. "As you know, Tikima's body was found in the French Broad not too far from here. Any way someone could have snuck onto the estate?"

He snorted. "With over eight thousand acres? Hell, yes. The police already asked me that." He looked at

Nakayla. "I understand your interest, but how does your friend fit in the picture?"

"My sister visited him in the hospital the morning before she died. He worked in criminal investigations for the military."

Luther's eyes narrowed. "You on this case officially?"

"No," I said. "I guess you could call me a friend of the family."

"And you can work looser than the police. Like lying to Jake to get to see me."

"There's that advantage," I admitted.

He leaned across the desk and picked at his ragged fingernails. "More power to you, but I don't know how I can help."

"When's the last time you saw Tikima?" I asked.

He grabbed a pocket calendar from beside his phone and flipped back a few pages. "May 29th. She came by that Tuesday afternoon."

"The Tuesday before she died," I said. "Was it related to her work?"

"I thought she was just touching base. Tikima would come by several times a year to make sure we were happy with Armitage's services."

"Jake doesn't speak highly of their guards."

Luther waved his hand at the space where Jake had stood. "He takes himself too seriously. I give Armitage the boring stuff—check-in deliveries, direct lost tourists to the main entrance, and watch for people trying to sneak in."

"Any reports of anyone sneaking in the night of June 2nd?"

"No. I gave the same information to the police." Luther glanced at his watch; not an exaggerated motion for our benefit, but I knew our time was limited.

"If Tikima wasn't here for business, do you mind telling us why she came to see you?"

"She had some questions about the old days. I knew her family worked here before the house was built. She was interested in employment records. How far back they might go."

"Do you keep those here?" I asked.

"No. They're at the company headquarters uptown. But I told her I doubted if they went back much further than thirty or forty years. She was looking for records from the teens and twenties."

"Did she say why?"

"Researching family history." Luther turned to Nakayla. "I understand your great-great grandfather worked with Olmsted in laying out the master plan."

"Yes. Elijah knew Olmsted from Chicago."

A smile broke through Luther's hard features. "That must have been something. The things they accomplished. Reshaping the land itself." His eyes brightened. "That was another thing Tikima asked. Had Vanderbilt ever exploited the mineral rights on his property?"

"Like mining?" I asked.

"Yes. But I've never heard of such a thing. Vanderbilt was interested in renewable resources like forests, crops, and dairy cows. They used to have a prize-winning herd."

"Did Tikima say why she was interested in mineral rights?"

"No. But there are a lot of rock hounds combing these mountains." He chuckled. "I thought she was probably setting me up for some security system to keep the tourists from stealing stones off the property."

"And you never had any contact after that Tuesday, even by phone."

"No. She thanked me for my time and said she'd check back in a couple months."

I figured we'd learned as much as we could. I got to my feet slowly, conscious that he'd noticed my leg. Luther stood and offered his hand. His grip was firm. Then he clasped Nakayla's, gently patting it with his left in a show of concern.

"I'm so sorry about your sister," he said. "I considered her a friend."

"Thank you." Nakayla put her left hand on top of his, keeping them bound together for a few seconds. Then she let go as she asked, "Mr. Rawlings? How long has your family worked for the estate?"

"This September I'll have forty years in. My grandmother spun wool for Mrs. Vanderbilt and my grandfather and my father worked for the dairy. Guess we go back to the late teens. Not as far as your family, but more than most. Our kinfolk certainly would have known each other."

I glanced at Nakayla and saw the tightening of her jaw. She knew their families would have known each other, but back in those days of Jim Crow and the KKK, would they have liked each other? A more ominous question crossed my mind. Was Tikima's death linked to old secrets from a bygone era?

FOURTEEN

"You still want your ice cream?" I buckled my seatbelt, prepared to go wherever Nakayla wanted.

"No." She checked her wristwatch. "It's three-fifteen. We have time to run over to Pisgah. I'd like to talk to that ranger."

"James Taylor?"

"Yes. Easy enough to remember." She started the car. "What did you think about Luther Rawlings?"

"He seemed straightforward. He didn't hesitate to tell us what Tikima was looking for."

"Did he?" Nakayla arched her thin eyebrows. "All he said was Tikima was interested in employment records and mineral rights. No names regarding whose employment or what minerals."

"Do you think he was lying?"

"I think there's a good chance he was incomplete with the truth. His job is to protect the estate."

"Second to protecting himself," I said. "If we get additional information that contradicts what he told us, we'll have to pay our good friend Luther another visit."

She cocked her head and stared at me. "You didn't completely trust him either, did you?"

I grinned. "Old habits die hard. I didn't want to prejudice you. Whenever I investigate with a partner, I want two brains working independently and arguing the case back and forth."

"Then believe me, you won't find anyone more in-dependent or argumentative in Asheville than me. Are we clear on that, partner?"

"Yes. That's one thing we definitely agree on."

We drove about twenty minutes, winding through valley roads and passing small strip malls and country churches. Then the area grew more congested. A Walmart appeared on our right.

"Welcome to the entrance to Pisgah National Forest." Nakayla put on her right-turn signal as we approached a major intersection. "Tikima and I hated when that Walmart was built. Until we got caught in a cloudburst while camping and bought ponchos and dry socks from their sports department."

We turned onto a narrower road and left the commercial sprawl behind. The forest closed around us and we drove a couple miles until we saw signs for the Rangers Welcome Center. We found a space at the end of the parking lot and walked past minivans and SUVs loaded with mountain bikes, kayaks, and camping gear.

The building looked well maintained and the grounds were landscaped with flowers and shrubs. Stone and wood construction created a rustic atmosphere. Inside, displays and interactive maps provided orientation to the trails, streams, and recreational activities the park offered.

Visitors of all ages wandered through the large space, collecting brochures and plotting their adventures. Surprisingly, the ranger at the information desk was free.

"May I help you?" The woman smiled at us. Her brown hair was braided in a long pigtail that drooped over her shoulder and touched the edge of her nameplate. Rita Carson.

"We were hoping to speak with Ranger Taylor," I said. "Is he here?"

"Not unless a fight broke out in the parking lot." Her eyes twinkled. "Just kidding." She pointed to the ranger insignia on her sleeve. "James has Enforcement written on his. He gets to carry a gun."

"So he doesn't have a particular station?" I asked.

"No, he has an office in administration. James is head of enforcement for this section of the park. Any crimes committed here come under his jurisdiction. But right now he's up at the Cradle of Forestry. They're having a chainsaw sculpture demonstration, part of the Lumberjack Festival this weekend."

"Can we talk to him?"

"That depends upon how loud the chainsaws are. And whether you want to pay the admission charge this late in the day."

Nakayla reached in her purse. "Admission's no problem."

"Good. But you pay up there." Ranger Rita took a notepad from the desk. "Give me your names and I'll have the base dispatcher radio that you're coming."

The Cradle of Forestry was almost ten miles farther into the park. Although we averaged only forty miles an hour, the time passed swiftly. For most of the journey, we traveled beside a cascading stream, often broken by waterfalls. At one point, we passed a line of cars parked along the road's shoulder.

"That's Looking Glass Falls," Nakayla said. "One of the most photographed sites in the mountains."

I caught a glimpse of mist boiling up from unseen turbulence and then a quick flash of whitewater tumbling over a slick rock face. "I'll have to come back sometime and explore. Good place to test my sports leg."

"You'd better do your testing away from this stream. If you fall in, it won't matter which leg you're wearing."

"I'll ask Hinnant if they make one that converts into a raft. Maybe collect a bunch of specialty legs—like golf clubs."

Nakayla didn't laugh and I decided to keep my morbid sense of humor to myself.

We paid six dollars each at the Cradle of Forestry entrance and obeyed multiple attendants as they waved us to a parking space.

"Vanderbilt established the Biltmore School of Forestry in the 1890s." Nakayla locked the car and we started walking. "He had brought in a guy named Pinchot to manage his forest."

"How do you manage a forest?"

"Avoid clear cutting, re-plant seedlings, and remove trees that hinder the growth of stronger ones. Remember Henderson Youngblood mentioned Vanderbilt's forestry in the journal."

One of the other things in addition to Elijah's murder we knew to be true, I thought.

"The Cradle of Forestry has reconstructed some of the original buildings," Nakayla said. "A German, Carl Schenck, followed Pinchot and developed the school to its full potential."

"Why'd it close?"

"I think Schenck went back to Germany just before the outbreak of World War One. Either he didn't want to return to America or he couldn't. And then Vanderbilt died in 1914." Nakayla nodded to the large building now visible at the end of the parking lot. "You can find everything you want to know in there."

Off to our left, a chainsaw roared to life.

"Right now everything I want to know is down there." I pointed to a trail that branched off toward the whine of the saw's engine. "Let's see if Ranger James Taylor has more than Carolina on his mind."

The even surface of the trail made walking easy for me. A late afternoon breeze cooled the air and for a second I thought snowflakes swirled around me. Several stuck to my lips. Sawdust.

We emerged in a small clearing where a blizzard raged. An enthusiastic crowd stood upwind of a chainsaw-wielding man who attacked an upright section of a tree trunk at least three feet in diameter. A cluster of Brownie scouts held their hands over their ears and watched in amazement as chips and dust spewed like the eruption of a geyser. Scattered on the sawdust-covered ground were a menagerie of freshly carved wildlife: a bear cub, squirrel, coiled rattlesnake, and doe with a fawn. Each sculpture stood at least a yard high and the detail exacted by the lethal blade created uncanny likenesses.

We started to circle around the clearing when I saw a hand wave behind the Brownie troop. Partially hidden by the spray of sawdust, the figure moved away from the crowd till I recognized a uniformed ranger. Shouting a greeting was useless so we waited for him to get closer. He had the energetic strut of a bantam rooster and the build of a pipe cleaner man, the figure Stanley and I made as kids out of the fuzzy wires our father kept with his tobacco humidor.

"James Taylor," he shouted above the noise. He took Nakayla's hand first and then shook mine.

A gust of wind suddenly whipped across the clearing engulfing us in a shower of sawdust. We jumped like we'd been drenched with a tsunami of cold water.

"Let's get closer to the exhibit hall," Taylor said, "where we can hear ourselves talk." He set off at a quick pace while Nakayla lingered with me.

I moved as fast as I could, but in addition to the artificial leg, I was plagued with woodchips sliding under my shirt and rubbing against my back. I looked at Nakayla. Her face was coated in dust. I must have appeared the same because she started laughing, laughing so hard she had to stop and catch her breath. For the first time, I noticed the dimples deep in her cheeks. Maybe the sawdust exaggerated them or maybe the sawdust for a brief moment covered the layer of sadness Tikima's murder had cast over her.

Ranger Taylor waited by a bench outside the exhibit center. He hadn't fared much better. Underneath his wood particle veneer, he looked to be in his mid-fifties, thin faced with crooked yellow teeth. These showed in a broad grin as he watched us approach.

"Well, you can imagine what kind of day I've had. Chainsaw sculpture is good for the tourists but I'll be digging woodchips out of my ears for a week." He pointed to the bench. "Take a load off. I'm used to standing."

I didn't know if he was being chivalrous to Nakayla or considerate of my obvious physical challenge, but I didn't argue. Nakayla sat beside me and Taylor stepped back a pace so that he didn't tower over us.

"Sam Blackman and Nakayla Robertson," he said. His expression turned serious. "You related to Tikima?"

"She was my sister."

"I was so sorry to hear what happened. Tikima had helped us with the security system here. I'd hoped to get her as a ranger someday."

"I think she'd have liked that," Nakayla said.

Taylor wiped sawdust away from his eyes. "Is there something I can do for you?"

Nakayla put her hand on my knee. "Sam's a veteran. A friend of Tikima's. He worked in criminal investigations for the military. We're unofficially checking with some of Tikima's favorite clients."

Taylor studied me. "About what?"

"About anything that might give the police a lead," I said. "You know how it is. When somebody close to you dies, you want to do something."

He nodded. "Sure. And I'll help any way I can."

"When did you see Tikima last?" I asked.

He thought for a second. "Must have been the end of May. Before Memorial Day Weekend because that kicks off our heavy tourist season. I try to get administrative things out of the way before then."

"You contacted Tikima?"

"No. She called me. Tikima knew our schedule and wanted to meet before the summer crunch. We lease equipment from Armitage and she pitched some upgrades."

"Nothing out of the ordinary?"

"No. I prodded her about becoming a ranger and she just laughed and said she was done with uniforms."

I decided to pursue another angle. "Does the national park stretch to the French Broad?"

"Close. Especially at the North Carolina Arboretum."

That was the second time today the arboretum had

been mentioned. Jake Matthews had linked it to the Bent Creek section of the river.

"At Bent Creek?" I asked.

"Yes." Taylor's eyes widened. "You think Tikima was killed at Bent Creek? I thought her body was found farther downstream."

"You tell me if that's possible. I saw the high water marks the river left from recent flooding and wondered if the police estimate took the current surge into account. Luther Rawlings says Tikima wouldn't have been on the Biltmore Estate property."

Taylor spit to his side. "Rawlings. Pardon my French, but he wouldn't know his ass from a hole in the ground." He took a step forward. "Did Rawlings say Tikima was killed on park land?"

"No. I'm just looking at all upstream possibilities. If it was park land, then it's your case."

Taylor mulled that over for a moment. "Was Tikima in her car?"

"At first the police thought no, but new evidence suggests otherwise."

"What new evidence?"

"Soil samples on the tires and a man's footprint on the driver's carpet."

"Who's working the case from Asheville?"

"Peters."

Taylor nodded. "He's competent."

"But Sam's the one who found the clues in Tikima's car," Nakayla said.

"That so?" He examined me closely like I might be withholding other information.

I shrugged. "Sometimes you get lucky."

"Give me a description of the car. I know it was some

kind of Japanese make. They all look the same to me."
He pulled a notepad and pen from his chest pocket and
blew sawdust off both of them. "I'll cross-reference it
with any vehicular reports my staff made around the
time she disappeared."

Nakayla gave him the information including the
Avalon's plate number.

Taylor flipped the pad closed and stuffed it and the
pen back in his pocket. "If I turn up anything, I'll send
it straight to Peters rather than have you take it to him."

"I understand. Nakayla and I are strictly low profile. Might be easier if you didn't mention we contacted
you."

Taylor grinned. "Gotcha. Everybody's got their turf
to protect."

I stood. "But I'd appreciate your telling us whatever
you learn after you talk to Peters."

Nakayla handed him her card. "Here's how you can
reach me."

Taylor read it. "Investigative Alliance for Underwriters. You two are quite the detective team. Tell me, did
Luther Rawlings ask for a description of Tikima's car?"

"No," I said.

"There you go." He spit again and our interview was
over.

INSTEAD OF TURNING back the way we came, Nakayla
drove us farther into Pisgah Forest.

"I want to take the Blue Ridge Parkway back to
Asheville," she said.

"Won't that be longer?"

"Not from where we are. The view is spectacular at
sunset, and we'll exit at Bent Creek."

"Then you've got my vote."

The ridges blocked the late afternoon sun and plunged the winding road into deep shadow. We climbed steadily until I saw a sign for the Parkway. Nakayla took the ramp and we came to the top of the mountain. Suddenly light streamed through the windows and off to the left the enlarged golden sun hung poised above the distant peaks. As we drove along the spine of the Appalachians, the mountain ranges looked like waves on the ocean. Gold-tipped and frozen, they rolled away from us on either side.

The Parkway made a slow descent with the panoramic vistas changing from right to left as we crossed from one side of the ridge summit to the other. Several times the road went through unlit tunnels where sudden crests were easier to bore through than build the road over.

Dusk had darkened the sky by the time Nakayla left the Parkway at the exit for Highway 191. As we traveled down the curving ramp, I saw a sign for the North Carolina Arboretum.

"I didn't know we had a state arboretum," I said.

"Over four hundred acres. At one time, it had been within Pisgah National Forest, but now it's part of the state's university system. Guess who first envisioned it?"

I named the only plant guy I knew. "Frederick Law Olmsted?"

"Give the man a prize. But the arboretum wasn't created until nearly a hundred years after he proposed it." She braked at a stop sign. "And there's the Bent Creek put-in."

Almost directly across the intersecting two-lane

highway lay a wide strip of dark sand beside the river. Kayakers were coming off the water and loading their boats onto roof racks and trailers. Nakayla crossed over and parked along the shoulder, leaving room for the exiting vehicles to pass.

"Want to take a look?"

I was halfway out of the car before she finished the question. Together we walked to the water's edge. Above the sounds of the kayakers and car engines rose the calls of frogs and katydids. Lightning bugs flickered along the opposite shore. Before us ran the wide river, inky black now that no light penetrated its surface.

I bent down and scooped up a handful of sand. The grains were coarse and dark. Those on Tikima's tires and carpet had been lighter. How much different would this sand look once it dried?

Upstream, a pair of headlights flew across the river. The Blue Ridge Parkway continued on, spanning the French Broad, oblivious to what might have happened beneath its stone arch.

NAKAYLA LET ME off at the front door of the Kenilworth. She offered to come up and fix me a late supper, but I wanted only a shower and bed. I itched from the sawdust and my stump ached from the exertion of the day's activities. She promised to pick me up at nine the next morning so we could visit the Gold for the Taking mine and the Woolworth Walk in downtown Asheville.

Once in the apartment, I stripped out of my clothes and dropped them into the washer/dryer combo off the kitchen. I removed my leg, hand-washed the liner and socks, and then hit the shower. Washing took twice as long since I had to steady myself with one hand at all times. I thought about the showers Tikima must have taken, her prosthetic arm probably left outside the door where my artificial leg now lay. I felt her presence around me.

The phone rang as I sat on the edge of the bed, drying my hair. Probably Nakayla or Peters. She'd given the detective the number.

I picked up the receiver from the nightstand. "Blackman."

"Nathan Armitage here." His voice was clipped and strictly business.

"Hi, Nathan."

"So you didn't go to Birmingham."

"No. I'm staying in town a few days."

"Yeah. Well, thanks for the heads up."

The files. Peters had interviewed Armitage about his client files and told him they were found in Tikima's apartment. Now Armitage was pissed at me.

"Look. Your files were at the scene of a break-in. Tikima's sister and I turned them in to the police. Peters told me not to say anything to anyone. You know how cops are with evidence."

"I'm not concerned about the cops. I'm concerned that you seem to be snooping into my clients' affairs. Luther Rawlings called me and said Nakayla and some hotdog were pumping him for information—a day after you did your civic duty and gave the police my files."

His accusatory tone punched all my wrong buttons. "Maybe I'm just speaking up for Tikima again when you won't. Do your own god-damned investigation." I hung up. If Tikima hadn't confided in Mr. B. C. Cure, then neither would I.

Although it was only a little after nine, I felt exhausted. As I crawled between the sheets, I patted the well-worn Bible Tikima kept on her nightstand. I'm not one for praying, but I told Tikima if she could put in a good word with the Big Guy, we could use a little help.

The ringing of the phone woke me. Tikima's digital clock read 10:14 p.m. I reached over the Bible and picked up the receiver.

"Blackman," I mumbled.

"Sam." Nakayla's voice was tight with excitement. "A man just called. He wouldn't give his name but he said if I wanted to know what happened to my sister I should meet him tonight."

"Where?"

"Riverside Cemetery. It's north of town near the Montford historic district."

The directions meant nothing to me. "Nakayla, that sounds like a setup. Why wouldn't he give his name?"

"He said he didn't know who to trust. That the police are covering up things and he has proof. He said he'd heard I'd hired a private detective and to bring him."

The skin on my neck was crawling. "I don't like it."

"Riverside's not that isolated. There are houses close by."

"And the river?"

"The French Broad."

The damn French Broad. Everything kept coming back to the French Broad.

"If you don't want to go, that's fine," Nakayla said. "I just wanted you to know about it."

"You're not going there alone."

"Sam, this might be our only break. I'm not going to lose him."

I ran my fingers through my hair trying to jump-start my brain. "Is he going to be at the entrance to the cemetery?"

"No." She hesitated. "He said to meet him at Thomas Wolfe's grave."

"Wolfe's buried there?"

"Yes."

I took a deep breath. "All right. Pick me up. I'll be downstairs."

"Thanks, Sam."

I could tell she was on the verge of tears. "Do you have a gun?" I asked.

"A little twenty-five automatic."

"Bring it."

FIFTEEN

"WHEN WE GET THERE, I want you to stay in the car." I gave Nakayla the order as she turned onto a side street of dimly lit houses.

"I'm not afraid."

"I know you're not. You're my runner. If this goes down bad, you get the hell out of here and call the cops. Pre-punch 911 so you can hit send and then floor the accelerator."

We came to a gate with a sign saying the cemetery closed at eight. A wrought-iron fence made going around impossible. We would have to leave the car, a development I didn't like.

"What do we do now?" Nakayla asked. "This is the only entrance."

"You stay with the car. I'd better go in on foot. Kill the lights."

She cut the beams. A half-moon cast a pale blue glow making shadows and objects nearly indistinguishable from one another.

"Are you sure?" she asked. "You've got to walk a ways."

"Yes. Are there any signs to Wolfe's grave?"

"No, but a few yards in, the road splits into three lanes. There's a rose marble marker that reads Riverside Cemetery. Take the middle fork, and then when the road forks again, the Wolfe family plot is on the right. If you come to a sign for William Sydney Porter, you've gone too far."

The name sounded familiar. "Who's he?"

"The author O. Henry."

Great, I thought. The writer famous for his surprise endings. "Have you got the gun?"

She reached in her purse and pulled out a black pistol. "There are seven in the clip." She handed it to me butt first.

"No. You keep it. Someone may frisk me. All I want is the flashlight."

"In the glove box." She put her hand on my shoulder. "For God's sake be careful."

"Careful's my middle name."

Actually my middle name was Clemens, as in Samuel Clemens, but we were dealing with enough writers for one night. I got out of the car quickly, minimizing the time the interior light flashed on. Nakayla rolled down the window so she could hear better. The air hummed with the noise of crickets.

"One more thing," I said. "If anybody drives up, you leave. It might be your mystery caller. Then come back in ten minutes. He should be in the cemetery by then. If I'm not back in twenty minutes, you go for help. Promise?"

"Promise." The word was barely a whisper.

"And turn the car around."

The flashlight felt hefty in my hand and was the black cylindrical style favored by the police. I kept it turned off, preferring to have my eyes adjust to the darkness. I climbed over the fence, my prosthetic leg turning what should have been child's play into a Herculean effort.

The old phrase "whistling past the graveyard" came to mind. However, the urge to relieve my built-up tension wasn't as strong as the urge to remain silent. I didn't want to come parading into a rendezvous with the equivalent of a target on my chest.

The road split and I took the middle lane. I descended a gradual slope, stepping off the pavement onto the grass where my footsteps would be muted. Rounding a curve, I saw the outline of an automobile pulled onto the shoulder. The shape of the car suggested a larger American vehicle, possibly a Crown Vic. I thought about Detective Peters and felt apprehensive that the police officer might be playing some double game.

The interior of the car was lost in shadow. If someone had seen my approach, he made no effort to reveal himself. I neared the trunk and saw extra radio antennae. The Crown Vic had to be a law enforcement vehicle. Was an officer planning to blow the whistle on a police cover-up?

"Hey," I said softly. "I'm here."

The only answer was the distant hoot of an owl. I eased toward the driver's door until I could make out the shape of someone behind the wheel.

"You all right in there?" I clicked on the flashlight. The narrow halogen beam pierced the side window and illuminated sandy brown hair matted with clumps of blood and torn flesh. I jumped back, repulsed by the grisly sight. Detective Peters' head was tilted forward on his chest, the side of his face coated with more blood that had congealed into a macabre mask.

I yanked open the door, hoping against the horror of the scene that Peters might still be alive. He toppled out of the seat. I stooped to catch him but the soaked fabric of his shirt slipped through my fingers, painting my clothes with blood as he fell.

Metal hit metal and I saw a pistol bounce off the car's threshold and hit the ground. Then the window of the open door exploded above my head. Dropping to grab Peters had saved my life.

The boom of a gunshot echoed through the hills. This wasn't the pop of a twenty-five caliber or the sharp crack of a rifle. Someone fired a forty-five or 357 Magnum.

I fell flat on the grass, rolling out of the pool of light cast by the car's interior. A second shot rang out. Peters' body twitched. The muzzle flash had come from about thirty yards away in direct line with the side of the Crown Vic. I dared not turn and run. My leg would slow me down and God only knew how many gravestones waited to trip me or how many men were after me. But I couldn't let my assailants move in for the kill.

I saw the pistol lying next to Peters. I'd be exposed for less than a second. I lunged forward, grabbed the gun, and scrambled away, half running, half crawling up a slope to the nearest monument. I crunched behind the stone slab, feeling the cool surface against my back.

The shooter fired again and the gravestone vibrated. Even a forty-five slug couldn't penetrate eight inches of granite. From the feel of the pistol, I knew I held a nine millimeter Glock. Not the stopping power of a forty-five, but enough to do serious damage. I lay flat on my stomach, gripping the gun in both hands. I had no idea if the clip was loaded or a cartridge was in the chamber.

I slithered around the edge of the headstone where I could see the car. A third shot fired; this time the muzzle flash was closer to me. I squeezed the trigger and the pistol kicked in my hand. The bullet might have been my last, but at least my enemy knew I was armed.

A blur of motion appeared, running low and zig-zagging away. In the moonlight, the shape was more shadow than substance, but I fired two more rounds to encourage his retreat. I hoped Nakayla had bolted at the first sound of gunfire. I didn't want her car blocking my attacker's escape.

An engine started. Headlights swept across a far knoll of gravestones as the killer sped into the night in a completely different direction. So much for Nakayla's one entrance. From the distance came the wail of sirens. The police were on the way. They would find one of their own had fallen. "Officer down," would spread over the radio and through the ranks like wildfire.

Suddenly my predicament became all too clear. The police would find me, Sam Blackman, beside the body of their comrade, smeared in his blood and holding a pistol that could be the murder weapon, now conveniently bearing my fingerprints.

For all my troubles, I was better off than Peters. I went back to the car, laid the gun on the seat, and then sat on the ground beside the dead detective. "Talk to me," I said. "Talk to me."

"Sam?"

I looked up. Nakayla stepped into the light, her small pistol clutched in both hands and her face wild with fear. But not the fear that should have sent her driving away and following my orders. This fear brought her out of the car and into a crossfire of bullets. Fear for me.

"Is he dead?"

"Yes. It's Peters. I found him in the car."

"It wasn't Peters on the phone. I'm sure I'd have recognized his voice."

"No. Peters was probably dead already. Someone used him as bait."

"Bait?"

"To lure us here." I picked up the flashlight from where I'd dropped it and got to my feet. I played the beam around the interior of the car. "See the blood's smeared on the floor of the backseat. And it's dried enough to be several hours old. I don't think Peters was killed here. The cemetery would have still been open."

"What do we do now?"

The sirens swelled and flashing blue lights winked through the trees.

I reached in the car and turned on the headlights. "Lay your pistol on the seat."

She stepped around Peters' body and set the gun beside the Glock. I grabbed her hand, intertwining my fingers with hers. Too late I realized Peters' blood now contaminated her skin. She didn't draw back but squeezed tighter.

"You shouldn't have taken such a chance," I said, and led her into the full intensity of the headlights.

"You're one to talk."

Two police cruisers raced through the cemetery. I let go of Nakayla's hand and then turned my palms to the approaching vehicles. Nakayla did the same.

"I'm one to talk all right, but I'll be damned if I know how I'm going to talk our way out of this mess."

The police cars slammed on brakes and swerved into a parallel angle that added their high beams to the Crown Vic's. All I could see was a blinding wall of light.

"We're unarmed," I shouted. "Detective Peters has been murdered."

The silhouette of a uniformed officer moved against the light. A second one followed. Both had arms extended bearing weapons. They moved slowly, like choreographed shadow puppets growing larger with each step. More sirens filled the air.

The second man bent over Peters. "He's been shot in the head." His voice quavered and I wondered if he'd ever seen a dead body before.

"There are two guns on the driver's seat," I said, forcing myself to speak calmly. "I used the Glock to shoot at the killer."

"Who was that?" the first officer asked. He turned to look in the car and the overhead interior light revealed a young man with dark hair, no older than his mid-twenties.

"Don't touch them," cautioned the policeman kneeling beside Peters. He stood and stepped forward, not trusting his partner to follow his order.

"I couldn't see who was shooting," I said. "I returned fire as he came at me. You can see where he shot out the side window."

The second officer studied the shattered glass. I blinked my eyes to clear my vision. The faces of the two patrolmen were identical. Twins in blue uniforms.

"What do we do?" twin number one whispered to his clone.

"You put me, Sam Blackman, in one car and my friend, Nakayla Robertson, in the other so we can't collaborate on a story. Then you get a tech crew and crime lab down here to scour the scene for evidence."

The Bobbsey twins looked at each other and shook their heads in unison.

"Keep your gun on them," the second man said. "I'll track down Uncle Newly." He walked back to a patrol car.

"Who's Uncle Newly?" I asked.

"Roy Peters' partner. Boy, is he going to be pissed."

WHILE MOST PEOPLE were in church at eleven o'clock Sunday morning, I was in jail. Not actually in a cell. I sat in an interrogation room nursing a cup of scorched coffee, but I was definitely in police custody. Nakayla's whereabouts were unknown. I assumed she was undergoing similar treatment.

The only small victory I'd enjoyed the previous night was when the officer who radioed Uncle Newly came back to say Nakayla and I were to be put in separate cars and kept clear of any other police until Uncle Newly arrived. The twins, who I now knew were Al and Ted Newland, had given me a look of respect. Somehow I'd known what Uncle Newly was going to say before the words were uttered.

Uncle Newly turned out to be Detective Curt "Newly" Newland. He'd arrived at the crime scene within twenty minutes, wearing a disheveled suit and shirt and his uncombed curly gray hair springing in all directions like tufts of crabgrass. And he was pissed.

I deduced that from his first words: "If I find out you had anything to do with Roy's death, I'll ream you so many new assholes you'll look like Swiss cheese."

I'd understood his anger and I'd told him so. Although I'd barely known Peters, the discovery of his body had left me numb. Peters and I'd had a rocky start, but mutual respect had forged a connection. There was no doubt in my mind that Peters meant to pursue Tikima's killer with all the resources he could muster.

The door to the interrogation room opened. Al and Ted entered followed by their uncle. It was nice to see a thriving family business these days.

"So, Mr. Blackman," Newland said. "Anything about your story you'd like to add or change?"

"Yes."

His tired face perked up.

"I'd like to be able to tell you who shot Peters and who killed Tikima Robertson. We're on the same side here."

He slid into a chair across the table. "Are we?"

I was losing patience. "Look, I've been fingerprinted so you could match me to the gun, had a paraffin test to prove I fired it, and let you enter my apartment without requiring a search warrant so you could get copies of the journal and the Armitage files I admitted making." I'd also asked them to bring me clean clothes since the blood-stained ones had been taken for evidence. "The only thing I'm not going to do is make a false confession while Peters' murderer gets away. Check the damn case file and the original journal and Armitage folders I gave Peters. They back up everything I've told you."

"There is no case file."

"What?" I looked from Newland to Al and Ted leaning against the wall. Their identical faces bore identical blank expressions.

"And we found no journal or Armitage folders in either his desk or logged into the evidence room." He paused. "You say Thomas Wolfe wrote this journal?"

I nodded. "Nakayla and I told Peters the handwriting

matched samples of Wolfe's." I wondered why Peters hadn't shared any of this with Newland. Then I remembered Peters had said his partner was on vacation.

"Thomas Wolfe," Newland repeated.

"And we discussed how it would be hard to know what might be fact or fiction."

"And then you found Roy's body near Thomas Wolfe's grave."

"That's why it was a setup. Whoever called knew that Nakayla and I couldn't resist that connection."

"Or Roy couldn't resist the connection if you said you wanted to meet him there."

"Peters wasn't killed there. I know it and you know it."

Newland smiled. "Chief Warrant Officer Sam Blackman. You must have been pretty good when you were in the service."

"Yeah. Amazing how much I remember since being discharged the day before yesterday."

"I'm not saying I believe or disbelieve everything you've told us. We're checking with Ted Mitchell, Jake Matthews, Luther Rawlings, and James Taylor. If they all corroborate your story, well, then that's a few more points in your favor."

"They're more likely to be suspects than I am."

"Maybe. What I have found on Roy's desk is a legal pad with these notes. He pulled a slip of paper from his suit coat. 'Check out Sam Blackman. Last person to see Tikima Robertson alive. Slips in and out of the hospital at will. Military trained. Hot-head.'"

"I won't dispute that. He probably wrote those sentences after our first meeting. I was upset because I'd found evidence in Tikima's car that your men had missed. I told him I thought the police had botched the investigation. Her car is now in the department's custody."

Newland nodded to Al and the young man went to check it out. I should have mentioned that earlier, but I didn't realize the case file had disappeared.

"So what's your evaluation of the people you spoke with yesterday?" Newland asked.

"No one seemed alarmed. I got the sense they told me what they knew. Ranger Taylor struck me as the sharper officer and he had undisguised contempt for the abilities of Rawlings. But Taylor's more astute questions could have been a ploy to determine what we knew. At this point I suspect everyone."

"Unfortunately, that includes people you didn't talk to," Newland said. "I know Roy well enough that if he'd had a hot lead he wouldn't wait until I got back Monday. He probably had the case file and documents with him. So he either talked to the wrong person, or you talked to the wrong person."

"If it was someone Peters interviewed, the missing case file would tell him about Nakayla and me."

"And how to reach you and what to say to sucker you in."

I took a deep breath, relieved at the possibility that the first consequence of my unofficial investigation might not have been Detective Peters' murder.

"Of course, you could have staged everything," Newland said, and the smile vanished.

"And my motive?"

"What's anyone's motive? You tell me that and we're a lot closer to solving this case."

"Read the journal. The murder of Roy Peters, Tikima

Robertson, and Elijah Robertson are tied together. Find the connection, Detective Newland, and you'll find your partner's killer."

There was a knock at the door and Al returned. He motioned for Newland to step outside. Twin Ted remained.

"How many Newlands are on the police force?" I asked.

"Just the three of us. But our father and grandfather were officers."

"Your father retired?"

He shook his head. "No. He was killed in the line of duty. Al and I were eight. Our mother didn't want us to join, but we Newlands can be hardheaded."

"Sorry," I said. I sensed Uncle Newly shared the hardheaded determination, and I suspected he'd promised his brother's widow he'd keep an eye on her boys.

"Yeah. Now Roy Peters' boys will have to grow up without a dad. One's twelve, the other's nine."

Newland came back in. "The car checks out. Crime lab also found casings from a forty-five at the cemetery. They're running them for prints but I'll bet my next paycheck they were wiped clean."

"What about a preliminary M.E. report?" Those usually take awhile, but we were talking about the murder of a police officer and everyone on the force would be chomping at the bit to get started.

"You're correct that the body was moved. We found a spot in a remote corner of the cemetery where the chain-link fence was cut. Two cars drove in from an adjacent recreational park. One was the Crown Vic. They knew the one spot where they would have clear access to a cemetery lane without being blocked by gravestones. The M.E. estimates time of Roy's death at closer to 6 p.m."

"Nakayla and I were with Ranger Taylor."

Newland nodded. "Yes. He confirmed you were together."

"So he's not a suspect?"

"Not unless you planned this together."

"What about Rawlings and Matthews?"

"We'll handle the investigation."

That probably meant Newland hadn't checked for alibis. He would proceed carefully and didn't want me tromping through his case.

I stood. "Am I free to go?"

"Yes. But don't leave Asheville. I'm holding you and Miss Robertson as material witnesses."

"All right."

Newland leaned forward, his hands braced on the table. "Watch yourself," he whispered. "And stay out of my case. Someone might think you know more than you do. They could still want you dead."

SIXTEEN

Nakayla and I stepped out of the police station and faced a wall of TV cameras and reporters.

"Mr. Blackman, what's your involvement with the case?"

"Miss Robertson, do the police have a link between Detective Peters' killing and your sister's death?"

"Mr. Blackman, any truth that you're a suspect?"

The questions came fast and furious—a verbal gauntlet we had to walk to reach the parking lot where the police had brought Nakayla's Hyundai. Neither she nor I said a word. I slammed the car door and nearly smashed a microphone in a reporter's hand.

"Let's get out of here," I said.

Nakayla started the engine and backed up, sending cameramen jumping for the safety of the sidewalk. She sped from the lot, drove two blocks to Mt. Zion Missionary Baptist Church, and then took a hard left down a hill and out of sight of the police station. She pulled over to the side of the road and stopped.

Her whole body was shaking. At first I thought she was crying, but when she looked at me I saw fire in her eyes, not tears.

"You know what that Detective Newland kept asking me?"

"No."

"Had Tikima and I argued recently and what did I

think of her friendship with you? He's working on a theory that I was the jealous sister."

I understood where Newland was coming from. Nakayla had set me up in Tikima's apartment and his initial lead was Nakayla and I standing over his partner's body. I would have used the same tactic myself in an interrogation.

"He tried to rattle you. Whoever killed Peters took the case file and Newland had nothing to go on. Once he got the copies of the journal and the Armitage files, and then checked out our story, he dropped his suspicions." I doubted Newland had completely crossed us off his suspect list, but I didn't want Nakayla to worry.

"So what do we do now?"

"Newland and the entire Asheville police force will work this investigation hard. One of their own is now a victim."

"You mean we're quitting?"

I thought about Newland's warning to stay out of his case and the fact that someone had tried to kill us. "Maybe we should give them a day or two. See what they turn up."

"Sam, they're going to do just what you said. Look for whoever killed one of their own. If that leads to Tikima's murderer, then it's secondary. And what about Elijah? You think they'll give a damn about an eighty-eight-year-old murder?"

"Newland ordered me to stay clear. He thinks we might be in danger. And when our faces are plastered all over tonight's news, people will be afraid to talk to us."

"Then we work the rest of the Armitage files this afternoon. Sam, you might trust the police, but somebody killed Peters and I know in my heart that motive goes back to Elijah. I can't get that old photograph out of my mind, the police standing beside the Klan at a graveside service. You think some of the police weren't under those hoods, not simply standing beside them?"

I thought about the twins, Al and Ted. "Our father and grandfather were policemen," Ted had told me. Maybe I was still on Detective Newland's suspect list. So what? Now he was on mine.

AN OLD PROSPECTOR held up a gold nugget that matched the tooth in his wide grin. "Gold for the Taking" read the cartoon bubble coming from his mouth. I'd seen the picture in Tikima's file. In person, the billboard towered over a parking lot nearly filled with cars and SUVs. License plates proclaimed a variety of origins from as far away as Oregon.

Nakayla found a spot straddling the edge of the pavement and a gravel shoulder. "So, we're going for the mineral angle, not security?"

"Yes." I'd starting thinking about new tactics sitting in the living room of Nakayla's bungalow in artsy West Asheville. Nakayla had wanted to shower and change clothes before we set off on our final series of interviews. "If Tikima asked Luther Rawlings about mineral rights at the Biltmore Estate, she must have asked a mineral question here. I'll say I was helping her when she was killed and she never got to tell me about her conversation. You're my assistant and I won't introduce you as Tikima's sister."

"Why not?"

"They might clam up if they think this has to do with a murder investigation. You've never met these people before?"

"No. Once in a while my insurance investigations crossed one of Tikima's clients, but not the Ledbetters."

Phil and Judy Ledbetter had been the names in the file. Now that the police held the Armitage folders, we were going from memory. Fortunately, Nakayla and I had reviewed the documents enough to remember everyone we planned to interview.

"Gold for the Taking" more accurately described what the Ledbetters were doing to the tourists. People sat on benches under what looked like a giant picnic shelter. Instead of tables, they faced troughs of running water. Each person had a bucket of dirt and a wooden-framed screen sieve. A scoop of dirt went in the sieve and then the flowing water washed away the loose soil, leaving stones that the Ledbetters claimed could be anything from rubies to emeralds. Kids, parents, and grandparents meticulously fingered through the remaining pebbles in search of treasure.

A poster at the entrance showed a girl in pigtails holding up what looked like green quartz. Underneath her photograph, the caption read: "Eight-year-old Jenny Pickens finds $25,000 emerald." The discovery Nakayla had told me about. Inset beside her picture was a newspaper article from the *Asheville Citizen*. The story was ten years old, but Jenny's smile still spurred on adults and kids alike.

We went to a stand at the far end where a man stood behind a counter. Stacks of buckets lined the wall in back of him, categorized by the gemstones most likely to be discovered. There were buckets labeled sapphires, rubies, garnets, topaz, and emeralds. Prices ranged from twelve to sixty-five dollars depending upon the size and gems likely to be discovered.

A disclaimer proclaimed: "Although all of our ore is from our gem-bearing sites, buckets have been enriched to make your prospecting more exciting." At least they were up front about baiting the tourists. From the occasional squeals of delight I heard from the families hunched over the troughs, I'd say it was a fair deal for everyone.

"Can I get y'all a bucket each?" The man in a full black beard and bib overhauls looked like he could have posed for the billboard. All he needed was the gold tooth.

"Is Phil or Judy in?" I asked.

"Phil's up at the mine. Judy's in the gift shop next door." He jerked a thumb toward the concrete walkway that went around his stand to the next building.

A wooden railing ran along the edge. I used it to steady myself as we headed for the white stucco gift shop. On the other side of the railing, the ground sloped down to a wide stream running parallel to us. Several people waded in the clear water, scooping sand into round pans and then swirling the current across it.

"Those must be the no-thrills prospectors," I said.

If the gift shop was supposed to feature mountain crafts and jewelry, then western North Carolina must have been annexed by China. Most of the merchandise was nothing more than trinkets. But along one wall, I noticed a glass case with both a motion detector and a security camera trained on it.

Here lay the legitimacy for Gold for the Taking, photographs of unearthed emeralds, some of them over a thousand carats and worth more than a million dollars. Several uncut gems were displayed under the glass. Even in their rough, quartz shape, I could see the green

coloring that would have me thinking dollars, not gold.
The photos went back in time, shaving the years off
the man identified in the captions as Phil Ledbetter. A
few earlier ones showed his father, Jimmy Ledbetter, at
the entrance of a mine, holding up a chunk of rock that
could have been nothing more than a piece of gravel in
the old black-and-white photograph.

"You folks look too dry to have been seeking your
fortune." A woman in a calico dress that could have
been a costume or straight out of her closet walked over
to us. Her gray hair was pulled back and her tanned,
weathered face had seen at least sixty summers.

"These pictures want me to buy a bucket of dirt,"
I said.

"Then you might want to sign up for a site dig."

"What's that?"

"You pay fifty dollars and Phil takes you to one of our
more promising digs. You keep what you find. That's
how little Jenny got her $25,000 emerald. Damndest
thing. She stepped on it."

"What about gold?" I asked. "Is that just in the
name?"

"No. Gold's what got this business started. Gold's
what the creek scavengers, that's what I call them, are
panning for. Phil's people bought over a hundred acres
back in the 1920s looking for the vein that dumps flakes
and nuggets into the stream. Tough luck. All they found
were emeralds." She laughed with the throaty rasp of
too many cigarettes.

"So, the reverse hasn't happened? They haven't
found the gold vein while looking for emeralds?"

"No. Different geological conditions produce gold.
The more emeralds you find, the less likely you'll find

gold. That's why buying so much of this mountain turned out to be the best thing. They got it cheap because the slopes were too rocky and steep for farming. They bought it for protection in case the gold vein traveled out rather than down."

"Why bother with the tourists?" I asked.

"Takes money to operate a mine. Significant emerald finds are few and far between. And when you hear the prices, they're usually after the gem's been graded and cut. Retail prices. Believe me, they're a long way from where we sell them."

I offered my hand. "You must be Judy. I'm Sam and this is Nakayla."

She smiled. "Sorry to talk your ears off. Is that how you knew my name? My motor-mouth reputation?"

"I work for Tikima Robertson." In my mind the statement was true.

Judy's mouth dropped open. "Oh, my God. What are you doing here?"

"Tikima told me she was going to talk to you. She wasn't able to file a report, and I thought maybe you could help us."

She looked at Nakayla and then at me. "What a terrible thing. She was such a nice person."

"And Tikima spoke highly of you," I said. "That's why she knew you'd be a big help to our mineral questions."

Judy tucked her lower lip under her tongue. She seemed uncertain how to reply.

"I don't mean to put you through her whole interview again. I just want the conclusions you reached. It means a lot to our client." I was at the end of my fishing line and afraid if I guessed at something more specific,

Judy would realize I was a fraud. "Maybe we should talk to Phil," I added.

"No. Phil wasn't here. I talked to her." Judy sighed. "It's kinda painful to think about, you know, with what happened."

"I understand."

"Tikima wanted to know about gold and precious gemstones. What we were just talking about." She eyed me suspiciously like I'd been pumping her for information all along.

"Right. About the conditions under which they might be found." I made a leap. "What did you think about the Biltmore Estate?"

Judy took a step back. "The old days?"

"Old and new."

"That was years ago and several mountains over. Our land might as well have been a hundred miles away."

"So you don't know if any precious minerals were ever found on the estate?"

Judy shook her head. "No. Like I told Tikima, the Vanderbilts had so much money they probably didn't bother to look."

The gift shop door opened and a wiry, gray-haired man in dirty dungarees entered. I recognized Phil Ledbetter from the newspaper articles in the display case.

"We're back," he said. "Charlie's unloading the buckets."

"Sorry, I've got to run," Judy whispered. She moved like a skittish deer and intercepted her husband. He stared at us for a few seconds and then both of them left the store.

"You get the feeling she didn't want to introduce us?" Nakayla asked.

"Yes. Maybe she didn't want Phil to know what we were talking about."

"Or maybe she didn't want him to know she'd talked to Tikima."

I thought about it. "Tikima was their security expert. If I were sitting on gold and emeralds, I'd want to know what she had to say."

NAKAYLA HAD TO circle the block three times before she found a parking space. Haywood Street in downtown Asheville was a happening place. The small park at its intersection with Patton Avenue had become an impromptu amphitheater with bands of bluegrass musicians vying to out-pick one another. Tourists took advantage of the sunny afternoon to roam the streets, soaking up the wayward fiddle and banjo notes and congregating at Malaprop's Bookstore and our destination, the old Woolworth's that housed an eclectic collection of artists and artisans.

We hurried from the car concerned that Sunday business hours might be shorter. Three people were on our list: Andy Culpepper, Malcolm Grant, and Herman Duringer. Nakayla doubted Culpepper would be there if he worked for the building's owners and we didn't know if the other two were employees or artists.

"There's usually a steady stream of browsers," Nakayla said. "If Grant and Duringer have booths, neither one will want to spend time talking with us."

"Then we'll need to get right to the point."

The store had preserved the original Woolworth exterior from the 1960s, but inside, the gutted space had been subdivided into a maze of booths like three-walled rooms—some with display cases between them and all using their wall space for hanging paintings, carvings, jewelry, fabrics, or photographs. We went to the main counter just inside the front door where people were lined up paying for their purchases.

"This will take too long," I said. "Let's ask one of the artists."

"Pottery by Delores" read the banner stretched across the back wall of a nearby booth. The middle-aged woman I assumed to be Delores saw us approach and nodded a greeting. She stepped back to give us room to admire her bowls, goblets, and pitchers without our feeling forced to speak with her.

Her work had a unique quality of imperfection. A slightly misshapen handle on a pitcher, a bulge on a chalice stem. The effect gave pieces in matching sets a distinguishing trait, a mark of originality. I liked what I saw.

"Do you ship?" I asked, though I had no address to give her.

"I'm sorry. Too risky. I have bubble wrap if you're traveling."

I laughed. "When I figure out a destination, I'll be back."

Delores winked at me. "I can tell any destination will be fine if you're traveling together."

This earth mother thought Nakayla and I were a couple. I felt my face blush and became more embarrassed. I'd never had an interracial relationship, but I didn't want Nakayla to think I had any prejudices against her.

"I don't believe I could get her to leave Asheville," I said.

"Gets in your blood," Delores said. "I came for a brief stay twenty years ago. They'll bury me in my own clay." She ran a strong stubby finger across the lip of a bowl.

"We actually came to see Andy Culpepper. Is he here?"

"No. He usually comes by on Saturdays."

"How about Malcolm Grant or Herman Duringer?"

"I know Herman's here." Delores pointed down the aisle. "Go all the way to the back, past Leroy the dulcimer maker. Turn right. Herman's the second booth on the left. Malcolm's two beyond him. Sometimes he's called away for a patient."

"Malcolm's a doctor?"

"A dentist. That's how he got into designing jewelry. From working with gold in his dental practice. Now he spends more time designing jewelry with Herman than with his patients." Delores gave Nakayla a sly smile. "A gemstone from Herman and a gold setting from Malcolm." She looked at Nakayla's ringless fingers. "Might be enough to lure you out of Asheville."

We left the matchmaker potter and wormed our way through the crowd.

"Gold and gemstones," Nakayla whispered.

"I'd say we've discovered the focus of Tikima's inquiry. She must have read something into the journal that we missed."

"I don't remember anything that gave the location of a mine. The Ledbetters' site is too far away and the Vanderbilts never had a mine."

"Unless the Vanderbilts never knew about it. Luther Rawlings said he has eight thousand acres to patrol. Maybe Elijah discovered gold and mentioned it to the wrong people. He was killed before he could tell Mrs. Vanderbilt."

"And someone's been concealing it all these years?"

"You don't think that's possible?"

She thought for a second. "No. Except with mountain people. A lot of them keep to themselves. There're all kinds of secrets back in the hills."

"And how many of those families go back to 1919?" I asked.

"Like Delores said, these mountains get in your blood. We can start with Luther Rawlings and Curt Newland. Their family trees are rooted deep."

Herman Duringer sat in a webbed lawn chair behind a glass-covered case. He was a portly man with tufts of gray hair encircling the bald dome of his head. His blue eyes darted through the crowd as he searched for someone to look over his wares. His gaze latched onto me, and Nakayla and I walked over.

Unlike Delores, Herman went right into his pitch. "If you don't see what you want, you tell me and I'll find it for you. I dig all my own stones, each one of the highest quality and guaranteed to come out of the Blue Ridge."

"We're interested in emeralds," I said.

"Excellent. North Carolina is known for emeralds." He slid his hand over the glass top and pointed to a set of dark green stones. "I cut these myself."

"Where are they from?"

"Hiddenite. Best emeralds in the state. Jamie Hill's property's the top source. Back in 2003, he found an emerald nearly two thousand carats. They say it's the largest in North America." Herman came close to salivating. "There's still a public mine down there, and I've always got hope."

"What about the Ledbetters?"

He wrinkled his nose. "Phil Ledbetter's more of a

carnie than a miner. He keeps his richest land for himself and foists the poorer digs on the hobbyists. I don't know any real rock hounds who dig there."

"What about the little girl who found the big emerald?"

Herman snorted. "Advertising. Wouldn't surprise me if Phil tossed the gem under the kid's feet. Uncut it might have fetched five grand. He's gotten ten times that amount from the suckers lined up at his troughs like hogs at feeding time."

I detected a tone of jealousy in his voice, but I didn't feel the need to defend Phil Ledbetter's smart business practices. "I want to ask you about emeralds and Tikima Robertson."

His eyes went wide. "Tikima? You know what happened to her, don't you?"

"Yes. I was working with her. She came to see you."

Herman suddenly seemed nervous. "You think that got her killed? The stones were nice but not that valuable."

My heart jumped a beat. We were onto something. "We don't know." I turned to Nakayla. "My colleague and I are trying to follow up on Tikima's efforts. I'm Sam Blackman and this is Nakayla."

If our names meant anything, he didn't react. The whole subject of Tikima had him on edge.

"She showed you the bracelet." Nakayla made the statement as a fact.

I was clueless where we were going, but I nodded as if I understood.

"Yes," Herman admitted. "She wanted to know if I could tell where the gold and emeralds came from. She said a relative was supposed to have made it."

"That's right. Her great-great grandfather."

"There weren't any identifying marks but the workmanship wasn't up to professional standards."

"What do you mean?" I asked.

"Have you seen the piece?"

"No," I said. "I heard about it." Like ten seconds ago.

"The emeralds weren't cut, they were polished. The true potential of a gem is revealed through the facets. Training and an artistic eye make the difference. These stones had either been tumbled smooth or hand rubbed with a whetstone."

"Could you tell where they came from?" I asked.

"I can't give you a precise global position, but the signature composition of the emeralds is consistent with western North Carolina. Slightly different from the gems unearthed in Hiddenite. These were definitely from this area of the Brevard fault."

"The what?"

"The major fault line running along the mountains. About a gazillion years ago, two prehistoric continents were smashing into each other, creating the Appalachian chain. The collision also created the wealth of minerals found here, products of incredible heat and pressure." He ran his hand over the top of his display. "The Appalachians are believed to be the oldest mountains in the world. The piedmont and coastal sections of North Carolina are nothing but the sediment of millions of years of erosion. Fissures and veins spread like a spider's web."

Herman recovered enough of his poise to laugh. "That's why so many of the pink and purple hair people flock to Asheville. For them, it's all about the crystals and the ancient vortex they say lies under the city."

"You believe that?" I asked.

"I believe in rocks. Something I can hold, something I can cut and polish with my own hands. And I believe Tikima's emeralds came from a source that could rival Jamie Hill's Hiddenite mine. I wish I knew where her relative got those stones. Maybe Phil Ledbetter's predecessors weren't so possessive."

"How long have your relatives lived here?" I asked.

"Since 1862. The first Duringer fled here from Charlotte to escape conscription in the Confederacy. He hid in the mountains. I prefer to think he was a man of principle, not a coward, which was more likely the case."

Nakayla bent over and peered at the gemstones set in gold rings. "Was the gold in the bracelet local?"

"Probably. The refining process left quite a few impurities. Malcolm Grant knows more about metal work. He designs all my settings. Tikima had him look at the bracelet."

"Is he here?" Nakayla asked.

"Two booths down. I'd introduce you but I don't dare leave my gems. You'll recognize him. He's got the cleanest teeth in the joint."

Malcolm Grant did have a bright smile. He was flashing it at two blue-haired ladies, many years ahead of the pink and purple vortex generation. Nakayla and I waited until he had answered their questions and boxed a gold brooch for one of them.

"Dr. Grant," I said.

He looked at me, trying to place the face, or at least the mouth.

"Yes?"

"We've never met. Herman suggested we speak to you. We're colleagues of Tikima Robertson."

Like Herman, Malcolm Grant froze for an instant. Tikima's name jarred him.

"I can't believe it," he managed to say. "I'd just seen her the weekend before she disappeared."

"She came to you about the bracelet."

He studied me closely. "I'm sorry. Who did you say you were?"

"I'm Sam Blackman. This is Nakayla. We were working with Tikima."

"She told you about the bracelet?"

"Yes."

He shook his head. "Tikima asked me not to mention the bracelet to anyone. I promised her."

Either Grant took his word very seriously or he had something to hide. Nakayla pulled her wallet from her purse and flipped it open to her driver's license.

"I'm Tikima's sister. The bracelet now belongs to me. I'd appreciate your sharing what you told her."

Dr. Grant took a sharp breath. He glanced down the aisle toward Herman, wondering what he might have already told us.

"What about the gold?" Nakayla asked. "We know the emeralds are native."

"The gold was excellent quality, but the workmanship was not." He gestured to several intricate pieces in his booth. "The refining left much to be desired and the shaping of the bracelet had more in common with a blacksmith than a goldsmith."

"But the gold?" Nakayla pressed.

"First rate. On a par with what used to be mined in Charlotte or the Reid Gold Mine. You know North Carolina was the largest gold producing state in the country until 1849 and that little discovery at Sutter's Mill in California."

"Could the gold have been mined in Asheville?" I asked.

"Possibly. But no mine that I know of. Might have been panned from a stream close to a vein."

"Why do you think my sister was so secretive?" Nakayla asked.

He shrugged. "Gold. The nature of the beast. If I thought I had a lead on where that gold came from, I'd be secretive too. Downright paranoid."

Except you're not paranoid when you wind up murdered.

WE HEADED OUT of Asheville to Arden, a small neighboring town and the site of Golden Oaks Retirement Community.

"Why didn't you mention the bracelet before?" I asked.

"I never thought about it until I realized Grant and Duringer made gold and emerald jewelry."

"Do you have it?"

"No. But I know where it is. Whoever broke into Tikima's apartment missed it. I checked."

"It's still in the apartment?"

"Unless you moved the Bible by the bed. You'll find it in an envelope after Revelations. Tikima figured crooks would never touch the Good Book."

A guardhouse and gate stood sentinel at the entrance to the retirement community, but the bar across the road was fixed in the upright position. The parade of Sunday afternoon visitors probably would have worn out the lifting motor.

Golden Oaks was built on top of a mountain, and the road switched back and forth as we climbed to the summit.

As we walked into the lobby, I saw my face on a television across the large room. I was slamming the door of the Hyundai. The set was too distant for me to hear the report, and the residents sitting on sofas and easy chairs in front of the TV seemed more interested in each other than the news. Nakayla and I watched the camera follow us from the police station till we disappeared beyond Mt. Zion Missionary Baptist Church. Then an anchorwoman appeared with a photo of Detective Peters over her shoulder. I had no idea what she was saying.

"And so it begins," Nakayla muttered. "I'll have an interesting day at work tomorrow."

I hadn't thought about Nakayla's need to get back to her job. Being unemployed meant I had no plans beyond the next interview.

The front desk was along the wall just inside the door. A woman with dyed blond hair sat behind it, her face buried in a romance novel. Both the hero and heroine on the cover had necklines so low they probably died of chest colds by the end of the book.

"Excuse me," I said.

The woman tore her moist eyes off what must have been a heart-wrenching paragraph. "Yes?"

"Is it possible to speak with Sandra Pollock?"

"Sorry. She's off. She'll be in tomorrow morning at nine. If you have a family member considering becoming a resident," she paused, realizing we had to be coming from an unconventionally blended family, "or a friend, you'll want to talk to Nancy in Marketing."

"No. We have a specific question for Ms. Pollock. Is it possible to speak with her by telephone?"

"It's against our policy to give out staff home numbers. But she'll be happy to talk to you first thing in the morning."

Finding Sandra Pollock at work after six on Sunday evening had been a long shot. I let the woman get back to her passionate whatever and turned to go.

"Hey! You're the people on TV." An octogenarian man in the lobby hustled on his walker with surprising speed. Behind him, several ladies stared at us. Evidently, the seniors had been more attentive to the news than I realized.

"I'm Ron Kline, but everybody calls me Captain." He circled around and clunked his walker down between us and the door.

"I'm Sam. This is Nakayla."

"So, the news lady said you found that poor detective's body."

"Yes."

"I saw a lot of bodies back in the war. Never got used to it."

"You were a captain?"

"Actually, I made colonel. But I always enjoyed being a captain the most. That's when what I did mattered." He leaned over the walker and took a deep breath. "Why are you up here, if you don't mind my asking?"

I looked to Nakayla.

"I guess this wasn't on the news, but Tikima Robertson was my sister."

He nodded vigorously. "That's what they said. Poor Tikima."

"You knew her?" Nakayla asked.

"Certainly. She worked for that security company, but she always took time to speak to us, especially the veterans."

Maybe Tikima hadn't stopped visiting vets, I thought. She'd just shifted her location.

"Did you see her shortly before she died?" I asked.

"Yep. Sure did. Not to speak to, other than hello. She'd come up to see the mayor."

"The mayor of Arden lives here?" Nakayla asked.

Captain chuckled. "No, the mayor of Golden Oaks. Harry. He's been here the longest. I'm the Captain. He's the Mayor. He's not a vet but Tikima took to him. She came to his hundredth birthday party last April. Maybe we should promote Harry to President."

"Is Harry here?" I asked.

"Sure. Where else would he go? I saw him at Sunday brunch. Only meal they fix on Sundays. He's probably in his apartment. D-133." Captain pointed across the lobby to a hallway.

"Thank you," I said.

"No trouble." The old man lifted his right hand off his walker and touched Nakayla's shoulder. "So sorry about your sister." Then he stood straight and saluted.

As we walked down the D-wing hall, Nakayla fought back tears. Captain had been a bittersweet reminder of her loss.

The door of number 133 had a brass name plaque: Harry Young—His Honor the Mayor. I gave two sharp raps with the knocker.

"Come in," called a raspy voice. "It's unlocked."

I opened the door and let Nakayla go first. A small kitchen lay on our left as we continued into the living room. A door on the right led to the bedroom. The apartment was tidy, and the elderly man sitting on the sofa wore a neatly pressed pink shirt and navy blue slacks. A wheelchair was turned facing him. He held a section of the Sunday paper and looked up, not at all surprised to see us.

Nakayla and I both stopped, speechless. Harry Young had only one leg.

"Thank God," he said. "I was afraid I'd have to come after you."

SEVENTEEN

"HENDERSON YOUNGBLOOD?" I blurted the name so loudly that Nakayla jumped.

"No. But I reckon I'm as close to being that boy as anybody could be." He waved us to sit in the armchairs facing him. "As close as Fred Wolfe was to being Luke in *Look Homeward, Angel*."

Nakayla and I sat. She hadn't said a word and the way she kept looking from the old man to me betrayed her anxiety. I knew what she was thinking, but Harry Young said it.

"I got your sister killed." The wrinkles in his thin face deepened. He choked back a sob.

Nakayla sprang from the chair and joined him on the sofa. She took one of his liver-spotted hands and pressed it between her own. "You gave her the journal?"

"When I realized she was Elijah's kin." He pulled his hand away and brushed the tears from his eyes. "I saw the news tonight. About that police officer. Leaving a wife and two boys."

"Do you know who's responsible?" I asked.

"No. I told Tikima to be careful." He eyed the way my left leg stretched in front of me. "You're the vet she went to see. The one that took on the brass up in Washington."

"Yes. But we only met once. She was still sizing me up and didn't tell me what she wanted." I glanced at Nakayla. "Someone broke into her apartment during the funeral, but they didn't take anything. Nakayla found the journal disguised as another book with my name on it."

"Then how did you find me?"

"My sister had the Golden Oaks file at her apartment," Nakayla said. "We came to talk to Sandra Pollock and learned Tikima had been visiting you."

Harry cleared his throat. "Would one of you get me a glass of water? I dry out when I'm talking and I expect y'all have more than a few questions."

I signaled for Nakayla to keep her seat. The sink was built into an island dividing the kitchen from the living room. I could see Harry and Nakayla as I checked the hanging cabinets for a glass. "Do you want ice?"

"Just plain water. I have a little problem swallowing if it's too cold. Right from the tap is fine."

I doubted a hundred-year-old man had much use for bottled water.

"Y'all eat?" he asked. "Make yourself a sandwich."

Nakayla and I declined and I brought him the water and a paper towel for a napkin.

He took a small sip and let it linger in his mouth. After he swallowed, he spoke a little stronger. "Where do you want me to begin?"

"Tell us what's true in the journal," I said. "Did Thomas Wolfe write it?"

Harry nodded. "That he did. But aside from my name and some dramatic exaggerations, Tom got most of it right."

"You told him the story?"

"Yep. Summer of 1937. I'd known Tom since we were boys. He was nearly seven years older, but Daddy did business with Mr. Wolfe and sometimes Tom would be at the monument shop. Tom had an eye and an ear. If he saw or heard something, he never forgot it. Like one of those VCRs they've got nowadays."

"But the events in the story happened in 1919," Nakayla said.

"That's right. So what's at fault is my memory, not Tom's. Why, they say the angel in *Look Homeward, Angel* is on a grave over in Hendersonville. Tom's daddy sold it in 1906. Tom was still five, but when he wrote about it, twenty years had gone by since he'd seen it. The description is remarkable."

"Nearly twenty years had gone by when you told him your story," Nakayla said.

Harry smiled. "That's true. But I wouldn't have been a good writer. Tom made that up about me. Math was my best subject."

"And he changed you to Henderson Youngblood," I said.

"My given name was Harrison Young. So close I don't know why he bothered. Except for my family, every other name he left the same. That's what got him in trouble with *Look Homeward, Angel*. People were too recognizable. Tom didn't come back to Asheville for eight years after that book was published."

I felt like I should be taking notes, but I'd come unprepared. "That's when you saw him again?"

"Tom first stayed at the boarding house with his mother, but so many people came to see him he couldn't work. He went to a cabin in Oteen where he could write."

Harry's sequence of events matched what Ted Mitchell had told us. The old man's memory was sharp.

"I'd missed seeing him in town. I worked for the Biltmore Dairy—had been since Daddy died—and I thought I'd take him some fresh milk and ice cream. I knew we'd have to eat it right then because the cabin had no way to keep it. Tom was glad to see me. We got talking about old times and our families and I told him the story about Elijah and the trip to Georgia. Tom had been at the university then."

Harry paused, took a deep breath and another swallow of water. "Tom got so excited he couldn't stop asking me questions. He wanted to know every detail. The ice cream melted in the tub and we talked past nightfall."

"And you told him everything up through Elijah's murder?" I asked.

"No. I went beyond that. I described the trip back to Georgia with Elijah's son Amos so we could bury Elijah with his kinfolk. And how Bessie and her family had disappeared."

"Disappeared?" Nakayla scooted closer, evidently hearing this story about her relatives for the first time.

"Yep. It was less than a month since Daddy and I'd eaten lunch in their farmhouse. The place was abandoned. Peaches were rotting in the wagon. Somebody had moved it out by the road. Amos had no way to reach them. Nearest neighbor said they'd gone north."

"When did your father die?" I asked.

"Two weeks after we buried Elijah. We found the cemetery where we'd helped him take his uncle Hannable. Amos and my daddy got a large rock from the stream and chiseled Elijah's name on it. They did the same for Hannable since Elijah had left it unmarked.

"One night Daddy took some supplies over to a funeral director in Brevard. He never came back. Sheriff found his Model T at the bottom of a ravine. The car had burst into flames. I overheard Mr. Galloway telling the sheriff my daddy must have been drinking. He knew better. My daddy never took a drop of whiskey. I never liked Mr. Galloway after that. He got meaner and short-tempered. He changed after his son Jamie returned from the war."

"The journal said his son had been killed," I said.

"That's what we all thought. Jamie had been shell-shocked and wandered off. At least that's what Jamie said."

"People thought otherwise?"

Harry shrugged. "You've seen combat. A man's whole unit is wiped out by a direct hit but he's unharmed? There were some in town said Jamie Galloway had been a deserter. He came back to Asheville and resurfaced as one of the returning heroes. He could have been hiding in the hills for months. People whispered and Mr. Galloway knew it."

I thought about what Herman Duringer had said about his ancestor evading service in the Civil War. "What happened to you and your mother?"

"Mother sold the property and we moved onto the Biltmore Estate. She started sewing homespun clothes. Mrs. Vanderbilt wore them to encourage the fashionable ladies to support the local dressmakers. Edith Vanderbilt was a woman without pretense and I don't regret one day of working for her. When she died in 1958, I stayed on at the dairy for Miss Cornelia. She'd married the British man Mr. Cecil whose family still owns the estate, but she'll always be Miss Cornelia to me. I retired when she died in 1976. Over all these years, the family's kept Edith Vanderbilt's promise to take care of my leg. But my skin's thin as tissue paper and I can't wear a prosthesis anymore. I get by with a wheelchair and a walker for hobbling around the apartment."

Harry's reminiscences about the Vanderbilts were interesting, but they didn't answer my main question. "If you told Thomas Wolfe more of the story, why'd he stop where he did?"

"Fred said his brother was unhappy with the way he had the boy writing."

"Fred?" I asked.

"Tom's older brother. Tom left the journal with him at the end of the summer. Fred gave it to me forty years later."

Harry was jumping decades so fast I couldn't keep up. "Why so long?"

"Because Fred and I didn't cross paths for forty years. I didn't know Tom had even written the thing."

"And you never saw Tom again?"

"No. He'd left the journal with some questions he wanted me to answer. Fred told me Tom was having trouble creating the story. He loved the events, but he didn't know where to take them. No one knew what happened to Elijah."

"So Thomas Wolfe couldn't solve the mystery," I said. "Even with a fictional solution."

"And he died the next year. He never came home again. Imagine, Tom dead before age thirty-eight and here I sit, a hundred years old."

I shifted in the chair, moving my leg to a more comfortable position. "I understand the comment written at the end about the kid's vocabulary, but what did he mean by 'Ask Harry about the mule'?"

"Fred said that was important to him. Tom wanted me to read what he'd written and tell him about the mule. All I know Junebug was found the morning after Elijah died, grazing in a lower Biltmore pasture with the cows."

"Wasn't that the normal pasture?" I asked.

Harry looked at me like I'd failed to add two plus two. "Elijah kept Junebug at his place. Junebug was only in a Biltmore pasture when Elijah was there."

Nakayla frowned. We kept coming back to the Biltmore Estate. But that was where Elijah worked, where he might have left Junebug during the day if he went off with someone.

"What about the mule's pack?" Nakayla asked.

"What?" Henry and I asked in unison.

"In the journal, Junebug's pack was missing. Did that happen?"

Harry pursed his thin pale lips. "I'd forgotten I'd told Tom. He must have set something by it."

"Maybe that was his question for you," Nakayla said. "About the mule."

"I only remember it because I was so surprised to see Elijah outside my window the Sunday morning after the trip to Georgia."

I understood how that would have been a vivid memory for a twelve-year-old boy, but Thomas Wolfe had seen the underlying significance. Someone had taken Junebug's pack.

The glimmer of an idea began to emerge from the murky mire of distant events. "How'd you get the journal from Fred?"

"I went to see him in Spartanburg. Back in 1977. Miss Cornelia had died the year before and I'd retired from the dairy. They were going to turn the barn into a winery. Milk to wine was too much of a new trick for this old dog to learn."

"Did Fred ask to see you?"

"No. One of his relatives was going down and offered to take me along. She knew we'd been friends and she could run errands while Fred and I talked. He was in his eighties and a real character." Harry laughed. "Fred smoked like a chimney and stuttered like a Model T with bad sparkplugs. He stayed in his pajamas and bathrobe the whole day. He sat in his easy chair with cigarette burns on the upholstery and carpet around him. It's a wonder he didn't burn himself up.

"We got talking about Tom and I mentioned our last conversation at the Oteen cabin. Fred got the oddest look on his face. He stood and went back to his bedroom. I heard him pulling out dresser drawers and a few minutes later he returned with the journal. 'Tom asked me to give you this.' He said it like his brother had dropped it off the night before. Then Fred told me what I've already told you—how Tom got stuck in the story."

"The journal must be worth something," I said. "Why'd you hold onto it for thirty years instead of selling it?"

Harry took a deep breath and stared at a photograph on the wall across the room. The scene was Asheville's Pack Square, probably in the 1920s and filled with antique cars and long dead people. For the first time I noticed the apartment was more of a museum. A plaque beside the photo proclaimed Biltmore Dairy Farms the winner of the Grand Champion Bull and Grand Champion Cow of the National Jersey Breed Show—1952. For a dairy man, I figured that was like sweeping an

Olympic event. Another picture over Nakayla showed a younger Harry standing in front of a barn with a Biltmore Dairy Farms truck beside him. Other photographs offered trips back in time for the old man. Thomas Wolfe, Edith Vanderbilt, and Cornelia Cecil were not paragraphs in an encyclopedia. They were flesh and blood, and his mind must have still heard echoes of their conversations and felt the clasps of their hands.

"Tom was my friend," Harry said. "So was Fred. That journal wasn't finished and I'd have been betraying them by letting people see it."

"But Tikima was different," Nakayla whispered.

"Tikima was different," Harry repeated. "Elijah's direct descendent, Harrison Robertson's granddaughter."

"My grandfather too," Nakayla said. "Harrison. Was he named for you?"

"Yes. Elijah's son Amos and I became good friends. He married and never went back to Chicago. We worked together at the dairy."

"Did you marry?" Nakayla asked.

"No. Too busy. Dairy cows don't leave much time for courting."

I wondered how much of that had been an excuse and glanced down at my artificial foot. Easy to think of yourself as incomplete and unattractive when you're missing a leg.

"I lost track of the family after Harrison died. Then six months ago, I met Tikima when she presented a program on security tips for seniors. Afterwards, I asked about her last name and made the connection. She came to my hundredth birthday party and I gave her the journal as a gift." His voice quivered. "I wish I'd burned the damn thing years ago."

"But you didn't," Nakayla said. "And Tikima found a link to Elijah's murder. I don't want my sister to have died in vain."

"I owe my life to Elijah," Harry said. "When I die, I'd like to know some justice had been served."

I knew justice would only come with evidence. "Did Fred offer any clues as to what Tom thought might have happened?"

"No. His niece's daughter returned and we had to leave." A twinkle sparkled in his eyes at the memory. "She'd brought Fred a strawberry milkshake from Baskin-Robbins. That had been his only request. She called me out to the kitchen where I saw a freezer so packed with strawberry milkshakes that we couldn't fit it in. Fred was like a squirrel hoarding what was most dear to him. He followed us out to the car and stood singing 'Give My Regards to Broadway' as we drove off."

Nakayla laughed. I found the story amusing, but not nearly as funny as she did.

Harry winked at Nakayla. "He doesn't get it."

"Get what?" I asked.

"Fred wasn't singing about New York," Nakayla said. "Broadway is a major street in Asheville and ends at Pack Square where Wolfe's Monuments used to be."

"That was the last time I saw Fred," Harry said. "Singing in his cigarette-burned pajamas on his front lawn. What a family."

I decided to pry some more memories out of Harry. "Do you know if Elijah made jewelry?"

"Jewelry?"

"Yes. Or worked with gold?"

"No. But Elijah was a jack-of-all-trades. I suspect he knew his way around the smithy at the estate. Why?"

"Tikima was asking questions about gold and gems the week before she died. Nakayla says there's a family bracelet Elijah is supposed to have made."

Harry scratched the thin hair behind his ear. "Tikima asked me what I thought Elijah was doing at the creek. That's where he brought me right after the bear attack."

"What'd you tell her?"

"That I'd never thought about it. But since then I've tried to recreate the scene in my mind. Junebug was there. Elijah had to take a shovel and pick-ax off her before I could ride. There may have been some pans—not cooking pans—the round flat ones. He could have been prospecting that stream."

"And then Junebug's pack disappeared," I said.

Nakayla leaned forward on the sofa. "With gold in it?"

"Maybe traces. Enough to spark someone's interest."

Harry whistled softly. "For all these years, I never made that connection."

"No reason you should have," I said. "You didn't know about the handmade jewelry. But Tikima did."

"So Elijah was murdered for gold?" Harry asked.

"As long as people have been mining for gold, they've been killing for gold. Maybe Mr. Galloway took the pack. Y'all were gone all that Saturday."

"But why take it?" Nakayla asked. "It would have warned Elijah."

"Maybe someone else then," I said. "Someone who wouldn't have been able to return it if Mr. Galloway was there."

"And maybe that's why Tikima wanted old employee

records from the estate," Nakayla said. "She was looking for a connection to Elijah and Galloway."

Harry took a longer sip of water and cleared his throat. "And she found one. Only she didn't know it until too late."

"We need to research genealogy," I said. "Nakayla, what kind of resources do you have at work?"

"We subscribe to a lot of services. Sometimes insurance fraud involves relatives so we access databases that hold birth and death records."

"Tomorrow you need to work it from both ends—Galloway and anyone Harry can think of from the past, and then the people we know Tikima talked with. We're looking for an intersection."

I felt energized by having something to do. Even Harry seemed eager. He gave us names of people he remembered as friends of Mr. Galloway and then people he worked with at Biltmore whose descendants were still employed at the estate. Both Luther Rawlings and Jake Matthews fit that category. I knew we needed someone whose family had a positive change of fortune, unless Elijah died without revealing the location of his strike. But if that was true, what was somebody desperately trying to cover up? The case continued to defy a clear course of investigation, but at least we had a starting point—and we had Harrison Young, perhaps the world's oldest witness.

We left him with a promise to stay in touch. Nakayla started the car.

"Wait," I said.

"What's wrong?"

"Whoever killed Peters has his files and his notes. I'm worried about Harry."

"His name's not in the file."

"But we managed to find him."

"Do we ask for police protection?"

"What do you think?"

Nakayla turned off the engine. "I don't feel too good about giving the police Harry's name."

"Me either." I opened the door. "Come on."

Without explanation, I led Nakayla back to the lobby. As I'd hoped, Captain was still watching TV with his bevy of beauties. I motioned him over and he used his walker to join us in a corner out of earshot.

"Did you talk to the mayor?" he asked.

"Yes. He was very helpful. Listen, Captain, you know we're trying to find out who killed Tikima."

"And we're praying for your success." He cocked his head toward the women by the TV.

"We might have put Harry in danger by coming here tonight. We haven't told anyone about him, but someone could come by asking questions."

"And they might want to hurt Harry?"

"They could try to force him to tell things he doesn't want them to know."

"What about the police?"

I shook my head. "Someone on the force might be involved."

Captain balled his right hand into a fist and waved it in the air. "Then we won't let that happen. No one will mention Tikima knew Harry and no one will say you were here."

"The lady at the front desk?"

Captain smiled. "She's one of us. I'll set her straight. And then I'll draw up a list of patrols. Old folks are always walking the halls. Teams of two should do it."

The fire in his eyes gave me a glimpse of what Captain must have been like in World War Two. I saluted him and he beamed as he returned the honor.

NAKAYLA DROPPED ME at the Kenilworth and planned to call me the next day as soon as she had something to report.

I went to the Bible on the nightstand and found the stiff old envelope taped inside the back cover. A string on the flap wound around a tab to keep it closed.

The bracelet was about an inch wide and hinged in three places. Tikima kept it unclasped and flat in the envelope, but when I fastened the clasp, the gold circle had four distinct sections separated by the hinges and clasp. Each had a green stone, polished smooth like Herman Duringer had described. On either side of the stones, ridges in the gold formed a design in relief. None of the patterns were alike, but they were similar in style in that they consisted of straight lines, curved lines, x's and o's.

The weight of the gold alone had to make the bracelet valuable. If Elijah had created it at the Biltmore smithy, he must have done so during hours when he was alone. I wondered if the Bible had been Elijah's and passed down from generation to generation with the bracelet.

I flipped to the front where the pages provided space for genealogical information: births, marriages, and deaths. The first name under deaths was Malachi, Elijah's grandfather and the first Robertson in the Georgia cemetery. The last was Harrison Robertson in 1983. Elijah's name had been entered for July 1919—not a specific day. Above his was Hannable Robertson, the uncle Elijah had gone to such trouble to bury.

I looked at the name a second time and a tingle ran down my spine. The date of death was July 2, 1917. The words *East St. Louis* were written beside it.

Hannable Robertson had died in one of this country's most horrible race riots.

Two years later, his coffin arrived in Biltmore Village.

Now I knew one thing for sure. The body of Hannable Robertson didn't lie in a grave in Georgia.

I marveled at the ingenuity of Elijah's scheme.

EIGHTEEN

"WE'VE GOT TO dig up Hannable Robertson's grave."

"What?" Nakayla sounded bewildered.

I'd called her on her cell phone and caught her as she entered her house. I realized how preposterous the idea must seem.

"The records in the family Bible state he died in 1917 in East St. Louis. I think Elijah used Harrison Young's father for the safe transportation of his gold."

"Slow down, Sam. I'm not following you."

"Then let me back up. Elijah had discovered gold and managed to either mine it or pan it from one of the streams on the estate. The Jim Crow laws were becoming intolerable and he planned to move to the home place in Georgia. For all we know, he might have been working his gold source for twenty or twenty-five years. Back to when he and Olmsted were first diverting streams and creating the landscape for the estate."

"But what about Bessie and Uncle Hannable?"

"Don't you see? Elijah gave Bessie enough gold to take her family north. The dinner in the cabin, the peach wagon blocking the view of the hearse—everything was set up for Bessie to get a share. As for Uncle Hannable, who would interfere with a black man's coffin, especially when they didn't know that it wasn't a white person being transported by a white funeral home?"

"What do you hope to prove?" Nakayla asked.

"The motive. If we find an empty coffin, or better yet, gold or traces of gold, then we'll know our theory is correct."

"And if we find a body?"

Her question stopped me. I was so sure of my deductions that the possibility of the coffin housing an occupant hadn't entered my mind. "Then I hope to God it's Uncle Hannable. Otherwise, we've really opened a can of worms." I regretted the worm analogy as I said it.

"So, we'll have to file a request for an exhumation with the state of Georgia?"

I'd had my fill of bureaucracies—from the V.A. to the U.S. Congress. "No. That would be a nightmare of red tape."

"You're saying we'll do it ourselves?"

"With Harry's help. He can guide us to the location."

"What about the research on the genealogy?"

"That can wait. I want to call Harry now. Can you miss work tomorrow?"

"Yes. I guess so. But digging up a grave…" She let the thought hang on the phone line.

"I know. But everything now points to that 1919 trip to Georgia. I think Tikima knew she'd have to go to extraordinary lengths to solve Elijah's murder. That might be why she came to me."

"Okay, Sam. Call me back."

"I will." I thought of something else. "Do you have any tools to dig with?" But Nakayla had already hung up.

I let Harry's phone ring, hoping he was in the apartment but needing time to reach the receiver.

"Hello." His craggy voice told me he'd been sleeping.

"Harry. It's Sam. You're not going to believe this."

I gave him a summary of what I'd found in the Bible and my theory of the trip to Georgia. "So we need to open that coffin, Harry. That way we'll know for sure."

"Can't be done."

"One night's all we need. We don't even have to lift it out of the ground."

Harry sighed. "I took Harrison there back in 1960 to show him where his grandfather was buried. Amos had lost the land to back taxes, but I thought maybe we could find the spot. People are hesitant to move graves. I'm afraid Elijah and his kin are at the bottom of Lake Lanier."

"Lake Lanier?"

"Yep. The government built a dam in the Fifties and flooded thousands of acres of farmland. Every road I remembered ended at the water."

Now I was the one who sighed.

"But I think you're on to something," Harry said. "Explains a lot of what happened on that journey. Elijah was a clever enough fellow to have pulled it off."

"Yeah," I said half-heartedly. "I guess we'll have to prove how clever some other way."

I hung up, deflated by Harry's news, and then called Nakayla to tell her the grave angle was a dead end.

As I took off my leg, I realized how foolish I'd been. What was I going to do? Hop up and down on a shovel? How would I and a hundred-year-old man with two good legs between us dig up a coffin in the middle of the night? Just as well that the family cemetery lay underwater. My gold fever had crowded out my common sense. Nakayla would have to find the genealogical connection and then we'd plan our attack.

I SLEPT TILL nearly ten—an indication of how much the events of the past few days had exhausted me. After a quick shower to clear my head, I hobbled around the apartment on my crutches, microwaving a bowl of oatmeal and browsing through Tikima's collection of books. *Exploring the Geology of the Carolinas* caught my eye. One of the authors was a professor of geology at the University of North Carolina at Chapel Hill. Tikima had earmarked a section on the western part of the state and I read in greater detail the story of ancient continents crashing into one another. Diagrams depicted the Brevard Fault that at one time made the action of the San Andreas in California look like the gentle rocking of a yard swing.

I was immersed in a section on gold deposits when the phone rang.

"Phil Ledbetter." Nakayla's voice crackled with excitement. "I was able to trace him back and guess who I hit?"

No Ledbetters made Harry's list of Biltmore employees so I was clueless as to the connection. "I have no idea."

"Galloway. Phil Ledbetter is the grandson of Jamie Galloway, the man who supposedly died in World War One. Ledbetter's mother was Galloway's daughter."

"But that property is the opposite direction from where Elijah prospected."

"How do we know that? Elijah and Junebug were all over these hills."

"But his body was found in the French Broad, Junebug was on Biltmore property—and Tikima might have been killed on the estate. The evidence doesn't support Elijah's involvement with the Ledbetters' gem mine."

"Look how bodies and cars have been moved around, Sam. And we've got the bracelet. Maybe an expert could match those emeralds to what Phil Ledbetter mined."

I didn't know enough about emeralds and gold to agree or disagree.

"And I've found something else," she said.

"What?"

"I'm going to show you. I'm in the car and I'll be there in fifteen minutes." Whatever Nakayla had discovered certainly boosted her spirits.

I put on my leg and quickly straightened up the apartment. Then I had an idea. I called information and got the number for the geology department at UNC. I expected to get voicemail, but the woman who answered transferred me to Dr. Kevin Stewart, the co-author of *Exploring the Geology of the Carolinas*. I hadn't thought through my approach but I decided to tell enough of the truth to get the information I needed.

"Kevin Stewart." The voice sounded younger than what I'd expected from a professor who studied old rocks.

"Dr. Stewart. My name is Sam Blackman. I'm calling from Asheville."

"Then I'm envious. It's ninety-five degrees down here. How can I help you?"

"Our family has a gold and emerald bracelet made in the early 1900s. We wondered if it's possible to determine where the gems and gold came from."

"Hmmm." He paused. "I assume you're talking about the geological source."

"Yes."

"That would depend upon their distinctive qualities. Ideally, you'd have a few samples for comparison—ones with a known origin. That would be especially true for gold. The geochemical fingerprint depends on what other trace elements are present."

"And the emeralds?"

"The best way to fingerprint them is with oxygen isotopes. Most natural oxygen is oxygen-16. That is eight protons and eight neutrons. But a small percentage is oxygen-18 with two extra neutrons. Emeralds from different sources will have different ratios of oxygen-16 and oxygen-18. When those ratios are the same, then it's a good bet you've found the common site. Even the rock around the emeralds will have the same ratio because everything crystallized at the same time from the same fluids." He laughed. "Are you still awake? This is when my students normally nod off."

"I'm still with you. But I don't have site samples. We think the gold and emeralds might have come from Gold for the Taking."

Dr. Stewart laughed again. "You sure they're not plastic?"

"A jewelry designer tells me they're high grade emeralds."

"Could be. The tourist bait at Gold for the Taking isn't worth much, but there's a rich emerald deposit somewhere on that property. I've seen some of the stones, but to my knowledge no one's been able to dig other than the owner. Ledbetter's his name?"

"That's right. So you might be able to match the emeralds?"

"If I had a sample emerald or even rock from the mine. Otherwise it's more likely I could tell you if they didn't come from there, not definitely prove that they did."

"What about the gold in the bracelet?"

"Highly unlikely that gold and emeralds would be found at the same site. Gold for the Taking's not known for much gold other than what's washed downstream. Gold's trickier because the extraction process and refining purifies the precious metal while obscuring its origins. If you had the ore, then you'd have a better chance."

I figured I'd gotten what useful help I could from Dr. Stewart and thanked him for his time.

"No problem. And if you get down to Chapel Hill, bring the bracelet. I'd love to see it."

Nakayla came into the apartment clutching a manila envelope. She went to the dining table, unfastened the clasp, and pulled out several sheets of paper.

"I spoke to a geologist," I said. "He doesn't hold much promise that we'll be able to identify the exact source of the bracelet's emeralds without a sample from the site."

Nakayla didn't seem interested. "Look at this."

She handed me a picture that had been downloaded from the internet and printed on standard paper. The website was Historical Graves of Georgia. The image quality was poor, but I could make out several large rocks behind a wrought-iron fence.

"What is it?"

Nakayla gave me a second sheet. The close-up showed a weather-worn gray surface with faint depressions that had once been distinct letters. MALACHI ROBERTSON.

"Elijah's graveyard," I said.

Nakayla grinned. "Brilliant, Sherlock. Glad you told me."

"How did you ever find it?"

Nakayla sat at the table and I took the chair beside her.

"I knew graves created problems. Native American burial sites and slave cemeteries usually have no descendants to insure their preservation and so historical societies and heritage foundations have lobbied for governmental protection. State laws have been enacted that make it extremely difficult to develop property containing a cemetery. I thought even in the Fifties, efforts might have been made to relocate graves lying in the proposed bed of Lake Lanier. Turns out these graves weren't moved at all."

"Harry was wrong?"

Nakayla slid me a third sheet. "Yes. But it's easy to see why. The lake changed so much of the landscape and it'd been forty years since he'd last seen the cemetery. The graveyard is at the edge of a county park. When the lake was formed, the stream became a cove and the water level rose nearly even with the graves."

I looked down at a wider shot of a green lawn with picnic shelters and barbecue grills. In the background, I saw the cemetery's fence and beyond, a wide stretch of water. Then I remembered the journal mentioned the graves were on a knoll above the stream. Elijah's people had chosen well. "You know where this is?"

She nodded. "Found it on the Hall County website." She tapped the papers in front of her. "I printed out Mapquest directions. It's about a three-hour drive."

I studied the pictures. "I don't know. A public park?"

"That's even better. It closes at ten. You said we only have to dig down to the coffin's lid."

But last night the reality of using a spade with only one good leg had come crashing down on me.

"Harry can hold the flashlight while we both dig." Any reservations Nakayla expressed earlier had been cleared away by her discovery.

"Do you have any tools?" I asked.

"No. But we'll buy them this afternoon. How soon can we pick Harry up in the morning?"

The idea of the three of us digging in a public place at two in the morning reminded me of Tom Sawyer and Huck Finn watching Injun Joe in the graveyard. That had gotten Tom buried in a cave, and I wasn't the Samuel Clemens who could write our way out.

"We shouldn't get Harry before nine," I said. "We'll say he's staying overnight with me. I'll tell the Captain so he can stand down his patrols." I stood and walked to the kitchen counter. I leaned against it with my back to Nakayla.

"What's wrong?" she asked.

I spun around. "Face it, Nakayla. I'm a damn cripple. We don't know how hard or rocky the ground will be. You're the only able-bodied man and you're not even—" I halted, realizing I'd be completing a sentence I'd regret.

"And I'm not even a man?" Nakayla's brown eyes narrowed. "Is that it?"

"No."

"The answer to my sister's murder may be in that grave. I'll dig with my bare hands if I have to." Her voice trembled and I knew there'd be no stopping her.

"Police or county rangers could swing by the park," I said.

"Then drop me off at midnight and pick me up in the morning. I can always hide behind a tombstone. You're not too crippled to drive, are you?"

Her words stung like a slap across my face.

"No," I said flatly. "I can drive." I could also think. The first rule of combat is don't launch an offensive undermanned. The second rule is that something always goes wrong with every plan. Have backup.

I returned to the table and picked up the map. Lake Lanier was almost halfway between the two cities. "All right. We'll do it. But I'm getting another digger."

"Who?"

"My brother Stanley. He can drive over from Birmingham."

"Why would he help?"

"Because I've got something he needs." I dropped the map and turned toward the phone.

"Sam. Wait." She stood. Tears glistened in her eyes. "You're going to let him settle the lawsuit?"

"That's my leverage. That's what he needs."

"No. You can't. That's too much to lose."

"Coming from a woman who's on her hands and knees clawing at the ground with her fingernails?"

Nakayla had to laugh at the absurdity of the scene.

"Someone fired a bullet that missed my head by inches," I said. "Somehow, I'd forgotten that. This is personal for me too. I won't tell Stanley any more than I have to." I smiled. "Besides, it'll be worth the money to see his face when I hand him a shovel in that graveyard."

NINETEEN

"MAY I HELP YOU?" The woman's voice sounded tinny coming from the small speaker beside the keypad.

"We're here to see Harry Young," Nakayla said.

"Come on through."

The crossbar next to the unmanned guardhouse lifted, and we began our ascent to Golden Oaks. The Hyundai's trunk contained three new shovels, a pick, and a ten-by-ten tarp. I'd also purchased a crowbar and a hammer, but I had no idea as to the condition of the coffin's wood after nearly ninety years in the ground.

Exactly one week ago, Tikima Robertson had been buried. Tonight, in another cemetery, I hoped to unearth the reason for her murder.

My call to Stanley the previous night had gone as well as I could expect. Thanks to Nakayla's insistence, my letter had arrived that morning, and, though I didn't back down from my position on the lawsuit, I'd written a profuse and sincere apology for the personal things I'd said. That probably kept him from hanging up on me.

When I asked Stanley to meet me in Gainesville, Georgia, he'd hesitated, saying anything we needed to discuss could be done over the phone. I said since writing the letter, I'd reconsidered my objections and would be willing to discuss them. But I needed his help with something else in return and I had to explain in person. I'd be in Gainesville at eight the next night. Otherwise, we'd leave things as they were and hope the lawsuit wouldn't drag on.

Stanley bit the bait. I just had to keep him hooked. I'd left him wondering when I'd told him come dressed for gardening.

Golden Oaks Retirement Center looked beautiful in the morning sunlight. Automatic sprinklers showered beds of begonias and impatiens lining the parking lot. A multitude of rainbows appeared in the fine spray as we drove to the main lobby. Nakayla found a visitor's spot and as we left the car, Captain came out the front door. He wore a pith helmet, a khaki safari shirt, and brown-checkered Bermuda shorts. Except for his walker, the old guy was ready to hunt crocodiles.

"Good morning, folks. It's a glorious day." His voice rang out like the town crier's. Then he dropped to nearly a whisper. "Hilda at the front desk said someone just buzzed at the gate for Harry. Glad to see it's you."

"We're going to take him out with us," I said. "Probably won't be back till tomorrow."

Captain's eyes darted left and right looking for eavesdroppers. "Part of the case?"

"Yes. But that's all I can say. I guess I'll need to sign him out."

Captain waved off the idea. "No. I'll take care of it. Anybody comes looking for him, we'll say he's not feeling well."

"Has somebody been by?" Nakayla asked.

"Not for Harry. Yesterday, Mr. Armitage dropped in on Sandra Pollock, the resident manager. I had Bertha stationed outside her office. He was asking about Tikima's visits, but Sandra didn't mention Harry."

So, Armitage was conducting his own investigation.

I regretted hanging up on him. Maybe Detective Peters was right. I am a hothead. I'd better cool down if I hoped to find Tikima's killer.

"Good," I said. "Don't be surprised if the police show up today."

"We're ready. Gertie and Harold are taking an exercise stroll up and down Harry's hallway. We'll still keep to our surveillance schedule while he's gone."

I shook my head in amazement at Captain's network of spies. His CIA—Corridor Intelligence Agency.

"If I might make a suggestion," he said. "Drive around to the rear of the building on the left. I'll wheel Harry out where he can get in your car unobserved."

"All right." I turned to Nakayla. "Have you got a notepad in the car?"

"In the glove compartment."

"Give Captain your cell phone number."

She went back to the parking space.

"Call us if someone comes looking for Harry. I'd like to know who we're dealing with."

"You've got it." He took the number from Nakayla and tucked it in the chest pocket of his shirt. "Give us about ten minutes." He swung the walker around and headed inside.

To the minute, Harry, Captain, and an elderly couple I assumed to be Harold and Gertie came out the rear door of Harry's wing. Harold pushed Harry in the wheelchair and Gertie carried his crutches.

We drove from the far corner of the lot and stopped by the access ramp at the curb.

I shook Harry's hand. "You can sit in the front seat with Nakayla where you've got more legroom."

"Don't be silly. I'm shorter and I only have one leg."

Harry wore a plaid cotton shirt and beige pants with the right leg tied up below the knee. "I'll be fine. You sit where you can stretch out that mechanical marvel."

I'd put on the sports model prosthesis and part of the articulating ankle must have shown as I got out of the car. Like Dr. Anderson had said, the feel was stiffer but the night's activities promised to be a good test.

Nakayla got Harry settled in the backseat and I thanked Harold and Gertie for their assistance. They wanted to help me fold and load the wheelchair in the trunk, but I didn't want them seeing the tools. God knows what they might have thought we were going to do with Harry. Nakayla anticipated the problem and asked a brilliant question—"Do you have any grand-children?" Osama bin Laden could have been in the trunk and they wouldn't have noticed.

As we pulled away, Harold and Gertie waved. Captain saluted.

"You've got some nice friends," Nakayla said.

"Yes, I do," Harry laughed. "Nice friends and nice to get out where they're not watching my every move."

I passed him the web pictures of the graves.

"That's them," he said. "Hard to believe after all these years. What are we going to do when we get there?"

"Have a picnic," Nakayla said. "It's a park. People will think I'm your nurse."

"Then we can check out what we're dealing with tonight," I said.

"And your brother?" Harry asked.

"He's meeting us at the Holiday Inn in Gainesville at eight."

"Does he know?"

"Not exactly," I said.

"Not exactly," Harry repeated. "Well, I hope he's more than a brother. I hope he's a best friend."

Stanley was definitely not a best friend. "Why's that?" I asked.

Harry chuckled. "That old saying. A friend helps you move. A best friend helps you move a body. This time tomorrow Lord only knows what we'll have done."

WE STOPPED AT a KFC outside of Gainesville and bought our picnic lunch. The park proved difficult to find, given the way roads wound in and around Lake Lanier's coves. We missed a few turns and discovered Georgia's street signage left much to be desired. The prevailing philosophy seemed to be if you don't know how to get where you're going, then you have no business being there. I was glad we were making our mistakes in daylight and not after dark. We were out in the country where moonlight and headlights would be our only illumination.

The wide picture Nakayla had downloaded turned out to be the whole park. No ball fields or tennis courts, simply a small boat launch used by fishermen and canoeists. A scattering of picnic tables covered the grassy knoll. Along a far edge near the lake's shore lay the wrought-iron fence cordoning off the small graveyard.

We claimed a picnic table and passed around a bucket of fried chicken, sides of slaw and hushpuppies, and plastic cups of lemonade. Harry sat in his wheelchair at the head. He lifted a drumstick like a baton.

"I remember Elijah telling me about fried chicken. Black folk cooked it as traveling food for trains or long car rides. When you couldn't stop to eat at restaurants, you had to fix something that would keep. Frying the chicken sealed it so it stayed fresh longer."

"Now I can eat anywhere I want," Nakayla said, "and what do I buy? Chicken."

But Colonel Sanders' secret herbs and spices tasted pretty good. Maybe the bright sunshine and cool breeze coming off the sparkling water had something to do with it. We took our time. Harry had to cut his chicken away from the bone and almost mince it before swallowing. Evidently more than cold liquids gave him problems.

For a Saturday afternoon, the park was sparsely populated. A few families with small children sat on blankets, preferring to let toddlers roam on the ground rather than imprison them in a car seat on a picnic bench.

We dumped our trash in a wastebasket and went over to the boat launch. Nakayla pushed Harry in his wheelchair on the concrete approach to the ramp. I stayed on the grass where I could practice walking with the new leg.

We watched a middle-aged couple unload matching yellow kayaks off the roof of a Saturn station wagon, the red-haired woman giving instructions, the curly gray-haired man ignoring them. Both seemed perfectly happy in their roles and I saw the marital wisdom of the two boats.

A gravel path looped from the ramp to the cemetery. The packed pebbles made pushing Harry's wheelchair difficult, and Nakayla veered onto the grass where the ride was bumpier but faster.

The pickets were about four feet high. A padlock clasped the gate shut. A bronze plaque beside the gate read—"Robertson Family Plot, Descendants Unknown."

Harry wiggled in his chair. "I'd like to stand. I want to see."

Nakayla pushed him closer to the gate. He grabbed the black iron bars with his bony gnarled hands and pulled himself up on his one leg. Nakayla and I stood beside him, ready to assist if he wavered.

"The last time I was here was with my father." Harry's words were barely audible.

Nakayla took his arm. "If we find Elijah deceived your father about the coffin, I hope you can find room in your heart to forgive him."

Harry turned and hopped closer to the fence where he could lean against it. "My dear. The gratitude Elijah and his kin showed my father and me wasn't deceit. We just didn't understand the full extent of our service." Harry smiled. "It will give me comfort to know we made a difference in the lives of Bessie and her family."

"And you're making a difference in my life too," Nakayla said.

The three of us stood in silence. Nakayla and Harry were probably lost in memories of family members gone forever. I was thinking how we would need to scale the fence. A six-foot stepladder could straddle the pickets and let Nakayla, Stanley, and me climb up and then use the support side of the ladder as a makeshift way down. Stanley had purchased a minivan when the twins were born. I'd find a Walmart or Lowe's open late enough to pick up the ladder tonight in his vehicle. Maybe call Stanley's cell phone and ask him to come at seven.

Deceit. The conversation between Nakayla and Harry hit home. I was tricking Stanley into helping me, but

I didn't care if he forgave me or not. He wasn't being altruistic like Harry's father, helping Elijah simply because he needed help. No, that wasn't quite true. Elijah had rescued Harry from the bear. A debt had been incurred. Stanley and I owed each other nothing. And yet guilt weighed on me. Was that what it meant to be family? To be in debt to each other? Or to recognize a shared debt to your parents? What does an orphan at any age owe his parents? But wasn't that the reason I'd given for making Galaxy Movers and its insurance company pay more money? Punishment for my parents' deaths, even at the cost of whatever fragile ties I had with my brother? The argument was circular. What would happen would happen. I was helping Harry and Nakayla. Their sense of family would be all the justification I needed.

"I wonder what the designs mean on the headstones." Nakayla leaned across the fence and pointed to the markings chiseled in the smooth space by the names. For the oldest monuments of Malachi and his wife Annabelle, the lines, curves, and circles weren't as eradicated as the names.

"All the designs share the same degree of erosion," I said.

"Maybe Elijah added them later," Harry said. "When his father died. They were here when I came the first time. They look like patterns to frame the names."

Like the ridges on the bracelet, I thought. A family marking. Maybe some alphabet born in the slave days when reading and writing were forbidden.

"We'd better go," I said. "There are a few more things we need. Then I want to get rooms at the Holiday Inn. A rest will do us good. We've got a long night ahead."

"NAKAYLA'S SISTER WAS the woman who was murdered. The victim the detective told you about at the hospital."

I'd just introduced Stanley to Nakayla and Harry after the two of us returned from Lowe's with the ladder and some plastic containers to hold whatever we found in the grave. We sat in my hotel room and I could tell Stanley was anxious. The contrast of the old one-legged white man and young black woman was strange enough, but the vague information I'd given him must have set his imagination running wild.

On the way to the store, I'd told Stanley that Nakayla's and Harry's families had known each other for over a hundred years. Harry knew of some family heirlooms stored in Gainesville that Nakayla should have. We needed to retrieve them from the property and that's why we bought the ladder and storage containers.

"Is no one living in the house now?" Stanley asked Nakayla.

She looked at me, wondering how to answer.

"There is no house," I said. "The items were actually buried on the property for safekeeping. Now that Nakayla is the sole survivor, Harry encouraged her to claim what is rightfully hers. Harry knows the spot."

Stanley looked from Harry to Nakayla. "Why would your family bury their own things?"

"Fear," I said before Nakayla could speak. "The KKK terrorized African-Americans who showed any hint of being successful. Harry helped Nakayla's great-great grandfather bury them years ago."

"Is this like silverware?" Stanley asked.

"Yes," Nakayla said. "I know it sounds strange, but Harry heard about my sister's death and got in touch with me. I'd prefer not to risk having someone see us dig it up, so Sam agreed to help me tonight. Thank you for helping us, Stanley."

Outside, a crack of thunder covered Stanley's "It's no trouble."

"Damn," I said. "We don't need a storm."

"It'll make sure no one's in the park," Harry said.

"We're going to a park?" Stanley asked.

Nakayla's cell phone rang. "Excuse me." She stepped out in the hall. A few seconds later, she returned. "Sam, it's for you."

Nakayla stayed with me as we walked across the hall to her room.

"Sam. This is Captain."

"What's up? Is someone looking for Harry?"

"No. The police are looking for you."

"They came to Golden Oaks?" I was baffled as to why Detective Newland would think I'd be at the retirement center. Had one of Captain's legions betrayed us?

"We saw it on the TV. The report said in light of new evidence the police want to re-question you and Nakayla. They put your pictures on the screen."

"Thanks, Captain. I'll deal with it in the morning." My mind raced. I didn't want us tied to a disturbed grave in Gainesville. I'd paid cash for the rooms and we'd registered in Harry's name. But I'd had to put the ladder and storage containers on my credit card. With the speed data can be collected, law enforcement agencies could be checking my bank transactions and placing me in Gainesville. "Captain, if we had to crash late tonight, is there a place at Golden Oaks we could stay?"

"The guest suite. Visiting families rent it. Tuesday night I doubt if it's occupied. I'll check and get the key."

"We might show up in the middle of the night."

"Don't worry about it. I get up to pee every thirty minutes."

I flipped the phone closed. "Do the police have this number?"

Nakayla nodded. "I gave it to Detective Peters. When I was in the interrogation room with Newland, I just gave my work and home numbers."

"Good. Turn off the phone and take out the battery. I don't want anyone to get a GPS fix on it."

"What's wrong?"

I gave her a summary of Captain's information.

"What do you think the new evidence could be?" she asked.

"I don't know. But they wouldn't go public with our pictures unless we were incriminated. Someone might be setting up a frame."

"If whoever killed Peters has his file, then he has my cell number."

"Yeah. We've got to move fast."

THE RAIN CAME down like a waterfall. Stanley's windshield wipers struggled against the deluge. We crept along staying as close to Nakayla's taillights as we dared. I kept glancing over my shoulder to see if we were being followed, but the double-back maneuvers we'd planned coming out of Gainesville seemed to have thwarted any surveillance. One thing I'd learned in Iraq: when you stop feeling paranoid, you'd better get the hell out.

"This is nuts," Stanley said.

"Yeah, I know. It's also important."

"Are you sleeping with that black chick?"

"Jesus Christ, no! I'm trying to find whoever killed her sister. Is that too difficult to understand?"

"No. Not when you tell me instead of weaving some fairy tale about buried silverware that we have to get to in a raging thunderstorm. But the most unbelievable thing is you giving up your dream of a big settlement from the lawsuit in exchange for transporting a ladder."

"Okay. Here it is. Harry's a hundred years old."

"That I believe."

"He knew Nakayla's great-great grandfather, Elijah, a man who was murdered just like Nakayla's sister. The killings are linked and what we're about to dig up could prove it and identify the murderer. I believe we might find gold or emeralds that Elijah hid. He was a miner."

Even in the dark I could see Stanley's eyes widen.

"A buried treasure?"

"Maybe. But it's Nakayla's and it's evidence. We have no claim on it."

Stanley slapped the steering wheel. "You're telling me you're chasing a hundred-year-old serial killer?"

"No. A family protecting a secret."

Nakayla turned left and I knew we were nearing the park.

"Why didn't you go to the police?" Stanley asked.

"Because the killers probably are the police. And if that's too much for you to handle, then you can turn around and leave."

"And the lawsuit?"

"Do what you want. I understand you've been stepped on as much as I have. But I've got one more fight before I go quietly."

Nakayla swung her car around and headed over the grass toward the graveyard. The stones behind the wrought-iron fence stood out in the rain like squat gray mushrooms frozen in time.

Stanley stopped short of the grass. "We're digging up a grave?"

"A fake grave. At least I think it's a fake grave."

"My God, Sam. You can't be serious."

"Solving a murder is serious business."

Nakayla stopped, her headlights focused on the gate. It was nearly eleven o'clock and I felt confident the storm would shield us for the rest of the night. A flash of lightning revealed the pale, sweaty side of Stanley's face. His mouth hung open as he stared at the graveyard.

"I'm a banker," he said, mystified that he'd somehow crossed into a parallel universe.

"And a damn good one." I unfastened my seatbelt. "If you don't want to drive the van on the grass, I'll need to get the ladder and the containers."

"I'm sick of being a banker." Stanley pressed the accelerator and the van lunged off the pavement. I bounced sideways on the seat, kicking myself in the shin with my prosthetic leg.

Harry stayed in the Hyundai, keeping the motor running to charge the battery and listening to the radio for any news about us. Stanley killed the van's lights and helped me position the ladder over the fence. We'd bought one with steps on either side so even I was able to make it over.

Stanley didn't hesitate. He dug the first spade of earth from Hannable's grave. I had to stop him until we could lay down the tarp alongside to hold the dirt. Then we cut away the sod first so when we refilled the grave, the grass could be laid back on top.

The storm proved to be a blessing in two ways: the

rain softened the Georgia clay as we dug deeper, and the downpour masked us from the lake, a potential problem had anyone been taking a midnight cruise.

Harry had told us the grave had been dug less than six feet and when we got to four, we should be careful. Stanley was digging close to the headstone, Nakayla in the middle, and I worked near the foot. I was slower than the others, having some difficulty with balance. But the deeper I went, the more adept I got at using the shovel. The weather was so miserable that we spent more time laughing at our predicament than complaining.

We must have been going for over an hour when Stanley let out a sharp short scream.

"I fell in," he said. "The ground just dropped out from under me."

"Stop digging," I said. "Grab the flashlight. If the coffin rotted away, a space might have been left. Maybe we can lift the dirt up from beneath. Two of us can work side by side. Climb out," I told Nakayla.

She and I scrambled up the muddy sides. The rain now served as a hindrance, pooling in the grave and blocking Stanley's view. He bent down and shone the flashlight into the opening left by the decomposed coffin.

"Bags," he said. He reached in and pulled one out. "It feels fragile. I'd better grab it from the bottom." He lifted out a sack about the size of a ten-pound bag of sugar and set it by the headstone.

Carefully, Nakayla plucked free the drawstring that had fused into the leather. She spread back the folds. In the beam of the flashlight, rich green crystals spread refracted rays in a hundred directions.

"Emeralds," she said. "You were right, Sam. We've

found emeralds." She held one above the grave for Harry to see. His ancient face was pressed against the windshield, grinning from ear to ear.

I fingered the stones, feeling the cool jagged surfaces. "And if we can match these to the Ledbetter mine, we'll have the Galloway family connection and the geological link."

"Here's another bag," Stanley said. "This one's heavier."

The collecting rain was deeper and the old leather was sopping wet. As he handed it to me, one side split and the contents tumbled onto the grass. Instead of emeralds, bars of gold spilled into the light.

"Bring the covered plastic containers," I told Nakayla. "Let's start getting these put away."

Stanley traded the shovel for the pickax and began using it as a hook to snare more sacks out of the small air pocket left by the coffin.

"Careful," I said. "Don't rupture them."

"I know," Stanley said, as if he'd been a miner all his life. "Instead of two of us digging at this end, we need to drain this water. Can you dig deeper at the foot and create a ditch below this level?"

Stanley's suggestion made sense. Nakayla and I concentrated on digging down and away. As the water flowed into our little reservoir, Stanley used the flashlight to search for anything left to recover. Then he cautiously dug down through the soil that had collapsed under him.

"Hello," he said. "This is different." From the mud he pried loose a square packet. He used the palm of his hand to wipe away the clay. "This is oilskin, not leather. Feels like papers inside."

"For God's sake, don't open it," I said. "We'll take it with us."

We made a final sweep of the grave, pulling the pickax across every square inch. A few times I stared through the glare of the headlights and saw Harry watching us. I wondered what he must think about this conclusion to his grand adventure begun so many years ago. This was just one mystery solved for him. I suspected what really burdened his heart could not be lifted until he learned what had happened to his father.

We spent another hour packing the bags of gold and emeralds into the covered containers and filling in the grave. The rain-swollen dirt nearly made up for the col-lapsed space of the coffin and when we replaced the sod, the ground was close to level. Of course, in a day or two, the earth would dry and sink, leaving an un-mistakable sign of our violation.

"Stanley, would you take the tools and tarp back to Birmingham in your van?" I asked. "I'll put the ev-idence in the Hyundai." Evidence. A bloody fortune was more like it.

The rain slackened as we loaded the vehicles. When we'd finished, Nakayla gave Stanley a mud-smeared hug. He and I shook hands and I slipped him the enve-lope I'd stashed under the Hyundai's front seat.

"Here's a copy of the letter I'm sending to Walt. I'll call him tomorrow and tell him to act on your behalf, not mine."

Stanley took it, but instead of rushing to the safety of the van, he held it up to the drizzle, turning it over and over until it was soaked. Then he ripped it in half and gave me the pieces. "We'll get those Galaxy bastards. If Ashley and I get tossed out in the street in the meantime, we'll just figure something out."

I didn't know what to say. "Thanks," was all I could manage. "Drive carefully. I'll let you know what Nakayla and I do next."

"Take care of yourself." And to Nakayla he said, "You watch my little brother. He missed out on his share of common sense."

I got in the backseat of the car despite Harry's objections. With Stanley driving behind us, we headed out of the park.

Suddenly, Nakayla's headlights bounced off the side of a black car blocking the exit. She slammed on her brakes, skidding along the wet pavement before stopping only a few feet from it. Before she could shift the transmission into reverse, someone yanked open the rear door and jumped in beside me.

The cold, wet barrel of a pistol pressed hard against my temple.

TWENTY

NATHAN ARMITAGE HELD the Glock automatic rock-solid. From the corner of my eye, I saw rain beaded on his black slicker, its hood drawn tightly around his face.

He reached his open left palm over Nakayla's shoulder. "Turn off the engine and hand me the keys. Sam, you and I are getting out. You'll tell your friend in the minivan to step in front of his headlights, his arms out to his side where I can see his empty hands. Otherwise, somebody's going back in that graveyard as a permanent resident."

"Then shoot me, you punk." Harry twisted in his seat. "Killing that innocent girl."

In the faint glow of the dashboard I saw Harry's lips convulse. He fired the only weapon he had. He spit in Armitage's face.

My mind screamed attack. Make a play for the gun before Armitage shot the old man. But the pressure of the muzzle never eased on my temple. Instead, Armitage took a deep breath.

"I haven't killed anyone," he said. "But someone murdered my employee and my friend. And someone killed Detective Peters and took my company files— files Peters had questioned me about on Saturday, only hours before he died." He turned to me. "You hung up on me that night. Then a few hours later you're discovered by Peters' body. Why wouldn't you talk to me?"

"Because we didn't trust you," I said. "And it's hard to trust you now with a gun to my head."

"The keys," he ordered.

Nakayla cut the engine and dropped the keys in his hand.

Armitage pulled the pistol back to his waist. "Who's the guy behind us?"

"My brother from Birmingham. The only illegal act he ever committed before tonight was drinking white wine with steak. He's unarmed."

"Let's go back and talk to him before he does something stupid. You get out first. Keep your hands above your head."

I stepped into the drizzle. Armitage walked behind, keeping me positioned between him and Stanley's headlights.

We'd crossed no more than ten of the twenty yards to the van when a blur of motion leapt from the darkness. A loud clang sounded and Armitage toppled forward, the pistol clattering over the pavement. Stanley stood in the headlights, raising the shovel for another blow.

"Stop! Don't hit him." I snatched up the Glock and pointed it at Armitage.

He groaned, a good sign that Stanley hadn't killed him.

"Stay face down," I ordered. "Spread your arms and legs."

Nakayla ran up beside me. I handed her the pistol. "I'm going to pat him down."

I did a thorough search for a second weapon, even checking his socks for a knife or small derringer. In the headlights I saw blood seeping along his cheek from under the hood. I feared he needed medical attention.

"Stanley, put the shovel back in the van, then help me get him to his car. I'll drive him to the Holiday Inn. We've still got our rooms."

"You know him?" Stanley asked.

"Yes. Tikima's boss. I think we're working on the same side."

Stanley's face fell. He stood in the rain, covered in mud from head to toe, holding his shovel like a medieval sword. My pudgy brother, who would never be mistaken for a hero, had attacked an armed man when he could have run away.

"I guess I screwed up."

"Stanley, you're as brave a combat soldier as I've ever known." And in keeping with the Captain, I saluted.

NATHAN ARMITAGE SAT on the bed propped against four pillows. A plastic trash bag packed with ice from the hotel's dispenser covered the back of his head. His bloody black slicker had been tossed in the Dumpster in the parking lot and his wet socks and shoes lay on the heating and cooling unit under the window.

The temperature in the room rivaled a tropical rainforest. We'd switched off the air conditioning and ran the heat and blower at full blast. Stanley and I sat wrapped in bath towels, the clothes we'd rinsed in the tub drying on the heater's vents. Dr. Anderson and Kale Hinnant had warned me to keep the prosthesis, sleeves, and socks clean and dry. They were neither. The scarred stump of my leg was red and swollen as a result. Fortunately, I'd brought extra supplies so when we left I could at least attach the leg to a fresh sleeve.

Across the hall, Nakayla waited for her clothes to

dry. She'd wanted to join us and talk with Armitage, but even though it was three-thirty in the morning, with our luck, someone would see and remember a towel-clad woman darting from room to room.

I'd persuaded Harry to take advantage of his dry condition and grab a few hours sleep. I didn't want the responsibility of a hundred-year-old man dropping dead from exhaustion. Nathan Armitage was already one casualty too many. I looked at him.

"You sure you don't want to go to the emergency room?"

"No," he said. "They'll just tell me I have a concussion and not to go to sleep for eight hours. And what am I going to tell them? I got hit in the head with a shovel?"

Stanley shifted uncomfortably in his chair. "You did a hell of a job tracking us."

Armitage shook his head and winced. "I put a locator on Nakayla's car. We do security work for trucking lines and install GPS devices to make sure the drivers stay on route. We can also quickly find a hijacked truck."

"When did you do that?" I asked.

"Sunday night. After Peters was killed, I wanted to know where you were going and who you were seeing."

"You've been tailing us ever since?"

"No. I watched your movements on my computer. Nakayla went to work and then to the Kenilworth apartment. But the drive south this morning caught my attention. I saw you stay in Gainesville and then heard the police were looking for you. I wondered if you were hiding or found a clue I'd missed."

His story sounded plausible. "And then you found us in the graveyard."

"I didn't know what the hell was going on. I didn't know it was a Robertson family cemetery."

"Why didn't you call the police?"

"The same reason you didn't. I don't know who to trust."

If Armitage was lying, he was damn good at it. I decided to level with him. I had his Glock and he had a knot on his head the size of a golf ball. He also had resources we might need and I'd rather have him with us than against us.

"We weren't digging up a grave. We were digging up evidence."

"What kind of evidence?"

"Some gold and emeralds that the great-great grandfather of Tikima and Nakayla buried in 1919. His name was Elijah."

Armitage whistled. "That's what this is all about?"

"Yes. We believe Phil Ledbetter and his wife are sitting on the mine Elijah discovered and that Ledbetter's grandfather killed him. Now we can fingerprint the source of what Elijah buried to match the Ledbetter property."

"So that's why Tikima pulled all those files," Armitage said. "Everything was related to gold or gems." He thought for a second. "But the Biltmore Estate?"

"Tikima thought the mine was on the estate. It's where Elijah worked and his body had been discovered in the French Broad. I think Tikima was picking Ledbetter's brain on possible mineral deposits. She might have told him too much of the story and he panicked. Or maybe she suspected something and went on his property Saturday night. We might be able to match the soil samples on her car. What I don't understand is why she had the Pisgah Forest file?"

"Easy," Armitage said. "That whole section used to be part of the Biltmore Estate."

Of course. I'd heard how Edith Vanderbilt deeded over a hundred thousand acres to the U.S. government. Tikima was investigating all possible sites where Elijah could have prospected.

"That's interesting background," Armitage said, "but evidence from 1919 won't convict anyone of Tikima's murder. And soil samples on a car aren't enough."

"I know. We'll have to set a trap."

Armitage nodded. "And the bait?"

The bait. What did we have? Gold and emeralds. Good to catch a thief, maybe. To catch a murderer who's already on guard, no. We needed something Ledbetter would see as incriminating—something to force his hand. We did have something else. The packet wrapped in oilskin Stanley found in the grave.

I stood, balancing on one leg and leaning against the chair.

"What is it?" Stanley asked.

"That oilskin you said contained papers. I want to see it."

"You can't go outside without your leg."

"You mean I can go out wearing only my leg?"

Armitage laughed in spite of his headache.

"I'll go," Stanley said. He pulled his clothes off the heater. "These are getting pretty hot. Another ten minutes on the grill and they'll be well done."

He disappeared into the bathroom for a few minutes and then came out wearing his shirttail out and his sockless feet stuffed into his unlaced shoes. "Back in a flash." He picked up Nakayla's car keys from the table by the TV and closed the door behind him.

"He didn't take the room key." I pulled the towel tighter around my waist and hobbled nearer the door where I could let him in.

"How'd your brother get involved?" Armitage asked.

The honest answer, bribery, reflected badly on both of us. "A favor. I neglected to tell him we'd be digging in a graveyard, but he didn't hesitate. Stanley surprised me."

"Tell me about it." Armitage lifted the ice bag from his head. "I think this has done all it's going to." He dumped the bag in the wastebasket by the bed.

A knock sounded. I opened the door and Nakayla stepped in. Her damp shirt and jeans clung to her like a second skin. The provocative shape of her body paralyzed me. I stood helpless, leaning against the wall with the irritated remnant of my leg dangling below the towel. I was embarrassed, and though nurses and even Tikima had seen what the rocket grenade had left of me, Nakayla sparked a different reaction—one that caught me off guard.

"I'm sorry," she said. "I thought I heard someone leave."

"Stanley's gone to the car. Come in."

She brushed by me, trailing the sweet scent of fresh shampoo.

"We need a plan before we leave," I said. "Whatever's wrapped in that oilskin might give us something to work with."

She looked at Armitage.

"I told Sam we need more evidence tied directly to Tikima's murder. If it's a property deed or claim to mineral rights, then maybe we can force Ledbetter into overplaying his hand."

There was a second knock and Stanley returned. He set the packet on the table. Armitage slid to the foot of the bed. Nakayla took my arm and helped me stand beside Stanley.

"Go ahead," I told my brother. "Open it carefully."

The oilskin had been tucked into itself. If twine or leather thongs had once bound it, they had rotted away over the years. Stanley turned the packet over at least four times slowly unraveling the oilskin. As each layer became exposed, the surface grew cleaner, raising our expectations that the contents would be well preserved.

Stanley lifted a square of yellowed parchment roughly six inches by six inches. "I think it's a single sheet that's been double folded."

"The creases will be weakest," I said. "Don't let them tear."

He laid the parchment in the center of the oilskin and opened it like a book. Then he unfolded it vertically and we stared at a one-foot-square document.

"A map," Nakayla whispered.

The creases divided the square into four quadrants and at the center where the creases intersected like crosshairs in a rifle scope, an ellipse was roughly drawn with the initials BFS written inside. The lower right-hand corner contained a compass legend with north designated toward the upper right. Lines that could be roads or streams had been drawn freehand and a smaller circle in the upper half had the initials PB beside it.

Nothing looked to scale, especially a shaded rect-angle with a few bushes drawn beneath it. Bluff was written above it. An X had been circled on the base line. We all knew what an X meant on a map.

"Elijah recorded the location of his mine," Nakayla said.

Armitage smiled. "I don't think he was marking a good fishing hole."

A few sentences were written in the lower left quadrant: 1200 paces NNE from PB. Behind rhododendron. Left of spring.

"Do you know where this is?" I asked Nakayla.

"No." She turned to Armitage.

"Nothing looks familiar," he said. "We could look at maps from 1919 for points of similarity. I don't know what BFS means."

"Biltmore Farms something?" I guessed.

"Maybe stable," Nakayla suggested.

"We don't need an old map," I said. "We've got Harry. The summer of 1919 he and his pony were all over those woods."

Stanley headed for the door. "I'll get him up."

While my brother woke Harry, Nakayla gathered my clothes and helped me into the bathroom.

"Thanks. I can take it from here."

"You got that right." She closed the door.

I put on a fresh sleeve and a reduced ply sock to adjust for the slight swelling the digging had caused in my stump. The warm clothes felt good and a glance in the mirror showed I wasn't a complete wreck. The discovery of the map invigorated me.

Stanley wheeled Harry to the table. The old man stared at the map, and then rubbed his fingertips over the surface. "Mr. Elijah still talking to me over all these years. I read these sentences and I hear his voice just like I hear Tom's in the journal."

"Is he telling you where he found his gold?" Stanley asked, cutting straight to what we all wanted to know.

"Biltmore Farms stable?" Nakayla prompted.

"No." Harry tapped the three letters in the ellipse. "Biltmore Forestry School." He moved his finger up to PB. "Pink Beds. We called it that because of the color of the blooms that grow, mostly on the rhododendron and laurel."

Nakayla and I had been there. Now I recognized one of the lines as the Davidson River that ran along the entrance highway.

"The Biltmore School of Forestry closed in 1913," Harry said, "but Elijah used to deliver supplies there from the village."

"When did that land go to the federal government?" I asked.

"Mrs. Vanderbilt sold it in 1915 or 1916. It wasn't till the 1920s that they took full control."

"And Elijah could have been working his mine for almost twenty-five years," I said.

"How much gold did you find in that graveyard?" Armitage asked.

I'd purposefully created the impression we'd discovered a sampling of gold and emeralds. "Not much. We know Elijah gave most of it away to relatives. That's the trail that led us to the cemetery."

"So when the government came in, Elijah got out," Nakayla said.

I patted Harry's bony shoulder. "Your timeframe works. Let's say Galloway or someone else found gold dust in Junebug's pack. He could have followed Elijah or forced him to give up the mine's location and then killed him."

"Ain't no somebody," Harry said. "I bet my life on Jamie Galloway. He'd probably snuck back earlier from the war, maybe on a merchant marine ship, and he'd been hiding in the hills. He was a mean cuss and a coward to boot. A bad combination."

Armitage shook his head. "But isn't the case against Ledbetter unraveling? The mine's not on his property. And I've never heard of any gold strikes he's made."

He raised a good point and the room fell silent.

Then the answer came to me in stunning simplicity. "This isn't the map of the gold mine. It's the emerald mine. Jamie Galloway and his descendants have been sneaking onto government land all along. That meant they had to have some way to explain the existence of the emeralds. So in the 1920s, Galloway buys some land with marginal gem and gold deposits. Every few years, they announce a major find and in the meantime the tourist trade provides income. They're laundering the emeralds and creating publicity for Gold for the Taking at the same time."

"And the journal and my sister's inquiries threatened the whole operation," Nakayla said.

"What do we do now?" Harry asked.

"We bait our trap," I said. "Nathan, have you talked to Ledbetter about Tikima's visit?"

"No. Peters told me to stay clear."

"We were here," I said, pointing to BFS on the map. "With a park ranger as our alibi. But since you haven't talked to Ledbetter, you can follow up saying you found a personal file of Tikima's at the office that refers to an old emerald mine near the Cradle of Forestry. You're going to give it to the park rangers, but first you wanted to check with him whether he'd ever heard of it."

Armitage looked skeptical. "It's sketchy at best, but if Ledbetter's guilty, it could panic him. I'll be sure and do this in broad daylight surrounded by tourists."

"I hope he'll head for the mine to make sure nothing incriminating exists."

Armitage smiled. "And we'll have it staked out."

"Yes. It'll be a nice collar for Ranger Taylor. He's got jurisdiction."

Stanley leaned over the map. "But if Ledbetter doesn't go to the mine?"

"Then we fall back on the geology professor's recommendation. We do an oxygen isotope test on Elijah's emeralds, the rock in this mine, and an emerald from Ledbetter's property. A three-way match traps him in the middle of the triangle."

"But that's not the first step," Armitage said.

"No." I placed my finger beside the X. "First we find out if this mine even exists. Which means Nakayla and I have to stay on the run from the police." I squeezed her hand. "Did you ever dream you'd be starring in Bonnie and Clyde?"

TWENTY-ONE

WE DECIDED TO switch cars as a precaution against a police road check. While Nakayla waited in the room with Harry and Armitage, Stanley and I pulled two emeralds and a gold bar out of the Hyundai and stored them in the glove box of the minivan. Nakayla and Harry would drive it back to Asheville, I'd take Armitage in his Lexus, and Stanley would get the Hyundai and its valuable cargo to Birmingham. He'd tell his wife the minivan had broken down and I'd lent him the car.

Armitage and Harry slept most of the way back. Nakayla and I stopped twice for coffee, but I was still feeling groggy when we got to Golden Oaks around eight-thirty.

Harry was delivered to Captain and his octogenarian security detail. I'd been tempted to accept Captain's offer of the guest suite, but Armitage said we could rest at his home for a few hours. His wife and kids were at their Pawley's Island beach house and he had plenty of room.

I expected the president of a large security company to live in some gated compound. Instead, Armitage's house was a rambling ranch on a street near the golf course of the Grove Park Inn. The furnishings looked lived-in, not some designer's ideal where you never leave a newspaper on a chair or your shoes under the coffee table.

Armitage led us into a spacious kitchen. Marble countertops separated the food preparation from the eating area. Sunbeams streamed through skylights. There was even a fireplace at one end with a grouping of chairs so host and company could converse while the meal came together.

"Breakfast anyone?" Armitage motioned us to the chairs as he stepped behind the counter. "I make a hell of an omelet."

"So do I," Nakayla said. "A guy with a cracked head shouldn't be cracking eggs."

"It's only a dull throb. I'm thankful Stanley didn't use the pick. But there's orange juice in the fridge if you want to pour some glasses and you can set the table."

Nakayla became the assistant chef and I settled into the softest chair I could find.

"What time do you think we should get there?" I asked.

"Between two and three. After the bulk of the pic-nickers leave and before campers start setting up for the night."

Bacon crackled on the stove. The aroma triggered hunger pains in my stomach.

"We should leave about one," Armitage added. "I suggest you get a couple hours of sleep. I'll prepare the backpacks."

Nakayla looked up from setting the silver. "Back-packs?"

"Sure. You want to look like hikers. No one would expect fugitives to be enjoying a trek through the woods. And we'll need flashlights, a compass, a hand pick, a camera, chalk, a ball of twine, a newspaper—"

"You're losing me," I interrupted. "Chalk, a ball of twine and a newspaper?"

"We don't know how deep this mine might be. We tie the twine at the entrance and roll it out as we go. The chalk may be needed to mark our route if the twine's not long enough."

"And the newspaper?"

"In case we find evidence we need to date. Digital camera stamps can be altered, but this way we have proof that whatever we found was in the mine as of Wednesday, June 20th."

My confidence in Armitage rose. His ideas sounded solid and practical. I should have realized Tikima wouldn't have worked for a jerk. And he was right about another thing. He made a hell of an omelet.

A FEW MINUTES after two, we pulled into the Pink Beds picnic grounds. No more than twenty cars were in the lot, leaving a wide choice of spaces. Armitage pulled the minivan to the far end where foliage screened us from the main highway. He and Nakayla got out and walked to the rear door.

I opened the glove box and slipped the two emeralds and gold into my pants pocket. I especially wanted the emerald crystals so I'd know what I was searching for.

I found Armitage showing Nakayla how to adjust her backpack straps. Two more backpacks lay on the floor of the van. They were more like book bags, but a respectable size for a day hike.

"Given the map's instructions of 1200 paces, I figure we've got nearly three-quarters of a mile." Armitage handed me the smallest backpack. "So, I hope you're not offended that you're toting two towels, matches, and some candles."

"Not in the least. And if I fall behind, keep going. I'll find you."

Armitage shook his head. "I'd rather we stay as a threesome. The Asheville police have probably scanned your photographs to the ranger station. They'll be looking for couples, a black woman and a white man. The three of us will break that pattern."

"Where's the map?" Nakayla asked.

"With Stanley," I said. "I memorized it because if we're stopped and searched, I want it safe."

Armitage agreed. "Simple enough to follow. The only problem is an exact starting point. Pink Beds is actually a small valley with a bog. But this is the way the road has always run and we know we're looking for a bluff." He pointed across the meadow beyond the picnic shelters where the terrain rose sharply. "I'd say it's somewhere along the northern ridge line where a north by northeast route intersects in less than a half mile."

"And there's the stream and rhododendron," I added.

Armitage smiled. "True. But up here they're hard not to find." He reached in the van. "I brought you this."

He held a long walking stick with a grip carved into the handle. "Solid hickory. It'll take some weight off that leg and give you a jaunty air."

"Oh, yeah. People will look at me and the word *jaunty* will immediately spring to mind."

Armitage flipped open a compass dangling from a cord around his neck. "North by northeast. So let's try a twenty-three degree heading and see how we do."

He set a comfortable pace. The heavy walking stick took the edge off the irritation in my leg and the cool breeze blowing down the valley carried the fragrance of the Pink Bed blossoms from the higher ground. The afternoon hike could have been relaxing if we weren't on the trail of a killer.

At the far edge of the meadow, ferns and ground vines fought for space as the grass gave way to the forest. Nakayla and I let Armitage pick the best route.

"Poison ivy," he said, steering us clear of a patch of waxy green vegetation.

"Ledbetter probably planted it," I said.

We entered a world of shadows where the dense canopy of hardwoods kept seedlings from growing. Although underbrush was thin, Armitage's course across the slant of the rising ridge became a challenge. Hidden depressions, exposed rock, and the constant strain of the uneven terrain slowed me down. I shifted the hickory staff to my right hand, bolstering my balance against the downward pull of the slope.

"Let's stop a moment." Armitage checked his compass and marked a distant tree for reference.

"How far do you think we've come?" Nakayla asked.

"About a half mile, though it's hard to accurately count paces. Our stride gets shorter as we climb."

"Should have been the same for Elijah," I said.

"That's true." Armitage set his backpack on the ground and took three water bottles from a pouch. "I recommend you take a drink now. The rest of the climb will be more strenuous."

"How do you know?" Nakayla asked.

"I've cheated us to the downside of the slope. We don't know how big this bluff is. Too small and we could pass above it. I'm counting on the stream to be our signpost since water flows downhill. The next creek we come to we'll follow to its source."

After about five minutes of resting, I felt the chill from the sweat evaporating off my body. "We'd better move on. I don't want to cool down too much."

"All right." Armitage repacked our water bottles. Then he unzipped another pouch, but didn't remove anything. He stood for a moment listening. "From this point on we're obviously not on a trail. Move as quietly as you can. Someone could be at the mine."

Nakayla and I exchanged glances. The walk in the park was over.

Armitage chose our way carefully, moving from tree to tree as he stayed true to the compass bearing. We'd gone about a hundred yards when the faint gurgle of a creek rose above the warbling birds and chattering squirrels.

A rocky stream no more than five feet wide flowed straight down the slope. Armitage stopped at the edge. "We shouldn't have to cross," he whispered. "The map said to stay to the left."

"You sure this is it?" I asked.

"No. But I'm not sure about anything. We'll give it a shot and we'll either hit the bluff or we won't." He started directly up the ridge.

Vegetation was thicker by the water, which made the ascent more difficult. I fell behind and let Armitage press on, too excited to wait for me. Nakayla slowed, never getting more than a few yards ahead and testing the ground for solid footing.

The stream shrank until it became no more that a gully. I looked through the trees and saw Armitage frozen in front of a clump of rhododendron. As I came closer, he turned, grinned, and pointed up.

About thirty feet behind the rhododendron rose a moss-ravaged rock, a good twenty-five feet high and fifty feet long. It wasn't a bluff to the scale of some of the major formations in the mountains, but it was clearly a wall of ancient stone that wind and rain had exposed over the eons. The bald vertical face had stopped the tree line, and in the small patch of open light, the rhododendron thrived. The creek disappeared under the thickest wedge of the pink-blossomed thicket.

"We crawl through that?" I asked.

"Shouldn't be too tough for a man who spent last night in a grave."

"Surely there's another way," Nakayla said.

"Rhododendron doesn't grow out of rock. There's got to be a gap at the base." I moved to the left, parallel to the bluff. The rhododendron couldn't go on forever.

When the rock ended and the slope became gentler, the hardwoods reclaimed the soil. With Nakayla and Armitage behind me, I climbed to the spot where the bluff and rhododendron began. I wedged between them and discovered a pathway a yard wide with the rock on my left and thicket on my right. Unless you pushed past the first few plants, you'd never see it.

"Come on. We can cut back to the stream." I hurried forward, using the walking stick as a third leg to speed me along.

"Some of this rhododendron has been cut," Nakayla said.

I looked to the right where bushes had been pruned away. Armitage's warning came back to me and I put my finger to my lips. Armitage signaled me to stop and then reached over his shoulder into the top of his backpack. He pulled out the Glock and waved Nakayla and me to one side.

"Keep her to the rear," he whispered as he passed me.

We followed close behind. The ground sloped down, revealing more of the rock face until we found the stream flowing out of a fissure. Through erosion, or millennia of freezing and thawing, or the incomprehensible pressures of continents colliding long before this spring ever bubbled to the surface—whatever the agent, the rock wasn't solid but split into an overlapping crevice wide and high enough for us to enter.

Light faded rapidly as we left the source of the stream and walked on a carpet of moss into a natural arch. Armitage stopped and, like Mary Poppins, pulled yet another necessary item from his bag. He clicked on a heavy-duty flashlight. The broad beam illuminated an iron door set into the back wall of our small rock chamber.

Its dimensions couldn't have been greater than four-feet-square, more what I'd expect Snow White's seven dwarves to construct to protect their mine. A padlock and latch worthy of Fort Knox meant we would either need an explosive or welding torch if we were to penetrate its secrets today.

Armitage relaxed. "Unless someone locked himself in, we're alone."

"Amazing Elijah found this place," Nakayla said.

"Must have been the stream. I suspect he found gems while panning for gold." Armitage stepped forward to examine the lock.

"Wait!" Too many months in Iraq sent alarms ringing in my brain. "It might be booby-trapped." I scooted by him, scanning the ground closely for any sign of a disruption in the moss or an out-of-place stone. A pressure plate wouldn't be that hard to rig, even in this confined space.

The lower frame of the door rose about six inches above the crevice floor. Anyone coming in or out would have to bend over and step up at the same time. The door opened outward and the hinges were visible but tamper-proof. I didn't see any wires running around the perimeter or contact points whose break could trigger a device.

I found something much simpler. Something that changed everything.

"Oh, my God."

"What?" Armitage focused the bright spot of the beam where my hand touched the rock floor.

I brushed my fingertips across the ledge where iron met stone. "Sawdust. Still tacky with sap."

"Ranger Taylor?" Nakayla's question held an edge of fear. She'd figured it out.

"What's going on?" Armitage asked.

I stood and showed him the particles on my hand. "There was a chainsaw sculpture exhibit last Saturday when we talked to Taylor. We got coated with this stuff. It sticks like glue. Taylor must have knocked his shoe against the rock going in. Jesus, how stupid can I be?"

"He was your alibi when Peters was killed," Armitage said. "So you were his as well."

"But once we learned the mine was on park property we should have figured Ledbetter had somebody on his payroll. We never had a good reason why Tikima pulled Taylor's file."

"Why did she suspect him?" Armitage asked.

"Because she discovered Ledbetter's my cousin." The angry voice came from behind us, amplified by the rock walls.

Armitage whirled around, his Glock at his waist.

A boom shattered the air with the force of a concussion grenade. In the confined space, I felt the sound as much as I heard it. Armitage fell backwards. I dove for Nakayla, pulling her to the ground. The world collapsed to the ringing in my ears, then the acrid smell of gun smoke so familiar to me. Armitage's flashlight had rolled behind him, lighting up the iron door. In the back spill, I could make out his body lying face up. The Glock had disappeared.

TWENTY-TWO

"Don't move!" A murky shadow passed us. Taylor picked up the flashlight. "Show me your hands."

Nakayla and I lifted them from where we lay.

He shifted the light to the hand with the gun, bent down, and retrieved Armitage's pistol. "Any more?"

"No," I said.

"Take off the backpacks and toss them to me."

Taylor unzipped all the pockets and dumped out the content. Then he ordered us to stand and face the wall. I didn't know if he was going to execute us or frisk us. I didn't want to take a chance.

"You know how we found this place?" I asked.

"Her sister," he said. "And that's bad luck for you."

"No. It was the map drawn by her great-great grandfather."

"Map?"

"That's where we've been. Digging up his secrets."

Taylor laughed. "I already know how to get here."

"So will the world when I go missing and my lawyer delivers a certain envelope to the police."

"The map's not with you?"

"I'm not stupid. You've been watching us, haven't you? Did you ever see us pull out a piece of paper? Parchment actually, drawn in 1919."

Now the silence was longer.

"Then I guess I'll have to retire to some exotic place

without extradition and you can take comfort in knowing someone will find your bodies."

My mind raced. Stay calm, I thought. What does he want to hear? "Or we could both retire very, very rich."

"Nice try, but there's not much left in this hole and Phil doesn't want another partner."

"That's Phil's bad luck because I'm not talking about this hole. And I'm tired of talking to this damn wall." I turned around and faced him. "Do you want to run like a rat the rest of your life or do you want a real fortune?"

"What have you got?"

"You can reach in my pocket or I can do it."

"Go ahead, but try anything and you'll wind up like your pal."

I pulled out the two emeralds and held them in his beam. "These can be proven to have come from this mine. More are with the map and they'll irrefutably tie you, Phil, and his gems to this site. We've got plenty of these and you and Phil can keep your little game going without having to come back here."

"So we still need Phil?"

"For the emeralds. But not for this." I took out the gold bar. It was about two inches long, an inch high, and an inch wide. I kept my fist wrapped around it until Taylor had steadied the flashlight. Then I opened my hand like a magician materializing a dove out of thin air.

Taylor took in a short breath. I had his attention.

"Gold and emeralds don't come from the same site. That's why there's a second map. Of course, we could do very well just selling this little guy. He's got plenty of brothers and sisters."

"Where'd you get it?"

"The key was in the journal, the one you took from Peters. But everything's been moved."

Taylor shone the spot straight in my eyes. "What's to keep me from beating the location out of you?"

"Nothing. Except I don't think I'll talk. The Sunnis tried. Cost me a leg." Taylor didn't know any different. "But if my lawyer doesn't hear from me tonight, the police will have the last word."

"And the woman?" He jerked the beam over to Nakayla.

"She's part of the deal."

"Phil won't like it. He killed her sister. And then he brings me the body, expecting me to clean up his mess. Same with the detective. Phil's a damn hot-head. He panicked. He shot at you in the cemetery. I told him to wait till we knew where the woman was and we could walk right up to you."

I sensed Nakayla stiffen beside me. She kept her face to the wall.

"You put Tikima in the river at Bent Creek?"

"Yes. The water level was high. We knew she'd be swept far downstream."

"Well, money has a way of healing hard feelings. That's what we've been after. Besides, I look at Phil as your problem."

Taylor and I stood staring at each other. He was probably thinking how he could kill me and get the gold.

"Check it out." I tossed the bar at his feet.

He stooped down without taking his eyes off me. Then he snatched up the gold. "How many brothers and sisters?"

"I don't know. The weight of a body. They were in the coffin Elijah buried in Georgia. You've read the journal. Now you know what we figured out. Except we got there first."

Taylor licked his lips. He looked at the bar again and this time his eyes lingered. "We'll see."

"What's that mean?"

"It means we'll see. Turn around and put your hands back on the wall."

I didn't argue. I'd played all my cards.

He patted me down first, then Nakayla.

"Okay. Stay put." He walked back to the door. The padlock clicked open. "You're going in there till I can think this thing through."

I wheeled around. "What's there to think about?"

"I don't like her being part of the deal."

"And I don't like Phil."

"Phil's on his way. I called him when I spotted you leaving the parking lot. I'll try and stop him, but I need to go back far enough to pick up a cell phone signal. Either I'll be back for you, or we'll rename this Blackman's coffin."

"All right. But let's put Armitage's body in as well. Somebody could have heard the gunshot and I don't want a hiker finding his body while you're gone."

"Even if it means you'd be rescued?"

"Don't you get it? I want my share of the damn money and you're not going to screw it up." I grabbed Nakayla. "Come on."

Taylor stepped aside. I scooped up the backpacks and items he'd scattered and tossed them through the door.

"Hold it," Taylor said. "Leave the walking stick. I'll take it."

The heavy hickory was the one thing I could have used as a weapon.

"Fine." I moved to Armitage and lifted him under his arms. He groaned.

"Still alive?" Taylor asked.

"Not for long. Get his feet, Nakayla." I backed through the door, careful not to trip over the things under our feet. "Dump him where he's not blocking the entrance."

Taylor leaned in shining the light to the side. I laid Armitage down as gently as I dared without looking concerned. "I like Armitage's coffin better than Blackman's coffin."

Taylor laughed. "Well then, stay close to the door. There are pits and shafts back in the quartz seams." He slammed the door, leaving us smothered by the darkness.

"Wait," I whispered.

The padlock clicked shut. I scurried toward the sound, feeling my way to the spot I'd dropped the candles and matches.

"Sam, what are we going to do?" Nakayla's voice trembled but she wasn't hysterical.

"Save Armitage if we can. Then be ready for Taylor."

The edge of my palm bumped a candle. I grabbed it and then swept my hand over the dry rock till I found the matches.

The flickering flame helped me find the second candle. Quickly I lit it and brought both to Nakayla. She sat cradling Armitage's head.

"He's barely breathing," she said.

I held a candle over him. Blood soaked the right side of his shirt.

"Went through the lung," I said. "He's losing a lot of blood. I can't do anything about the internal bleeding." I ripped off my shirt and wadded it into a ball. "Roll him on his side. The exit wound is usually worse."

He still wore his backpack. I noticed the blood flow had clotted against the fabric. "Stop. The canvas is working like a bandage. Don't pull it free." I unzipped a pouch under him and found the ball of twine. I tried a longer one and pulled out the handpick. Now I had a weapon.

Nakayla slipped my wadded shirt inside Armitage's and applied it like a compress. His shallow breaths gurgled, but at least he was breathing. I knew he was going into shock.

"Stay with him." I left a candle beside her and took a few steps away from the door. The mine was about seven feet high and ten feet wide, but narrowed as it disappeared beyond the reach of the light. With the pick in one hand and candle in the other, I walked deeper into the mountain. Quartz crystals bounced the candle rays back at me. Scars of past excavation showed where the emerald hunters had gouged the wall. I'd gone no more than thirty feet when the first support timbers appeared. The shaft now sloped downward and narrowed to about eight feet in width. Then it split. The left side continued while the right went only a few yards and ended at a black abyss.

I leaned over and the candle light revealed the tops of rocks and boulders more than forty feet below. Had this shaft been dug or had it been a natural fissure like the one at the entrance? I suspected I was looking at a convenient hole for dumping the rubble from the second shaft that must have followed the emerald-bearing seam.

I took a few steps into the narrower way, now only a yard wide and less than five feet high. Chunks of quartz underfoot made walking with my sensory-dead prosthesis difficult. I turned back and noticed a notch cut in the wall behind one of the support timbers. By tucking up beside the rough-hewn wood, I could be shielded from view. My only chance to get the drop on Taylor would be the element of surprise.

I hurried to Nakayla. "How is he?"

"Coming in and out of consciousness. He mumbled a few words but I couldn't understand them."

"Keep steady pressure on the wound." Then I told her the plan.

I tied the twine around Armitage's leg and unwound the ball as I walked toward the pit. At the edge, I threw it over. Several seconds passed before the line slackened and I knew the ball had hit bottom. The hole was deeper than I thought. I tugged to tighten the cord to Armitage and then dropped it to the floor. If Nakayla played her part right, Taylor would see the twine leading to the pit and assume I had fallen, taking his golden dreams with me.

Three times I practiced running from my hiding place. It took about three seconds to cover the distance around the split passages. If I waited too long, Taylor would see my body wasn't at the bottom. If I sprang from my nook too soon, Taylor would spot me before he was at the pit. I'd get one swing with the handpick and I'd show no mercy.

"I'm ready," I shouted.

Nakayla blew out her candle. "I'm praying, Sam."

"And I'm sure Tikima's putting in a good word for us. But the more terrified you sound, the better. Taylor's got to believe I tumbled down that shaft."

"Thank you for what you've done." The sob in her voice told me no acting would be necessary.

"I wouldn't have missed it. Now no more till we're on the other side of this." I pressed back against the rock and extinguished the candle.

Total blackness engulfed me like a hood. Without sight, my other senses intensified. I heard Armitage's quick breaths, I smelled the dusty staleness of the trapped air, I tasted metal in the back of my throat as fear dried my mouth, and I kept touching the sharp point of the pick, reassured by its hardness.

I had no idea how long I stood there. I tried to push down the thought that Taylor had left us buried alive. Our only other option would be to take the pick to the door. The thick iron looked formidable. If it didn't yield, I'd have to attack the rock around it.

My good leg began to cramp. I took a few steps to keep the muscles loose. Then I heard the rattle of the lock.

Even the slight amount of light coming from the open door was enough for my dilated eyes to see the jagged edges of quartz opposite me. I had the vision advantage as long as I didn't look directly into the flashlight beam.

Nakayla screamed hysterically. "Something happened to Sam. He tried to find a way out, unraveling string behind him. I heard him cry. Then nothing." She broke down in sobs.

"God damn it."

The voice wasn't Taylor's. Phil Ledbetter had come with him. There would be no deal.

"Stupid son of a bitch," Taylor said.

A jerky pattern of lights flickered over the quartz as both men ran to the pit.

I took a deep breath. When the beams were masked by the wall between us, I leapt forward, raising the pick beside my head. Rounding the turn, I saw them peering over the edge. Taylor stood closer to me. He twisted at the sound of my footsteps.

I swung the pick as hard as I could, aiming for the broadest target. The head drove through his side, cracking ribs with the impact. Taylor toppled backwards, flashlight and gun falling from his hands.

I tried to wrench the pick free, but the point had sunk so deep that if I held on, I'd be pulled into the pit with him.

Ledbetter dove at me, butting my stomach with his head and knocking me to the ground. He didn't have a gun but swung his flashlight like a blackjack trying to crush my skull. I blocked the brunt of the blow with my forearm and used the momentum of his swing to roll him over. He kept rolling and wound up on top of me. I could feel my good leg dangling over the pit.

He raised his arm to strike again, but this time I grabbed his wrist. I yanked it down and sank my teeth to the bone. Blood gushed from severed veins. He yelled and struck the side of my head furiously with his other fist. I brought my good leg up under him, opened my mouth, and kicked him as he tore the bleeding wrist free.

He slid over the lip of the pit but managed to grab my artificial foot with his uninjured hand. I felt his full weight tugging on my stump. I started to slide and frantically grabbed at the rocks around me.

Hands snared me under the arms. Nakayla's thin fingers dug into my bare skin. "Kick him off," she shouted.

"Let go of my left arm but hold on to the right."

I reached down and pushed the release. The leg broke free of the sleeve.

Ledbetter's scream echoed in the cave a few seconds after the rocks split his skull.

Nakayla helped me to Armitage. She relit the candle. "You're bleeding."

"But I'm breathing. And so is Armitage." Gently I wedged my hand into his backpack and found what I wanted. "Here's his cell. Get out of here and call Detective Newland. Tell him we need air med evacuation if possible and mountainous terrain rescue. Tell him to call the rangers. Don't come back unless you're with a med team."

"Do I tell him what happened?"

"Just say Armitage was shot and the situation is not hostile. If he wants to call you back after a medical team's been dispatched, fine. But don't tell him about Stanley or the gold and emeralds. I'll handle that. Now get out of here."

She bolted through the door.

"Can you hear me, Nathan?"

His tongue flicked between his dry lips.

"You're going to be all right. And not a word about the gold and emeralds or my brother."

His tongue flicked again. I put steady pressure on his wound.

For the first time in a long time I started praying.

TWENTY-THREE

"WOULD YOU LIKE another cup of coffee?" Al Newland held the pot beside me.

"No, thanks. I'm all coffeed out." I was back in the interview room at the Asheville Police Department, three-thirty, Thursday morning.

"Uncle Newly said to tell you Mr. Armitage is out of recovery. Looks like he's going to pull through."

"That's good. Where is your uncle?"

"Talking to Ledbetter's wife. How about a dough-nut?"

In sharp contrast to my last visit, the men in blue had become valets whose sole ambition seemed to be my happiness.

"I'm fine. Really."

"Uncle Newly always thought that Ranger Taylor was a little piss ant. He said it was divine justice that you pinned him like a bug."

A knock came from the door and Detective Newland entered. "How are you holding up?"

"Tired and sore. I'd like to get my leg." The med team had taken me to the hospital where I'd had my beaten face treated and bandaged. They'd wanted to keep me overnight but I'd thrown a fit. Newland had brought me here, given me a shirt, and listened to my story. Now I needed to get out and tie up loose ends.

"Ted's on his way back from your apartment. He said

he found everything you wanted." Newland slipped into the chair across the table.

"Thanks. Can I see Nakayla?"

He nodded. "In a few minutes. Your statements are being typed now. You know the drill. Got to keep you separated till they're signed."

"Anything on Ledbetter's wife?"

Newland smiled. "Everything. She's babbling like a brook. She's lived in fear of the guy for thirty-five years and isn't going to jail to protect his memory. She knows the mine scheme goes back to her husband's grandfather, but claims she doesn't know about Elijah's murder. I'm inclined to believe her."

"The map we found in Georgia is proof enough for me. I figure Jamie Galloway killed Elijah in 1919 and started working the mine himself. Then as the park service took over, he had to find a way to sneak the emeralds out. When he got enough money, he bought land he claimed to be the source of the gems. I guess the family's been working the real site a little at a time for over eighty years."

"What about the gold?" Newland asked.

"Gold?"

"In addition to two emeralds, we found a small bar on Taylor's body."

I shrugged. "Interesting. I wonder if they had another mine."

Newland cocked his head and looked skeptical. "Any other ideas?"

"Have a good geologist examine it."

"Right." His eyes told me he had more questions but he let them go. "We found Peters' files and the journal in Taylor's house." Newland paused and cleared his throat. "I know you've had some rough cards dealt you, Sam, but you did a hell of a job on this case. The whole force is in your debt."

"I'm sorry I had to hold things out on you."

Newland grinned. "Yeah. Like I really wanted to know you were digging up a grave in Georgia."

"Fake grave."

"I'm just glad it was Nakayla's family. Chief Buchanan will be making a request that the Georgia authorities look the other way."

"Thanks."

Newland clasped his hands in front of him and rubbed his thumbs together. "I'd appreciate a favor."

"What?"

"The chief wants to hold a news conference at ten. This story is going to break across the nation."

"I don't doubt it. An emerald mine in a federal park, a crooked ranger, a murdered police officer."

"You've got a national reputation, Sam. For not backing down to anyone."

"For being a hothead I think someone said."

Newland laughed. "That too."

"I promise I'll stay clear."

"No. Chief Buchanan wants you there. You and Nakayla. He wants you to tell the whole story. You're a trained investigator, not an amateur who solved a case."

"I get it." The police chief had a legitimate concern. How inept would they look if some local yokel broke the case?

"We're not trying to tell you what to say, but we want to minimize any impression that you were a suspect."

"The sawdust." In the aftermath of my confrontation with Taylor and Ledbetter, I'd forgotten the police had been searching for me. "You found sawdust in Peters' car."

"Yes. You told us you hadn't been in the car. We matched sawdust from the front and back seats to particles we collected in your apartment."

"Ledbetter killed Peters and then got Taylor to move the body just like he did with Tikima. They tried to set me up by luring me to the cemetery."

"Looks that way."

"And when Nakayla hit a genealogical link from Ledbetter back to Galloway, we stopped searching. Jamie must have had two daughters."

"Yes. Judy Ledbetter confirmed her husband and Taylor were cousins. So, are you okay with the press conference?"

"Yeah. If you'll get me to my apartment in time to catch a few hours sleep."

"I'll take you there and pick you up personally."

I passed on Newland's offer of a ride to the press conference, telling him Nakayla would bring me. He didn't know her car was in Birmingham with Stanley and I wanted to keep it that way.

At seven, I called a taxi. I'd told Nakayla to be ready at nine, but I had a few things to do before then.

The driver took me to a Waffle House. He promised to return in an hour.

Nakayla's cell phone and the apartment's landline could be monitored, but I doubted if any surveillance extended to the graffiti-covered pay phone by the jukebox at the Waffle House.

I placed an order for a waffle with a side order of link sausages, and then asked the cashier for five dollars in quarters. The first call went to Stanley. I told him to watch cable news and keep Nakayla's car out of sight. He should also tell his wife no one must know about his trip to Gainesville. Then I asked him for Walt Misenheimer's home number. My call to Stanley lasted less than two minutes.

My conversation with Walt was even shorter. "Can you get hold of the Galaxy lawyers and their insurance company reps this morning?"

"Maybe. I'm headed to the office now."

"Tell them to watch the news. If they haven't settled our case by tomorrow, I'll be making a public statement about the death of my parents. The suit is now six million."

"What's going on, Sam?"

"I am. At ten."

My last call was to Harry. I gave a summary of what had happened and said we were keeping his name out of it.

"Fine with me," he said. "As long as you and Nakayla got them."

"The truth will come out. What was your father's name?"

"Luke. Why?"

"Cross-checking some things in the journal for the police."

"I guess Tom changed it because he'd used Luke for his brother Fred."

"You and Captain watch today's news, and remember, mum's the word. We'll be out to see you soon."

Chief of Police Ty Buchanan set up a platform in front of the station. At nine-thirty, reporters, cameramen, and TV microwave trucks were already assembling beside Pack Square. I was struck that we stood at the spot Harry Young had witnessed Asheville's young men rallying for World War One. Along the square's perimeter had once stood W.O. Wolfe's monument shop. I felt history closing in a circle around me.

Four chairs were behind the podium. Detective Newland, Nakayla, and I were called by Chief Buchanan to join him. He opened the press conference by revealing the killers of Tikima Robertson and Detective Peters. He commended the diligence and professionalism of his department and then announced the case couldn't have been broken without the assistance of Nathan Armitage of Armitage Security Services, Nakayla Robertson, Tikima Robertson's sister and an investigator for the Investigative Alliance for Underwriters, and Sam Blackman, former Chief Warrant Officer for the United States Military and fearless advocate for what is right and just. "I'd like for Sam to share in his own words what happened yesterday in the dramatic encounter with the men who murdered Miss Robertson and our beloved Detective Roy Peters."

I stood and walked to the podium, completely at ease with my leg and with what I had to say.

"Eighty-eight years ago, a terrible crime occurred..."

DETECTIVE NEWLAND WHISKED Nakayla and me into the privacy of the police station and away from the barrage of questions Chief Buchanan and his public information officer fielded. I knew from the embrace the chief had given me that he was thrilled with my performance and was delighted to reclaim center stage.

"Can I take you up on that offer for a ride?" I asked Newland. "We took a taxi here."

"My pleasure. I forgot we still have the minivan registered to your brother."

I'd figured that fact would pop up. We'd left Stanley's vehicle at Pink Beds. "He let me borrow it. I'm supposed to move to Birmingham."

"Think twice about that. The chief would hire you in a heartbeat." Newland pressed the exit bar on a door and we stepped out into a side parking lot.

"I do have a favor to ask you," I said.

"You got it."

"This case isn't closed."

Newland stopped. "The gold?"

"Luke Young."

"Who?"

"The man who drove the coffin to Georgia. A few weeks later he was killed in a car crash. No witnesses, just a charred wreck at the bottom of a ravine near Brevard."

"That's close to the emerald mine," Newland said.

"Yeah. And I don't like coincidences. We'll never know for sure but I think Jamie Galloway was an army deserter hiding in the forest. His father knew Luke Young had taken Elijah to Georgia, and Luke had probably asked old Galloway about the pack missing from Elijah's mule. Luke Young was the only loose end who could tie the Galloways to Elijah."

"What's your evidence?" Newland asked.

"I don't have any. That's why I'm counting on you to find some."

NEWLAND STOPPED THE unmarked police car in front of the Kenilworth's front door. "Let us know if you need anything." He twisted where he could see me in the back seat. "I'll get your other leg back as soon as I can."

"And the journal," I said. "That belongs to Nakayla."

She sat beside Newland in the front. He offered his hand. "That's a promise."

"One more thing," I said. "Can you keep this address from the press? I'd like to sleep about four days."

"No problem. If something comes up, how shall I reach you?"

"My cell," Nakayla said. She opened the door. "Call anytime."

For a second, Newland appeared surprised that Nakayla wasn't going to her house. He quickly recovered. "Thanks. And if anyone bothers you, let me know."

We watched him circle the wide lawn and disappear.

"What now?" Nakayla asked.

"Call a taxi. We're going to the hospital."

NATHAN ARMITAGE HAD been moved out of intensive care, a good sign that the bullet must have passed through with minimal damage.

I knocked on the door and someone called, "Come in."

An attractive woman with short brown hair sat by the bed. "You're Sam Blackman."

"And this is Nakayla Robertson. Are you Mrs. Armitage?"

She nodded and then started crying. "The doctors said you saved Nathan's life staying with him in that cave."

"He had the keys to the car," I said.

She laughed through her tears.

Armitage rolled his head on his pillow. His complexion was pasty and his face unshaven. IVs went into both arms and a chest drainage tube dripped pink fluid by his waist. He opened his eyes and struggled to focus.

"Sam?" he whispered hoarsely.

"I'm here. Nakayla's with me. Don't try to talk."

He shook his head. "They told me you got them."

"We got them, Nathan. You, Nakayla, and I. I know you took that bullet just to avoid the press conference."

He gave a weak smile and then turned to his wife. "Helen, give us a moment."

She frowned. "The doctor doesn't want you to exert yourself."

"Fine. I won't do any heavy lifting."

She got up.

"We'll keep it short," I promised.

Helen closed the door behind her.

Armitage licked his dry lips. "I haven't given a statement yet."

"Good. Nakayla and I made no mention of Stanley, Harry, or the gold. We said we found a map in the empty coffin and two emeralds. The police don't know about the others. I said Elijah must have given everything to his kinfolk. The police are testing the two coffin emeralds and the ones Ledbetter claimed to have found on his property. They'll all be tied to the Pisgah mine. Newland and the police chief will have rock-solid evidence to close the case. Stay with our story and we'll be fine."

Nakayla stepped beside me. "Where's this going, Sam?"

"To you, I hope. The emeralds and gold belong to you. We'll find a way to convert them into cash."

"But we were all in this together."

"Harry," Armitage whispered. "Give my share to Harry."

"And Stanley and I will be fine," I said. "Harry's father performed an act of kindness for Elijah. You and Harry should split it."

"Will he take it?" Nakayla asked.

"Probably not. So you'll have to throw him one hell of a one hundred and first birthday party, the likes of which this town has never seen."

Armitage coughed, and then motioned us closer. "Better make it a one hundred and a half. At one hundred, Harry shouldn't buy green bananas."

NAKAYLA SPENT THE night at the apartment. We figured the press would be camped outside her door. I threw a blanket and pillow on the sofa and insisted on sleeping there. As I lay trying to surrender to my exhaustion, my mind wouldn't let go of one prickly fact: emeralds and gold aren't found at the same source. Why had Elijah left a map to the emeralds but not his gold? I visualized the parchment unfolded from the oilskin, pressed flat on the Holiday Inn table with the creases dividing the hand-drawn treasure map into four sections—four quadrants. Looking at each one isolated from the other, I saw lines, curves, and circles, a pattern I'd seen on four gravestones in Georgia, a pattern repeated in miniature that I'd held in my hand.

"Nakayla?"

"Yes?" She answered from the bedroom, no trace of sleep in her voice.

"Bring me the bracelet in the Bible, please." I'd laid my prosthesis on the floor and didn't want to hop across the room to her door.

She came out wearing one of her sister's oversized tee-shirts and holding the bracelet. "What is it?"

"Get me some sheets of paper and a pencil."

I copied the designs from the four segments of the bracelet onto four pieces of paper. Then I matched the drawings like dominoes, connecting lines wherever they lined up. The result yielded a circle with an X at the center and a series of lines and curves around it.

"What are we looking at?" Nakayla asked.

"The site of your great-great grandfather's gold mine. He'd carved segments of it on the family tombstones and then duplicated it on the bracelet."

"But where is it?"

I pointed to a thick line across the top of the joined papers. "I think this is the French Broad. The circle with BH split across the upper pages is the Biltmore House. This wavy line is the entrance stream and the circle with the X is the mine. It's beside the spot where the stream veers to the right from the road."

"On the estate?"

"Yes. The stream Elijah and Olmsted diverted. The one Elijah discovered held a secret in gold."

"What do we do?"

"Tomorrow we check it out."

Nakayla stroked the side of my head where Ledbetter had pounded me with his fist. "And tonight?" she whispered.

"We put this bracelet back in the bedroom."

"We?"

I gently wrapped my hand around the nape of her neck and pulled her to me. "We." I kissed her lips, then whispered, "if you'll help me."

TWENTY-FOUR

THE CELL PHONE kept ringing, but I couldn't tell its location. *When the Saints Go Marching In* seemed to be coming from everywhere. I sat up in bed. Light streamed through the window. The clock read nine. I'd slept for nearly ten hours.

I patted the sheet beside me. The warm spot told me Nakayla had been there only a few minutes ago. Then I heard the banging of pans in the kitchen.

The phone started again and I found the culprit on the desk by Tikima's computer. "You want me to get that?"

"Yes. Tell them I'll call back. How do you want your eggs?"

"Scrambled." I snatched up the phone. "Hello."

"Sam. Misenheimer just called." Stanley sounded giddy.

"Yes."

"There was a fax waiting for him at his office this morning. Six million dollars, Sam. Galaxy is settling for six million dollars."

"An insult. I hope you told Misenheimer they could stick their offer where the sun don't shine."

Silence, as if Stanley had disappeared from the face of the planet.

"Hey, brother, I'm kidding."

"SO YOU WANT me to pick you up later?" The cab driver turned in his seat, hoping to secure a guaranteed fare.

"No," I said. "You can take us back now."

His eyes widened in amazement. "That's it? You're not going in for tickets?"

I looked out over the valley where the stream of cars and the stream of water split. Then I looked at the building beside me, constructed on land excavated and leveled from the side of the hill. Visitors flowed in and out in a non-stop procession, leaving money at the Biltmore ticket counters and buying a glimpse into the gilded age of days gone by.

"Some other time," I said.

"Tomorrow's Saturday. It'll be even worse," the cabbie warned. "This place is a gold mine."

NAKAYLA PARKED HER Hyundai in a Golden Oaks visitor spot. The day before, Stanley had picked up his minivan and left both her car and its contents. We'd leased a public storage place and in a few weeks I'd travel to New York City where gold and gem buyers knew a value and didn't ask a lot of questions.

I clutched the plastic evidence bag close to my side and followed Nakayla into the lobby. Captain and his harem weren't in their usual positions by the television. Just as well. Nakayla and I wanted to see Harry without any fanfare.

I knocked on his door.

"It's open." Harry called out the same greeting as the first time.

He sat on the sofa, the morning paper in his lap and his wheelchair within reach. His face lit up. "Sherlock Holmes and Dr. Watson."

"More like Laurel and Hardy," Nakayla said.

"You're not in the news today." He tossed the paper into the seat of his wheelchair.

"It's been a week," I said. "The snarling pack moves on."

Nakayla joined him on the sofa and I brought the evidence bag from behind my back.

"Detective Newland loaned me something. He's violated policy so don't say you saw it here."

Harry stared at the bag, uncertain what to make of it.

"Detective Newland found this in a cigar box in Phil Ledbetter's house. Something his wife said belonged to his grandfather."

I opened the bag. The silver was black with tarnish.

Harry reached for the pocket watch, a slight tremor running through his hand. He pried open the case. I knew what he'd read inside: "For Luke on his eighteenth birthday. This watch is a gift from his parents. Time is a gift from God." Harry ran his forefinger over the etching.

Nakayla and I let him cry. Even after all these years, the pain of knowing his father had been murdered must have cut through him like a knife.

After a few minutes, he handed the watch back. "Do you think they'll give it to me?"

"Without question."

"Sam made sure," Nakayla said. "He's receiving a substantial insurance settlement for his parents' deaths. Part of the money's going into a trust for Detective Peters' children. The police will be very appreciative."

Harry shook his head. "How many generations have suffered because of the Galloway family's greed?"

"We can't make the past right," I said. "But we can

do something about the future." I glanced at Nakayla and she nodded her approval. "I'll be using my money to invest in gems and precious metals. Over time, I'll be able to launder the gold and emeralds for you."

Harry laughed. "Over time? Like my father's watch says, time is a gift from God. I think I've stretched his generosity as far as I can expect."

"That's why we'd like to set up a foundation," Nakayla said. "Something that will outlive you. Sam and I were thinking a fund for amputees, veterans who need extra help with job training or rehabilitation. My sister would have liked that."

"A foundation for amputees?" Harry leaned forward and the tears seemed to evaporate from his eyes.

"Yes. Sam and I will both contribute."

Harry searched our faces. "Do you think we could include children? I'd want to help children."

And in his bright eyes I saw the spirit of the twelve-year-old boy in the journal, shining clearer than any of Thomas Wolfe's marvelous words could describe.

NAKAYLA TURNED THE car left coming out of Golden Oaks.

"Where are we going?" I asked.

"One more stop."

We took the Hendersonville exit off I-26 South onto Highway 64 and followed the franchise-laden boulevard into town. Nakayla drove across Main Street and made a few turns until 64 headed toward Brevard. Suddenly, she pulled onto the wide shoulder and stopped. We were beside a cemetery.

"What's this?" I asked.

"Oakmont Cemetery. Come on. This won't take long."

"Seems like I can't get away from graveyards."

We crossed the two-lane blacktop and walked through the gravestones.

"That's it up ahead," she said.

A monument was cordoned off by a wrought-iron fence, not unlike the one around the Robertson plot in Georgia, but twice as high. Climbing over this barrier would be tough.

The grave dated from 1905 and marked the final resting place of the Johnson family. An angel topped the pedestal for Margaret Johnson, wife of Reverend H.F. Johnson. The elegant marble figure stood ghostly pale against the crystal blue sky.

"This is it?" I asked. "The angel Thomas Wolfe's father had at his shop?"

"That's the common wisdom. It made quite an impression on a five-year-old child."

A five-year-old child whose love of stories would one day lead him to create a journal, a story he would never finish, but whose truth would bring healing through its completion. I knew that I was part of that healing, and that I was whole, if not in body, then in soul. I understood nothing else mattered.

"If the angel's looking homeward, then why not to the sky?"

Nakayla took my hand and centered me directly in front of the angel. The sightless eyes gazed down on me and the smooth marble lips held the trace of a smile. The right hand was lifted to the heavens, not pointing the way, but blessing those beneath.

"Home is where the heart is," Nakayla said. "She came from the stone of the earth. She is looking homeward."

Just like me. I pulled Nakayla close.

* * * * *

Get 2 Free Books,
Plus 2 Free Gifts—
just for trying the Reader Service!

HARLEQUIN
INTRIGUE

YES! Please send me 2 FREE Harlequin® Intrigue novels and my 2 FREE gifts (gifts are worth about $10 retail). After receiving them, if I don't wish to receive any more books, I can return the shipping statement marked "cancel." If I don't cancel, I will receive 6 brand-new novels every month and be billed just $4.99 each for the regular-print edition or $5.74 each for the larger-print edition in the U.S., or $5.74 each for the regular-print edition or $6.49 each for the larger-print edition in Canada. That's a savings of at least 12% off the cover price! It's quite a bargain! Shipping and handling is just 50¢ per book in the U.S. and 75¢ per book in Canada.* I understand that accepting the 2 free books and gifts places me under no obligation to buy anything. I can always return a shipment and cancel at any time. The free books and gifts are mine to keep no matter what I decide.

Please check one: ☐ Harlequin® Intrigue Regular-Print   ☐ Harlequin® Intrigue Larger-Print
                              (182/382 HDN GLWJ)   (199/399 HDN GLWJ)

Name	(PLEASE PRINT)
Address	Apt. #
City	State/Prov. Zip/Postal Code

Signature (if under 18, a parent or guardian must sign)

Mail to the **Reader Service**:
IN U.S.A.: P.O. Box 1341, Buffalo, NY 14240-8531
IN CANADA: P.O. Box 603, Fort Erie, Ontario L2A 5X3

Want to try two free books from another line?
Call 1-800-873-8635 or visit www.ReaderService.com.

*Terms and prices subject to change without notice. Prices do not include applicable taxes. Sales tax applicable in N.Y. Canadian residents will be charged applicable taxes. Offer not valid in Quebec. This offer is limited to one order per household. Books received may not be as shown. Not valid for current subscribers to Harlequin Intrigue books. All orders subject to approval. Credit or debit balances in a customer's account(s) may be offset by any other outstanding balance owed by or to the customer. Please allow 4 to 6 weeks for delivery. Offer available while quantities last.

Your Privacy—The Reader Service is committed to protecting your privacy. Our Privacy Policy is available online at www.ReaderService.com or upon request from the Reader Service.

We make a portion of our mailing list available to reputable third parties that offer products we believe may interest you. If you prefer that we not exchange your name with third parties, or if you wish to clarify or modify your communication preferences, please visit us at www.ReaderService.com/consumerschoice or write to us at Reader Service Preference Service, P.O. Box 9062, Buffalo, NY 14240-9062. Include your complete name and address.

HII7R

Get 2 Free Books,
Plus 2 Free Gifts -
just for trying the Reader Service!

READERSERVICE.COM

Manage your account online!
- Review your order history
- Manage your payments
- Update your address

We've designed the Reader Service website just for you.

Enjoy all the features!
- Discover new series available to you, and read excerpts from any series.
- Respond to mailings and special monthly offers.
- Browse the Bonus Bucks catalog and online-only exculsives.
- Share your feedback.

Visit us at:

ReaderService.com

RS16R